Jennifer De Leon

Border less

A Caitlyn Dlouhy Book

 New York   London   Toronto   Sydney   New Delhi

for migrants everywhere

A atheneum An imprint of Simon & Schuster Children's Publishing Division • 1230 Avenue of the Americas, New York, New York 10020 • This book is a work of fiction. Any references to historical events, real people, or real places are used fictitiously. Other names, characters, places, and events are products of the author's imagination, and any resemblance to actual events or places or persons, living or dead, is entirely coincidental. • Text © 2023 by Jennifer De Leon • Jacket illustration © 2023 by Krystal Quiles • Jacket design © 2023 by Simon & Schuster, Inc. • All rights reserved, including the right of reproduction in whole or in part in any form. • Atheneum logo is a trademark of Simon & Schuster, Inc. • For information about special discounts for bulk purchases, please contact Simon & Schuster Special Sales at 1-866-506-1949 or business@simonandschuster.com. • The Simon & Schuster Speakers Bureau can bring authors to your live event. For more information or to book an event, contact the Simon & Schuster Speakers Bureau at 1-866-248-3049 or visit our website at www.simonspeakers.com. • Interior design by Irene Metaxatos • The text for this book was set in Caslon 540 LT Std. • Manufactured in the United States of America • First Edition • 10 9 8 7 6 5 4 3 2 1 • Library of Congress Cataloging-in-Publication Data • Names: De Leon, Jennifer, 1979- author. • Title: Borderless / Jennifer De Leon. • Description: First edition. | New York : A Caitlyn Dlouhy Book, [2023] | Audience: Ages 14 up. | Audience: Grades 10-12. | Summary: Caught in the cross hairs of gang violence, seventeen-year-old fashion designer, Maya, and her mother set off on a perilous journey from Guatemala City to the US-Mexico border. • Identifiers: LCCN 2022037593 (print) | LCCN 2022037594 (ebook) | ISBN 9781665904162 (hardcover) | ISBN 9781665904186 (ebook) • Subjects: CYAC: Mothers and daughters—Fiction. | Fashion design—Fiction. | Gangs—Fiction. | Urban violence—Fiction. | Guatemala (Guatemala)—Fiction. | Mexican-American Border Region—Fiction. • Classification: LCC PZ7.1.D39814 Bo 2023 (print) | LCC PZ7.1.D39814 (ebook) | DDC [Fic]—dc23 • LC record available at https://lccn.loc.gov/2022037593 • LC ebook record available at https://lccn.loc.gov/2022037594

no one leaves home unless
home is the mouth of a shark
you only run for the border
when you see the whole city running as well

—Warsan Shire, "Home"

Prologue

As she turns the corner onto her street, she feels instantly uneasy. There is no one around. Not the tortilla lady selling her last docena of the day, or some guy on a motorcycle whispering into his girlfriend's ear, or a tired señor coming home late from work. The avenida is empty, save for a stray dog whose ribs Maya can make out even in the dark.

A surge of relief—she is home! Then, about to unlock the door, she sees it is already open a crack. She takes a step backward, instantly wary—pushes the door open carefully. She hears someone laughing. Who is *that*? Mama would never deliberately miss Maya's big night. They've both been looking forward to the show for two straight weeks. Mama would never—she would never miss it. . . .

"Mama?" Maya calls out hesitantly. The kitchen lights are on—and what is that strange smell? Smoke—cigarette smoke.

Again, a laugh. A man. A man laughing. Not a celebratory kind of laugh, not one that has been watered with jokes or chisme or . . . This laugh scrapes her from the inside.

Maya drops her bag soundlessly. Smoke, and bottles clinking, and men—two?

She takes a step, then another, quietly, quietly, until she can peek around the corner into the kitchen. There, at the round table with the plastic tablecloth—the one with mother hens feeding little chicks, a pattern repeated—sits her mother.

Tied to the chair.

Two men in black masks and gray hoodies surround her. Maya fixates on one—the one gripping the gun. *No, no, no.* He holds it to the back of her mother's head. Mama! Her face is wet with tears. A gag covers her mouth. Teal. *Their* fabric.

"Mama." The word escapes in a tangled whisper. As if she hears, Mama glances up.

Shakes her head ever so slightly. *Don't talk. Don't say anything.*

Maya briefly registers Luna whimpering somewhere, but she can't, she *can't*, look away from her mother's face. It is her face too.

1

Two Weeks Earlier

Maya felt about tomorrow the way she did at the top of a roller-coaster ride, right before it dropped—she both wanted to fall, feel the wind on her face, and to hold on, hold on, before everything changed.

"So, mañana is the big day?" her mother asked. It was late. She leaned against the bathroom doorframe and tightened her fuzzy pink robe at the waist. Her hair was wrapped in a white towel. The smell of shampoo lingered in the air.

"Yep," Maya said. She fluffed her pillow, trying to get comfortable on the mattress she shared with her mother and with Luna, who was inching her way underneath the covers, tail wagging. Every evening Maya and her mother lay the mattress down on the living room floor, and every morning they lifted it back up and tucked it between the sofa and the wall. In this way, the living room became their bedroom and vice versa.

"Don't be worried. I have a good feeling, mija," her mother said, toothbrush in hand.

Tomorrow the director of Maya's high school—the best fashion school in Guatemala—was going to announce the top ten designers of the year. These ten would then get to showcase three looks each in the annual fashion show. Two weeks from now! This was the first year Maya was even eligible; you had to be at least in your second year at the institute and be sixteen. She—finally!—was both.

"Are you worried about Lisbeth?" her mother asked before spitting out toothpaste in the sink.

"A little . . ." Maya snuggled against Luna.

Now her mother returned with a jar of Pond's lotion. "What's meant to be is meant to be." Maya watched as she rubbed cream onto her cheeks. Okay—strange. That lotion was a morning smell, one that belonged next to coffee and oatmeal and folded newspaper pages on the kitchen table. Not to evening.

"Hey, what's going on? You never shower at night."

"Ay, mija. You have talent. And you work harder than most girls at that school."

"And you're changing the subject. Why are—"

"I have an early appointment. No time to shower in the morning." Mama waved her hand dismissively. "Anyway, you have *real* talent."

Maya managed a small smile. It was true that she could tear a yard of fabric with nothing but a steady hand and a ruler, and she knew a dozen different hand stitches by heart. Though she preferred La Betty, her sewing machine. Tucked in the corner underneath the swaying light bulb, its loyal presence—along with Luna, who liked to sit on Maya's feet while she sewed—kept her company whenever her mother had to work late.

Dresses were Maya's favorite. Tops a close second. Fixing hems, shortening skirts, creating pockets, closing pockets—she could practically sew those in her sleep by the age of ten. She couldn't afford the fancy fabrics sold in the Mercado Central in the capital, so she improvised with the scraps her mother brought home from the factory, stitching them together. Soon she began including other materials. She began using, well . . . trash. Not trash from the dump. Trash in the sense of: plastic cups, scratched CDs, tablecloths. Even crayons and playing cards. Anything and everything. So Maya's mother enrolled her in a sewing class, and she was sold. And it was this method of hers—the pinching of this and that here, that and this there, from cotton to denim to linen, and patterns from polka dots to stripes—that became her signature style. She learned about it on Instagram—it was a whole thing. Since then, trashion has been her passion! Now she prayed it was enough to win her a spot in the fashion show.

As her mother worked the Pond's into the creases at her neck, the steam from the bathroom glowed behind her. "I'll finish up in a sec. You go to sleep."

"Okay—good night."

"Good night, mija."

Maya set the alarm on her cell phone for six thirty a.m., placed it facedown beside her, and curled into the sheets. "Besides . . ." She spoke into the darkness. "You're right, Mama."

"Right about what?"

"If I don't get it this year, there's always next year."

Silence. Except for Luna snoring.

"Mama? Did you hear me? This is when you say, 'Yes, mija, definitely.'" Maya swore she could hear her mother swallow.

"Sí, mija," she said at last.

Well, that wasn't exactly encouraging, Maya thought, fighting sleep. And just as she closed her eyes, she spotted a quick-moving shadow. Her mother, making the sign of the cross. Her mother. Carmen. Her only family in the world. The two of them finished each other's sentences, ate halves of the same sandwich, shared clothes, sunglasses, sneakers, sometimes makeup on special occasions. They even shared the same dream: to open their own shop one day, not just a tailor shop, but an actual label. They'd need to come up with a good name. . . .

The next thing Maya knew, it was morning. On the kitchen counter was a plateful of scrambled eggs and a slice of buttered white toast, a wicker basket full of pan dulce beside it. Her mother had already left for her appointment. Appointment for *what?* Maya wondered.

2

The Finalists

"Maya! Hurry up!" Lisbeth called from Maya's doorway.

"One second."

"Mira vos, that's what you said five minutes ago."

"I can't find my lucky scissors—you know I can't go to school without them."

Lisbeth paused. "You know, I never realized how creepy that sounds." Then she laughed. "Have you looked on the roof?" She stepped inside and immediately checked herself out in the framed mirror hanging on the wall. She had the best eyebrows in all of Zona 7, thanks to the fact that she spent hours working on them.

For once, Lisbeth wasn't being sarcastic. As small as Maya's house was, it had a secret doorway in the bathroom. It was a trick door, because although it looked like a closet, it wasn't. It led to a staircase that spiraled to the roof, and from there, you could see the whole neighborhood. The wide paved roads and uneven sidewalks. The few palm trees that never dropped coconuts—at least none that Maya had ever seen. And the entire colonia, the rows of pastel stucco houses adorned with black iron bars over the windows, looking like eyelashes thick with mascara. In the distance stood the skyscrapers that marked downtown Guatemala City.

"Maya!"

"Okay, okay. I'll look for them later."

Lisbeth was right. Lisbeth, who was practically a sister. Not that they looked anything alike. Maya was short, with thick black hair down to her butt, whereas Lisbeth was tall and slender and had curly hair that had its own agenda, which was why it was usually braided, loose or tight, depending on her mood.

Now they linked arms and speed-walked to the bus stop. On the corner, a woman with white hair tied in a bun, wearing a hoodie, a long skirt, and sneakers, called out, "¡Atole de elote! ¡Atole de elote!" A line of five people were already waiting for the sweet corn drink the woman was ladling into Styrofoam cups from a pot balanced on a crate. The steam swirled around her wrinkled face, and the sugary smell tugged at Maya.

Lisbeth read her mind. "No time. Come on!" She pulled at Maya's elbow.

As the bus bumped its way through morning traffic, Maya stared out the smudged window at a woman who balanced a wide basket full of red and orange mangoes on her head, walking toward the market. Another lady held a tub full of magenta carnations individually wrapped in plastic. Maya's abuela always said that women carried the country. No joke.

It'd been her grandmother who'd introduced Maya to the world of fashion—well, sewing. Abuela never wasted a single scrap of fabric. She'd use even the leftover slivers, to make little pockets inside handbags, or to crochet flowers or sweet brooches she could attach to anything—purses or lamps or pillows, a headband, backpack, scarf. Maya had a distinct memory of her grandmother sitting by the lamp one evening, creating a ruffle by carefully rolling a piece of pink felt from one end, slip-stitching the layers together along the bottom edge as she rolled. In the dim light Maya saw little flashes firing from her hands, the needle moving this way and that under the lamp. It was harmony, the way her grandmother pressed and rolled and pressed and rolled. And before long, she handed Maya a pink rose. Magic. And then Abuela's constant cough morphed into cancer and she passed away three years ago. Maya and her mother cried all through the forty-eight-hour vigil, and when it was time to close the casket and say goodbye for real—the ceremony had taken place waaaaay high up on the mountaintop in San Marcos—Maya stuck a tiny pincushion she'd made, in the shape of a strawberry, her grandmother's favorite fruit, inside the casket so she could take it to the afterlife.

The bus stopped abruptly, jolting Maya back to the present. They were finally at Salomé Fashion Institute. Maya and Lisbeth elbowed their way off the bus and practically flew up the stairway. By the time they reached the top—it was steep!—Maya's quads were burning. But in just a few minutes, they'd know!

From street level, the school looked pretty grand. Three

stories high, it sat beside a movie theater that was converted to an auditorium for fashion shows. The all-girls school was the most modern Maya had ever attended; it had the best bathrooms, and the fanciest classrooms, with smart screens instead of whiteboards. If she hadn't gotten a scholarship, there would be no *way* she could have attended this school. When she and Lisbeth turned fourteen and, like all Guatemalan teenagers heading to secondary school, had to decide what they'd study—prelaw, premed, education, dentistry, computer science, graphic design, business . . . the list went on—they hovered around the idea of fashion. Lisbeth could afford it, no question. She had an aunt in Mexico City—crazy rich—who sent her family money all the time, not only on birthdays and Christmas. But Maya and her mother, not so much. Then her mother found out about the scholarships, and that was that. Sort of. Keeping up with the courses was no problem, but whereas Maya pulled out notebooks and pencils from her backpack to take notes, most of the other girls slid out iPads with sleek digital pens. But with Lisbeth by her side, Maya was just fine. Notebook or iPad, she was *here*.

Inside the main hallway, a crowd had already formed by the bulletin board. Judging from the nervous whispers, Maya could tell that señora Guerrero, the director, hadn't posted the list yet. And what if Maya's name *wasn't* there? Maybe last night her mom had just been trying to prepare her for the possible disappointment. She always told Maya, "You want something, mija. Get it. It's yours. I couldn't have it, but you can." Mama was fully on board; she believed in her daughter. And she worked so hard to pay for the part of the tuition that the scholarship didn't cover. She was also a wizard with a needle, but she was usually so wiped after spending the day behind a machine in the factory that she didn't want anything to do with sewing once she got home. Even still, some evenings, she hemmed pants or stitched bags for customers in the neighborhood. Every stitch meant another centavo. Maya helped too.

"Ladies!" señora Guerrero called out, snapping everyone to attention. La directora was waltzing down the corridor, heels click-click-clicking, waving a sheet of paper.

"¡Ay, Dios! ¡Ya me muero!" Manu, who'd transitioned last year and was one of Maya's favorite classmates, whisper-yelled.

At least thirty others made way for la directora like the parting of the Red Sea. Prayers and little squeals filled the air. Lisbeth gave Maya's arm an excited little pinch. Señora Guerrero adjusted her emerald-green-rimmed glasses and cleared her throat importantly before pinning the paper onto the corkboard. Why couldn't she have just posted the list online? This was so . . . old-school. And dangerous! Everyone pounced forward, and the list instantly fell to the ground. Just as quickly, señora Guerrero moved away from the frenzy. Eventually one of the girls managed to pick up the paper. Lisbeth!

"Everybody, quiet!" Lisbeth bellowed. "I'll read it out loud."

Señora Guerrero's eyes went wide. She opened her mouth to say something but must have changed her mind, for she spun and retreated to her office.

Maya's chest rose and fell.

Lisbeth yelled, "Quiet!" once more, and this time everyone

listened. Then she began reading the names. "Angela Vira-montes ..."

"Yes! Thank you, God!" Angela gasped.

Her friend hugged her. "¡Ay, Dios!"

Lisbeth paused, a hand on her hip. "I'm only going to keep reading if you are *all* quiet. I mean it. And save the prayers. This is not church, okay?"

A few girls laughed. But Maya only had room for one emotion right now: *fear.*

Lisbeth went on. "Diana Pérez." She raised a perfect eyebrow. They were all silent. Well, silent-*ish.* Diana made fists and did a little dance with her shoulders, whispering, "Yes-yes-yes!"

"Ana Mendez," Lisbeth read next, her voice flat. No surprise there. Her father donated a ton of money to the school. Every year he had VIP seats at the fashion show. Ugh.

More names. *Lucia ... Flory ... Gabriella ...* Until it was clear there was only one more name to be called. Lisbeth twisted her mouth the way she did when she wanted to tell the truth but was finding it very difficult ... and Maya knew she hadn't made it. But then Lisbeth lifted her chin and practically screamed, "Maya Silva!"

Maya covered her mouth. Maya Silva. That was her. She was on the list. She was on the list!!!!

But that meant Lisbeth—biting her lips, face gone pale—hadn't.

The paper swished to the floor. A few girls actually began to cry.

Maya approached Lisbeth in the now thinning crowd.

"Hey," Maya said carefully.

"Hey," Lisbeth said. She gave a sad little shrug.

"I'm sorry—"

"Congratulations." They both smiled. "No, really. You deserve it, Maya. I'm happy for you."

Maya reached in for a hug. "Oye, thanks." Relief swept over her. Maybe this didn't have to be weird after all.

"Let's get some air before class, yeah?" Lisbeth made a beeline for the concrete steps leading to the front entrance. Maya followed.

Then silence. Awkward silence. Maya felt *so* bad for Lisbeth, she had no idea what to say.

"Ana Mendez? Really?" Lisbeth said at last, not even trying to keep her voice down. "Her designs are so . . . basic."

"I know, right?"

"No—like, does she have *any* original ideas? She copies everyone else. Remember the dress with the diamond cutout above the belly button? She only made that dress *after* Rosa Sánchez made a dress with a rectangular cutout in the same place. Like, who does that?"

"Ana Mendez does, I guess."

It was enough to make them laugh. Even if it was a wilted one, it was still a laugh. And that was something.

"Hey, you wanna go off campus for lunch today? Get something at San Martín?" Lisbeth asked.

Just the thought made Maya's mouth water. The sesame loaves and the glazed donuts and the cinnamon rolls. Mmmm. But that bakery was sooooo expensive. She could get a dozen pieces of pan dulce at her neighborhood bakery for the price of one croissant at San Martín. El Centro bakeries with El Centro prices.

As if reading her mind, Lisbeth offered, "My treat. To celebrate!"

Maya grinned. She really did have the *best* friend. "Okay," she said. "Let's go. I'll meet you outside after third block?"

Lisbeth smiled. "You got it."

Maya sat through the next few classes feeling electrified. It was almost impossible to concentrate. She'd made the list. She'd made it! She sent Mama a text, but oddly, got no response.

After third block, she passed a kaleidoscope of bulletin boards on the way to the bathroom before meeting Lisbeth. Tacked-up posters announced everything from upcoming sessions—Pattern, Drapery/Folds, and Portfolio Prep—to a flyer about a women's weaving cooperative called Trama Textiles, whose mission was to create work for fair wages for the women of Guatemala. *Everything* looked interesting—she had made the list!

On the way back out of the bathroom, Maya reached for the door just as it swung open, hitting her smack in the face. The pain was blinding—she staggered backward. When the pain subsided and she could see again, who was there but Ana Mendez.

"Ay, I'm so sorry!" Ana cried out.

Maya managed to blink. Was she bleeding? She touched her eyes, nose, mouth. No blood, thankfully. But her forehead throbbed. She already felt a knot swelling. Great.

"It's okay." Maya forced the words out.

"And—hey! Congratulations on making the list!"

"Thanks." Maya looked down at her ballet flats, saw Ana's four-inch wedge sandals. "You too—"

But Ana wasn't done. "Especially," she went on, "because, well, you know, you're a scholarship student."

Maya shot her a look. "What's that supposed to mean?"

"Nothing! Oh no—I didn't mean to . . ."

Didn't mean to *what*? Was she implying that Maya was like, a charity case? Maya cleared her throat. "I am. And I work really hard and try to come up with *original* ideas." She couldn't help emphasizing the word *original*.

"Even if you use trash," Ana said matter-of-factly.

"Exactly."

"And that's really something!"

It seemed *Ana's* talent was insulting Maya and then immediately complimenting her.

"Anyway, I gotta go." Maya squared her shoulders. She'd rather win on her own merits any day. "I'm happy for you, Ana. Good luck at the show," she added, and slipped by her, out the door, resisting the urge to cross her fingers.

She wasn't trying to be snarky. She really wasn't. It was just that it was hard to accept backhanded compliments from someone like Ana. Maya's father—if he were alive—would never have tried to influence people like Ana's father did. Her mother had always emphasized how ethical Papa was, how he believed deeply in right versus wrong, almost to a fault. Actually, *to* a fault. A deadly one. Maya knew the story by heart, how he'd been walking with a friend to a fútbol game. Mama was six months pregnant with Maya. And this guy on a bike cruised up and tried to rob them. Her father tried to reason with him. The man pointed to Maya's dad's wedding ring. Her father kept talking about how the man could turn his life around—there were people who could help him—and then, the man fired twice. Her father died right there on the street, with his ring still on his finger. Maya has seen the ring on a ribbon inside a baby sock in her mother's bureau.

Nope. Her father would have wanted her to win on her own merits.

Outside, Maya breathed deeply to shake the memory. The smells emanating from the food trucks, already setting up for lunch even though it was only ten o'clock, were knee-weakening. Sizzling carne asada and peppers and onions, layered with diesel fumes and the bundles of fresh wildflowers being sold out of plastic buckets along the sidewalk. She looked for Lisbeth—probably near the ice cream truck. And yep. There she was—with some guy? A guy in tight jeans with holes at the knee and a long-sleeved shirt. His hair was spiked with gel, and his sunglasses hid the top half of his face. Who *was* he? And Lisbeth, she was totally flirting with him.

"Hey." Maya tapped her on the shoulder a little hesitantly. "Ready to go to San Martín?"

The guy looked over, didn't bother introducing himself. So Maya didn't either.

Lisbeth did that twisty mouth thing again. "Oh . . . oops, well, we just bought some ice cream." The man at the cart was indeed holding out a Styrofoam cup with one strawberry scoop and chocolate sprinkles. And *two* spoons. Okay—clearly Lisbeth knew this guy. It wasn't like she'd be sharing ice cream with a total stranger.

"Maya—" Lisbeth began.

"Who's . . . this?" Maya didn't mean for her question to have such attitude. Okay—yes, she did.

"Who am *I*? Who are *you*?" He took off his sunglasses. His eyes looked bloodshot.

"This is Oscar." Lisbeth put her hand on his arm. A tattoo peeked out from around Oscar's wrist.

Maya caught Lisbeth's eye. *Oscar?* How had she not mentioned an "Oscar" before?

"And this is Maya. My oldest friend in the world," Lisbeth went on. Maya held her stare, waiting for more.

Oscar gave a short nod, then took the container from the cart dude and began eating the ice cream like someone was about to take it away from him. Then he suddenly said, "What did the French teacher say to her student?"

"Um—what?" Maya glanced at Lisbeth.

"It's a joke." He paused, spoon in midair. "I'm auditioning for a spot in a comedy show. Here, actually." He gestured toward the movie theater beside the fashion institute.

"That's where we met," Lisbeth explained. Met? When? Ten minutes ago? Obviously, Maya was going to ask her a zillion questions later, and that was just one of them.

"I think I have a real shot, you know. But you have to try out first. So, what do you think?"

"Think about what?" Maya felt like she had entered an alternate reality.

"What did the French teacher say to her student?" Oh, wow, he was serious.

"I don't know," Maya said hesitantly. "What did the teacher say?"

"The student doesn't know. He can't understand her!" He laughed and laughed and shoveled in another huge spoonful of ice cream.

Lisbeth laughed too. "You're stupid." She play-punched him in the stomach.

Whaaaa? Okay, she definitely met him more than ten minutes ago. "That's . . . kinda funny. Anyway, I'd better just eat at school," Maya said. "Later."

Oscar grabbed Lisbeth's hand.

"Maya—I'll text you!" Lisbeth said cheerfully.

Maya took the steps back up to the school in twos. At the top, she pivoted to see Oscar whisper something to Lisbeth, who cracked up, her hand on his chest.

3

Maya's structural design teacher was drawing shapes on the whiteboard, reviewing the principles of balance, proportion, and emphasis. Maya took notes, careful to capture every detail, forcing herself to concentrate on the importance of contrast and how to achieve it within a range of designs. Her mind kept drifting back to Lisbeth putting her hand on Oscar's chest. She took her phone out and checked for a response from Mama about the big news. Nothing. So strange. Then Maya sent a quick text to Lisbeth without the teacher seeing.

???

give u deets later ☺

lol

xo

The buzz of Lisbeth's reply caught everyone's attention, so Maya put her cell on silent and scooched forward in her chair. The teacher then began talking about the relationship between the physical structure in a given piece of clothing, and how contrasting visual elements could be intensified depending on the shape of the garment. Again, Maya's mind drifted. But this time toward an idea. She could showcase up to three looks at the fashion show. She had plenty of designs, of course, but what *else* could she dream up? And in two weeks, no less? In the margins of her notebook she sketched and sketched and came up with—a corset top. What could she use to make it structurally interesting? Coffee filters, chip wrappers, newspaper. No, no, no. A corset required something sturdier. Cardboard, maybe?

"Maya?" the instructor asked. Shoot! She must have asked a question!

"Present," Maya said instinctively. Everyone laughed. Her cheeks burned.

"I suggest you pay attention, señorita."

Just as Maya was saying, "Sí, señora," she heard a girl in front of her whisper, "And *she* made the list." The friend made a *pffft* sound.

Maya shot them a dirty look. Lisbeth would say they were just jealous. Two years ago, when the school offered Maya the scholarship, the admissions letter mentioned how they had seen great promise in her work. *That* was what mattered.

On her way home, Maya planned to head right over to Lisbeth's after dumping her bag. Texting wasn't going to do it. She needed every last drop of the story. How did she and Oscar actually meet? Did he walk up to her? What did he say? And when? Her thoughts bumped this way and that as she stepped around oil stains on the cracked sidewalk, past the man in the baseball hat selling fresh orange juice from a rickety cart underneath the shade of the few trees left in her colonia. Then—ooof!

"*Oh, I'm so sorry!*" Maya cried. She'd bumped into a woman carrying a big woven basket on her head. A few dozen chuchitos tumbled out, and Maya immediately knelt to help the woman pick them up. The corn-husk-wrapped bundles were still warm.

"Está bien," the woman assured her as they popped each chuchito back into the basket. None had unfolded—the señora had skills.

"Thank you for your help," the woman said as Maya brushed her knees off. "And don't rush, mija. Remember, you shouldn't pick fruit before it's ripe." With a wink and a smile, she handed Maya a chuchito before moving on down the sidewalk.

"Gracias . . ." Maya held the little tamale in her hand. The warmth spread through her palm like a gift. Wait! That was it! She quickly unwrapped the chuchito and examined the corn husk, massaging the material. She would use corn husk to create the corset. *Perfect.*

Maya ran to catch up with the woman. "Please, can I buy ten?"

The woman's eyes went wide. "Really?"

"Yes, please." Maya handed her a twenty-quetzal bill. It was an entire week's worth of side sewing jobs, but . . . the corn husks—it was a great idea, she just knew it.

The woman, ecstatic, balanced the basket on one knee.

Then, licking her fingers, she pried a plastic bag from a bundle hanging on her belt and placed ten chuchitos inside. She tied a knot at the top and handed it to Maya with a flourish. "A la orden, señorita. God bless you."

"Thank you! You too!" Maya ran the rest of the way home, floating from the news of the fashion show and now this discovery. Chuchitos!

She instantly went to work, Lisbeth forgotten. Hands practically quivering, she unwrapped the corn husks from each chuchito, placing the tamales tucked inside on a plate. The corn husks she lay flat on the kitchen table to see what she was working with here. They would need to dry before she did any cutting. Where *were* her lucky scissors when she needed them the most? She'd look again later; right now, she was in the zone. She arranged and rearranged the corn husks, making mental calculations, thinking about which direction the fibers of the husk would stay sturdiest. She heard her mother turn the key and walk into the house. Maya glanced at the clock—she'd been doing this for two hours!

"Ay, mija! You're home. Gracias a Dios." Mama made a cross over her chest, like she did every time she came into the house and saw Maya. Wisps of hair hung into her face; worry spread like a mist around her.

"Love you, too," Maya said, her fingers sticky with fabric glue. She'd just started dabbing dots of glue onto the edges of two corn husks to make a larger piece of fabric.

She watched the tension fade from her mother's face. But it was never fully gone—especially considering all that had been happening in the colonia lately. A kidnapping. A shooting.

Even people they knew. Like Juan Morales, who lived just a few avenues over, murdered. A gang shot him in the back. The bloodstain was still there on the sidewalk, and the memorial cross that someone—probably his mother—had taped to the lamppost along with purple carnations was still there as well. The petals had wilted long ago.

Maya's mother scrunched her nose. "Why does it smell like chuchitos in here?"

"Long story." Maya wiped her hands on a rag and gave her mother a kiss on the cheek. Then she reached for her sweatshirt on the kitchen chair. Wow. Just thinking about Juan Morales had made goose bumps sprout on Maya's arms. And lo and behold—underneath her sweatshirt, her lucky scissors! Maya held them to her heart.

Mama cocked her head in curiosity, then sat and took off her shoes. "Mija, be careful with those scissors," she said, as she changed into her slippers.

"So, you clearly haven't read my text . . . ," Maya began in a cheery voice.

Her mother's face went bright, her eyes even brighter.

Maya could barely hold in a telltale grin. "Yup. I have some good news. . . ."

"The show! You're on the list!"

"I'm on the list!"

And then they were jumping up and down, hugging. In these moments her mother felt more like her sister, and Maya loved it. Good news turned on her mother's happy energy so high it seemed to light the whole world. Like last week, when she'd found the one-hundred-quetzal bill she thought she'd lost in the wash when really it was just tucked in her bra. You'd have thought she'd won the lotería.

Pulling the calendar off the wall, Mama grinned mischievously, flipped one page, and circled the date with a red pen. Two weeks! Maya let herself feel a shimmer of excitement.

"Which of my designs do you think I should show? I can choose three. Or should I make up all new ones? The pantsuit, no? Or maybe the exposed-zipper jean dress? Or this new one here I just started; it's why it smells like chuchitos—"

"Definitely, definitely, you should show the pink frilly quinceañera dress. You already have that one made, anyway. You can then focus on creating the other ones. You don't have a ton of time, mija. Am I allowed to help?"

It was sweet of Mama to offer, but no, it was understood that parents—or anyone—weren't allowed to help the finalists. Not that Mama had any free time. She was working so much lately; her last gig nearly wiped her out: a wedding dress for a wealthy family's only daughter. Besides, Maya *wanted* to work on her designs. The quince dress was her favorite—she'd made it from plastic tablecloths. "Ooh. You think so?"

Her mother nodded with certainty. "Absolutely. It's one of your signature looks."

"Maybe I could fluff it up more? Add a hoop petticoat or something—make it more dramatic, you know, for the runway?" See, she *had* paid attention to the structural design lesson today.

"¡Eso!"

This was just the beginning for them; Maya could feel it in her bones. She'd gain exposure from the show and build her portfolio and who knows, maybe they could get hired by a trade designer or finally open up their own shop or—

Her mother interrupted her thoughts. "What about Lisbeth?"
Maya nearly flinched. Shook her head.

"Okay. Well, así es. She can still be happy for you, right?"

"She is! But you reminded me—I should check in with her."

"Vaya." Mama looked around and took in the pile of
chuchitos. "I'll heat up dinner and then you can tell me the
grand plan"—she pointed at the spread of corn husks on the
table—"behind these."

Maya texted Lisbeth.

So, tell me everything!

His name's Oscar.

☺ I know.

I really like him.

When did u meet him?

After school last week when u were
with ur mom

. . .

Maya?

I'm happy for you.

> And I'm happy for YOU! You made the list!

They'd always been honest with each other. Like the time Lisbeth had gotten blond highlights that were overbleached and she ended up looking like a skunk (sorry, it was true). Maya had told her exactly that, even if it hurt. And Lisbeth had cracked up—she thought so too!—thanked Maya, and went straight back to the hair salon. They trusted each other. So Maya took the plunge.

> I just don't get why you didn't tell me before today

> Honestly—didn't know it would last this long

> It's been a week lol

> I know—just . . . it all happened so fast

> Oye, vos—it's cool. Just, next time, tell your most favorite friend in the universe.

> . . . you got it

> Hey—will u be one of my models?

> Of course! ☺

> Great! Talk later. Dinner w/ mama

Maya didn't tell Lisbeth that she'd gotten this . . . sketchy vibe from Oscar. She knew it would sound judgy, but some guys just gave off the wrong vibes, she thought as she started gathering her materials off the kitchen table.

Her mother placed a hand on Maya's back. "I was thinking we could eat on the roof, before it gets dark."

"Sounds great." Maya loved eating outside. Plus, she wanted to tell her mother about the corset idea.

They carried warmed-up chuchitos and water bottles up the secret staircase to the roof, where a little table, beside two beach chairs that were always open, waited for them. Pink-streaked sky, the smell of wood burning in the distance, and her mother beaming at her—Maya still couldn't believe she was on the list!—it *was* like a little celebration. She could hear señora Hernández on the street below calling, "¡Patojos! Hurry up!" to her grandchildren for dinnertime. The bells of a slushy cart tinkled not too far away. As the sun dipped lower, it bathed Maya and her mother in an orange glow. Her mother bit into a soft chuchito, an S of steam curling around her beautiful, lit face.

Then what sounded like a gunshot went off in the distance. Her mother went rigid. For a long moment, they moved not even a centimeter.

"The situation, mija . . . ," her mother began.

The situation. Maya groaned. She'd grown up hearing about "situations." Always a "situation." The economic situation. The political situation. The gang situation. That was the one Mama meant now. Gangs were slowly taking control of colonias near and far. They had started demanding money from people in some of the neighborhoods—simply to be able to come and go without harassment. The ones who didn't pay up were sorry. Plenty sorry. A family from the next neighborhood over, the Padillas, had refused to pay, and so the maras literally took their front door. As in, they removed it entirely. And when señor Padilla replaced it, the maras took it again. This went on until señor Padilla gave in. He could not keep replacing doors; it was cheaper, in the long run, to pay. And the Padillas were some of the luckier ones. They lost a door, not a limb, or a loved one.

And, of course, there was Juliana.

It had been over a year since Maya had last seen her. It'd been at Maya's favorite corner tienda, the one with a painted yellow curb, the wobbly plastic table with mismatched chairs, the ones you could sit in only if you bought something. It was where Maya would hear all the good gossip, mostly delivered by Lisbeth. That was where she'd been sitting, sharing a bag of TorTrix chips, coconut candies, and a Big Cola with Lisbeth, when out walked Juliana, who was, like, the sweetest girl *ever*. In primary school they all used to play hair salon together— even attempted to start a business when they were nine years old, but then a girl at school got lice and that ended that. Maya had lost touch with Juliana since then; she attended a different secondary school. Then, about a year ago, Juliana started hanging out with a marero, a gang member. Pretty soon Maya had heard she was skipping school, and more and more often, when Maya *had* seen her at the park or the mall, she looked spaced out, stoned.

So—the last time she saw Juliana, she was coming out of the tienda, holding a Coke, her hand shaking. She'd waved hesitantly to Maya and Lisbeth as her boyfriend loped after her. He'd cut his eyes toward them, spat, then hopped on his motorcycle, revving it. Maya had felt totally awkward, no idea what to even say to Juliana anymore. But as she passed them, Juliana had unexpectedly offered Maya a stick of gum. "I remember how you always chose gum as your prize on Fridays in school," she'd said.

Maya did remember that. It surprised her that Juliana had too. The motorcycle engine coughed black smoke right into their faces. "Juliana!" the guy barked. Lisbeth covered her ears.

"Coming!" Juliana had said quickly, almost urgently, pressing the stick into Maya's hand.

"Thanks." Maya took in Juliana's dyed blond hair, its perfect blowout, nothing like the double French braids she'd worn as a kid before their hair salon idea.

Juliana swung a leg over the back of the bike, tucked herself against her boyfriend. Waved once more. Maya slid the gum into her bag for later.

"Well, that was weird," Lisbeth had said after Juliana and her boyfriend left in a roar.

"Beyond," Maya said.

A week later, Juliana went missing. A few days after that, her kidnappers, who apparently were part of the most notorious gang in Guatemala, demanded a huge ransom, or else ... So her family handed over the money and saved her—*thank God*—and then sent her to a private school in Costa Rica.

And maybe a week after *that*, Maya found the gum she'd

forgotten about inside her bag. A pang arrowed through her—
Juliana—she'd been so nice to give it to her. Maya was about
to throw the gum out. Then, at the last second, she opened the
foil. When she did, her heart stopped. Written in pen inside the
wrapper: AYUDAME. *Help me.*

Mama cleared her throat. "The situation, it's getting worse,
mija—"

Maya cut her off. "I know, Mama." Obviously she knew, but
what was she supposed to do except stay focused on school
and stay out of the gangs' way? Which she did. If only Juliana
had . . . No. Maya shook her head. It wasn't fair to think that
way—it wasn't Juliana's fault.

And now, Mama nodded, but the look on her face meant she
had more to say. They ate quickly, Maya fast-forwarding Mama
through her corset idea, the celebratory mood broken. Maya
could tell her mother was listening for the next gunshot. Truth?
So was she. They were back downstairs five minutes later. As
Maya prepped coffee and pan dulce, their nightly tradition,
she thought about that gunshot. Who had it been aimed at?
Who pulled the trigger? And why? Her mother brought over
the mugs, back to beaming happily at Maya, her good news
of the day. Maya wrapped her arms around Mama, giving her
a big bear hug. Even after a day's work, she always smelled
sweet, a mix of honey and toast.

Later, though, as she dried the dishes, Maya couldn't get
Juliana out of her mind. What if Maya had stayed in touch with
her after primary school? She thought back to what her mother
had said about Lisbeth. A true friend would feel happy for her

friend. So maybe Maya should give this Oscar guy a chance. She could at least try. Even if his jokes weren't funny. Like, at *all*. Still, something gnawed at her. She couldn't stop her mind from comparing Juliana and Lisbeth. . . . And *that* wasn't fair; she knew Lisbeth was smarter than that. And she couldn't assume Oscar was a marero. Fair or not, though, Maya was going to find out, just to be certain.

4

12 Days to Go

The next morning Maya was ready to ask Lisbeth for major details about what she liked in Oscar. Only, she didn't have the chance. Lisbeth texted to say she wouldn't be taking the bus, that Oscar was picking her up. Well, now Maya had some extra drawing time. Plus, she decided she'd head to school an hour early each morning until the show. Every minute and every stitch counted!

The studio was quiet, peaceful, as she sketched an oversized belt that she could use to accessorize one of her dresses, then made a list of items she might use to construct it with—paper plates, chip wrappers, socks whose partners had been lost in the dryer. Maya loved the studio. She was given free rein to work on her designs and got to use all the equipment the school offered—including iPads she could sign out, with cool fabric simulation apps like Digital Fashion Pro and Drape.

She had studio first period as well (Lisbeth did too—where was she?), so Maya gathered up random fabrics and materials, held them to the light, and massaged them between her fingers, trying to figure out which would be best for the belt. She was in the zone. She couldn't tell if five minutes had passed or fifteen.

"Helloooo? Maya?" Lisbeth slid into the seat beside her, holding a coffee. "Wow, you're super focused."

"Hey!" Maya put down a piece of corduroy, lowered her voice. "Tell. Me. Everything. Does Oscar have a car? Or a motorcycle? Spill, girl."

At that, Lisbeth lit up. "A car. Tinted windows. And the stereo system! Mira vos, you really have to come with us next time."

"I don't know if he'd want me tagging along—"

"Sure he would! He's actually supersweet. Last night I told him how my stepmom was on my case about not making it into the fashion show—she literally brought up the price of tuition, vos. Saying how it's too expensive for someone not serious about fashion."

"Noooo . . ." Maya felt instant fury. Lisbeth's stepmother was always pulling BS like that.

Lisbeth nodded slowly. "Yeah. Thankfully, my dad shut that conversation down. But you know my stepmom. She's not exactly . . . subtle. So—I told Oscar all about it, and he offered to drive me to school. And he bought me this!" Lisbeth raised her coffee, the scent of caramel syrup making Maya want a sip. Lisbeth knew her so well, next saying, "Try it!"

It was as good as it smelled, Maya thought as Lisbeth

proceeded to download all things Oscar. Still, a question tugged at Maya: Why hadn't Lisbeth told *her* about her stepmom?

Lisbeth went on and on about how Oscar couldn't stop kissing her, even in public. The way he sent her a good-night text and a joke before bed . . . "And he graduated from high school last year in San Lucas and now he works fixing computers. Helps his brother, who has a tech job or something like that. I guess his brother is *really* good with computers and he's trying to teach Oscar everything he knows. They turned their garage into, like, a little computer café. They have beanbags and little mesas and everything," Lisbeth explained.

"Cool." Now Maya was starting to feel guilty that she'd judged Oscar so quickly. *Lisbeth is not Juliana. Lisbeth is not Juliana.* Then, "Hold up—you've been to his house?"

Lisbeth whisper-squealed, "Yes!"

Maya glanced at the clock. They'd been talking so long that there were only twenty minutes left of studio. "Oye, I have to look over my notes for an exam I have next period. You?"

"Design II. Where I'll apparently be wasting away tuition quetzales," Lisbeth said, a wisp of hurt clouding her face.

"Lisbeth . . ." Maya lifted her backpack.

Lisbeth drained her coffee, aimed the empty cup at the wastebasket, and—perfect shot—tossed it in. "It's fine, for real, for real. But anyway . . ." She switched to a teasing voice. "Oscar has a friend."

Maya dropped her backpack on her foot. "Ow! A friend?" Okay, she wasn't going to get any studying done right now.

Lisbeth nodded, beaming mischief. "He wants to meet you. His name is Sebastian."

"Por favor."

"What? Come on, Maya. He's cute."

"Cute like Oscar's funny?"

Lisbeth cracked up. "Mira vos. Seriously. I've seen a picture of him. Live a little!"

Maya's cheeks flushed. Thing was, she didn't actually know how to "live a little," at least when it came to guys. Whenever she met a guy her age—at the mall or the carnival or a fútbol game—her voice always seemed to disappear. Literally every time. It was pathetic. And yeah, it was a sore spot. And Lisbeth knew it.

"Sorry. Never mind." Lisbeth picked up a piece of lint on the table and massaged it into a little ball. "I just thought we could all hang out together."

Maya quickly reconsidered. Yes, she had to work on her designs, but this way, well, she'd get to hang out with Lisbeth, and—okay, she was going there—she could keep tabs on this Oscar guy, and . . . *and* what if this Sebastian guy was actually okay? "Fine. How about we meet up at the corner tienda after school?"

Lisbeth shrugged. "Oscar *hates* corner tiendas. He says they're so basic. Like only little kids with crushes hang out there."

"Okaaay. How about the mall? Or is that too 'basic'?"

"Oh, come on, Maya. Don't be like that."

"I'm not being like anything." She shoved the jumble of fabrics back into the clear plastic bins where they were stored. Put her notebook in her backpack.

"We could go to his house . . . to the computer café . . ."

"No way. I don't know him like that."

"All right." Lisbeth twisted her mouth. "Well . . . you know what's not basic?" The bell rang. Maya started walking toward the door.

"Your roof. Maybe . . . we can all come over after school?"

Maya's mouth fell open. Her mother would *kill* her if she had guys in the house. Especially guys she barely knew. But Lisbeth was her oldest friend . . . and that flash of hurt across her face just now . . . But, no. Nope.

"Your mom won't be home, right?" Lisbeth made a pouty face.

"No . . ."

"Porfa, Maya? We don't have to hang out too long. Just, like, half an hour."

"Half an hour," Maya repeated, the words escaping before she could take them back.

Lisbeth pounced, a green light. "¡Eso!" She gave Maya a fist bump as they both left the classroom. "I'll tell Oscar. Gotta run to class!" When the second bell rang, she jogged down the hall, phone already out.

Maya stared after her, her throat tight. No taking the offer back now.

She'd been home not even ten minutes and already changed three times—kept her black leggings but swapped her button-down denim shirt for a more fitted red T-shirt with a scoop neck, then back to the denim shirt over a black tank top, then finally landed on a flowery halter top that showed off her shoulders and her tan. Cute, but not thirsty cute. Then she cleaned up the morning dishes and scraps of fabric on the kitchen floor. The mattress was secure behind the couch, good.

They would only be inside for a few seconds before heading up to the roof, so technically it wasn't like she was having boys *over*. Not *really*. Her phone pinged. Lisbeth. They were already here!

"Hey," Maya said, opening the door. Impossible, but Oscar's hair seemed to have even wilder spikes. And he had on another long-sleeved shirt despite it being, like, boiling out.

"Hey." He stepped inside without an invitation; Maya had to move out of the way or he would have walked right into her.

Lisbeth was all smiles, her hair in loose waves, so pretty. *Be happy for your friend. Be happy for your friend.*

"Maya! This is Sebastian," she said, all singsong cheery, jokingly tugging the arm of the other guy in the doorway.

"Come in," Maya said, nudging Lisbeth. What if a neighbor saw?! She quickly closed the door behind them.

Only then did she get a better look at Sebastian. Like Oscar, he also wore ripped jeans and sneakers, but his red T-shirt (good thing Maya had changed!) with some graffiti design in English on the front, was short-sleeved. He had thick eyelashes and was more built than Oscar. Okay, he *was* cute. Okay, truth. He was *really* cute.

"Maya, right?" he asked. His voice sounded nothing like Oscar's to-the-point, snappy one, an inflection there she didn't recognize.

"Hi," Maya said. It was all she *could* say.

Luna nosed out from her spot under the sewing machine.

"Who's this?" Sebastian knelt right down, held a hand out. Luna gave it a sniff, then a lick. "Aren't you a friendly girl," he said, happy all in his voice. He picked Luna up; Maya barely believed it. Luna, a totally reserved cocker spaniel, never let anyone other than Maya or her mother hold her. And now . . . Luna was trying to lick Sebastian's chin.

"Aw . . ." Lisbeth cooed.

"Let me hold it," Oscar said, yanking Luna out of Sebastian's arms. Startled, Luna yipped and snapped at Oscar's hand. Maya reached out, but Oscar fired out, "Ow!" like it was a swear and dropped the dog before Maya could grab hold of her. Luna scrambled to the corner, trembling.

"What the hell?" Maya bolted toward her, but she refused to come out.

"Nice, pendejo," Sebastian said to Oscar.

"Whatever, Dog Whisperer."

Lisbeth laughed, but it sounded forced. She tucked herself into Oscar's arm.

"Sorry," Oscar mumbled. "You know—I used to actually be afraid of dogs. For real! One bit me when I was a little kid, and after that I would run and hide whenever I saw one."

Maya tried to imagine Oscar as a boy hiding behind his mother's leg.

"Really . . ." Lisbeth kissed him on the cheek. He kissed her back. Within seconds they were making out.

Sebastian stepped toward the sewing machine, La Betty, and slowly ran his thumb along the knobs and wheels. Maya watched as he gently twisted a dial and returned it to its original setting. He leaned in and stared at the spool of thread and needle clamp with such intensity that she felt like she was interrupting him when she asked, "Do you sew?" Her heart was beating so fast she swore he could hear it.

With that same intensity, he took her in—not her body or her face or her apartment, but *her*. Finally he stood up and said, "No."

Maya caught her breath. Who *was* this guy? Already, he seemed so different from Oscar. Already, she wanted to know him more.

"It's crazy, though. That, like, clothes come from this little needle, this . . . what do you call it?" He picked up a spool, and Maya instinctively reached for it. Their fingers touched and she blushed.

"Carrete de hilo?" she asked, tilting her head.

"Carrete de hilo," he repeated. "Yeah, I don't know that phrase in Spanish."

Maya was going to ask more and more and more, but Oscar practically yelled, "Hey, you guys wanna check out my new stand-up opening? I'm gonna start like this. Maya, you listening?" As if a minute ago he hadn't nearly killed her dog.

"What? Oh, um, yeah." Ay, no. Not another joke.

"I went to buy camouflage pants . . . but I couldn't find any."

"Wow," Maya heard Sebastian murmur.

"Get it? They're camouflaged so they were hard to find," Oscar went on, raising his eyebrows.

"Is this when I laugh?" Maya said. She didn't mean for it to come out rude, but at that, Lisbeth and Sebastian genuinely laughed. Maya felt a little rush of adrenaline. But Oscar scowled before saying, "You got anything to drink?"

He'd taken off his sunglasses and was now checking out the place. Her place. Her home. He stared at the framed photograph of Maya's parents on their wedding day, the one where their arms were linked as they sipped champagne. When Oscar touched it, Maya's shoulders tensed.

"I'll grab some water bottles," Lisbeth offered.

"And I wanna go check out this roof I've been hearing so much about," Oscar said. Would her roof live up to his expectations? And did she even *want* him seeing it? Damn, why had she opened her big mouth in the first place?

"Go on up," Lisbeth told Maya. "I'll be right behind you."

Luna stared at Maya balefully from the corner.

"Yeah, sure." Maya looked away from Luna and led them through the bathroom to the secret door, up the spiral staircase.

At the top, Oscar put his sunglasses back on and lifted his face to the sun. "Wow. Nice view!"

Sebastian peeked over the edge.

"You scared, hombre?" Oscar fake-pushed Sebastian, and Maya gasped.

Oscar turned to her. "You know he's my cousin?"

"Really?"

"Yeah. This pendejo was just deported. Tell her."

"I was just deported," Sebastian said in a deadpan voice.

"No," Oscar said. "Tell her for real."

Lisbeth arrived with the water bottles like she was their personal waitress. Oscar sat in one of the beach chairs and pulled her onto his lap.

"Sorry . . . You were . . . deported? From where?" Maya asked, distracted.

"Los Estados." That explained the slight accent. And why he didn't know the term for "spool." Sebastian pointed out across the roof to the north, as if he could see his previous home from here. "San Jose. It's in California. I was only one when my parents crossed. Never got my papers. The laws kept changing and it just got harder and harder, you know? So now I'm back." He reached for a bottle of water. "Thanks," he said, twisting it open.

California! What was it like in the United States? Was the rest of his family still there? Was he going to try to go back? How? Everyone had heard stories—on the news and in the colonia— about people riding trains or what people called La Bestia north through Mexico. Hiring coyotes to cross them over the border, or trying on their own. Stories of people carrying nothing but a backpack full of canned tuna and bottles of water, surviving in the desert for days. Or not. Drowning in the Rio Grande. She found herself suddenly worrying if Sebastian could even swim when Lisbeth murmured, "Stop!" Maya glanced over—Oscar was tickling her; Lisbeth was squirming and tickling him back.

This she couldn't watch, so she turned to Sebastian.

"So, how long have you been back?" she finally asked, her voice, miraculously, working.

"Like two months. Too long." He hesitated. "I mean, I guess it's all right here and all. It's just, I never got to say bye to anyone. My dad. My friends. I was playing basketball with them one afternoon, and the next morning I was in a detention center. By the end of the week, I was gone. They took my phone, everything."

"You miss home?" Maya bit her lip. Obvious question.

He took a sip of his water. "Of course."

"Now he's stuck here," Oscar added, looking over, sounding almost happy about it. "Like a real cabrón."

Sebastian took out his phone and recorded the view. Then

he snapped a few pictures. "What's your number?" he asked. "I can send these to you."

"Well, I see you got a new phone." Wow, she was excelling at stating the obvious.

"Yeah."

They punched their numbers into each other's phones.

"Maybe my cousin isn't such a pendejo after all," Oscar said, cracking up, his arms now tight around Lisbeth's waist.

Maya watched for Sebastian's reaction when suddenly they heard sirens. Oscar stiffened. "Oof!" Lisbeth yelped. Maya imagined flicking him off the rooftop if he ever hurt Lisbeth, and the very idea made her smile, until the siren's wail grew so loud she could tell it was on their street. She peeked over the wall. A police SUV was roaring up the street and—what?!—was stopping right in front of the house. Oscar practically slithered to the deck. Sebastian crouched as well, fitting his body behind the low wall that surrounded the rooftop.

A moment later someone pounded on the front door. "Open up!" an officer yelled. Maya and Lisbeth exchanged terrified looks.

"Señora Pérez! Open up!"

Señora Pérez? She lived two houses down. Relief and worry wrestled inside her. Relief won. They weren't looking for her. Or for her mother. They were at the wrong house.

Maya leaned over the wall and, in a wobbly voice, called down to the officer. "Wrong house. She lives in the yellow one." She pointed to the left.

The officer glared at Maya. Said nothing. Drove two houses down. Banged on *that* door.

They all sat frozen for another minute, Maya guilt-stricken—had she caused señora Pérez harm by pointing out her house? What did they want with her? She was the kindest woman in the colonia. Finally Maya said, "You guys should probably go."

"Fuck yeah. We'll be back, though." Oscar tapped Lisbeth's butt and reached for her hand to help him up.

Sebastian popped up easily. "Later," he said to Maya.

Ironically, only after they left did Maya start trembling. She hoped señora Pérez was all right. And what was up with Oscar and Sebastian? They were totally spooked.

That evening Maya sat on the couch and sketched versions of the quince dress with different petticoats. The fabric was the issue here—she needed something that wouldn't pucker the plastic tablecloths. As she sketched, she watched a home makeover show with her mother, one of their favorites, even if it was in English. It was the one where people are given a brand-new house, people who had their homes trashed in hurricanes or something like that. Yet Maya was so distracted by the police pounding on their door earlier that she wasn't able to focus on her designs or the show. After dinner she hadn't turned on La Betty like usual, even when Luna barked at it and then at Maya, willing the two of them to make up. Plus, she kept checking her phone for messages from Lisbeth . . . or (maybe!) Sebastian. She also couldn't help herself—she kept looking at his contact info on the screen—good thing *he* couldn't know how often!

Her mother noticed. "¿Qué te pasa, mija?" she asked, still staring at the screen.

"I'm just tired," Maya lied.

"Sometimes it's good to take a break. But after that, back to work! Así es la vida, mija. Besides, the show will be here before you know it."

Maya watched as the television couple jumped with joy at the sight of their newly remodeled home, complete with a garden and a swimming pool in the backyard. "This is the house of my dreams!" the woman sobbed. Maya had studied English in primary school, but she picked most of it up from watching television. There was never any reason to speak it, but she could understand plenty.

Her mother hit pause on the remote control and turned toward Maya, drawing in a deep breath before saying, "You know, I've been thinking, like the lady on the TV said, about *dreams*. I'm so proud of you for being a finalist, mija. And well, I think we should celebrate and go to San Marcos this weekend."

Hmm. Normally, a little trip didn't sound horrible. Not at all. But maybe instead of San Marcos, they could go back to Xetutul! There was a water park, and roller coasters. But no. Aside from it being super expensive—she'd only ever been there twice in her whole life—she needed to work on her looks for the show. But maybe . . . "San Marcos, Mama? But without abuela? We haven't been back since . . . Well, the last time was the funeral."

"I know." Her mother began braiding Maya's hair. "It won't be the same. But really, I'm ready to go back."

Her mother had grown up in San Marcos. Met Maya's father there. She pictured her parents sharing horchatas and tostadas and walking around the fountain in the main square as they held hands before sitting on one of the stone benches.

"You just want to go because it reminds you of Papa," Maya teased. Then she pictured Sebastian. On the roof. Today. She couldn't help wondering if he'd snuck any pictures of *her* on his phone. Would she and Sebastian ever hold hands?

Outside a car revved its engine and a couple of people started yelling. Mama's breath caught, even though this kind of thing happened all the time. Her mother shifted on the couch, causing Maya to have to shift too.

"What is it, Mama?" Maya's jaw tightened.

"Mija . . . the situation."

Not again with the situation!

"Don't roll your eyes—listen to me. We need to go away for a couple of days. Things are . . . hot around here." She lowered her voice, as if someone was eavesdropping. "People are saying that the gangs are taking over our avenida. So just . . . trust me, okay? We'll go to San Marcos this weekend."

"Hold on. So are we going to celebrate, or to skip town?"

"Shh! Maya . . . let's just say, a little bit of both."

She unpaused the TV and tucked a lock of hair behind Maya's ear, like she used to when Maya was little. "It'll be okay, mija. This is when you say, 'Okay, Mama.'"

Maya sighed. "Okay, Mama," she said, wishing she meant it.

Then she checked her phone for a text, a photo, anything.

No new messages.

5

11 Days to Go

It was only a four-hour bus ride to San Marcos on Saturday, but as soon as they disembarked, her mother changed. She wasn't constantly looking around, eyes darting here and there. She strolled instead of hurry-walked. Even the timbre of her voice shifted, matching the slowed-down accent of the high-lands. She let her hair down, literally. Her mother usually wore it in a braid wrapped into a bun at the base of her neck, but not here. Here, she let it waterfall down her back; she looked ten years younger. They got a small room in a hotel just two blocks from the main square. It was a little more expensive than others farther away, but this way they could walk every-where and not have to rely on taking tuk-tuks. Her mother was always thinking ahead, planning. Which made it all the more . . . strange that she had forgotten to go to the bank before they'd left Guatemala City. Immediately after leaving their bags at the hotel, they had to hunt down a bank where Maya hadn't even known Mama had an account. Maya hated waiting in long lines, so she chose instead to sit on the stone steps outside, facing the park. Moments later, her mother practically floated out of the building, whistling and taking Maya's hand. With that errand settled, she seemed more relaxed than Maya had seen her in, like, forever.

The longer they walked, marigolds dotting the mountain, the more Maya had to agree that it was a nice break from the humid, honking-car, oil-stained streets back home. The air here was crisp, no petrol fumes, no rotting garbage. If she had been keeping score, San Marcos would have just won a point.

Another point? Paches—tamales made from potatoes instead of corn—made only in the Western Highlands. Maya and her mother bought a pair from a local stand and ate as they strolled, checking out the latest shops that had popped up along the main square. Thirsty then, they shared a large rosa de Jamaica drink and people-watched on a stone bench. There were a lot more people wearing traditional Mayan clothes here than in the capital. The cloth was beautiful—her abuela had told her it was usually dyed in buckets or woven on huge wooden looms. Maya had to resist the urge to walk up to someone and touch it. *That* would go over well!

Just as the sky spilled lavender, they found an outdoor restaurant overlooking the fountain. Around them the laughter from a group of kids on the sidewalk echoed and the spicy smell of carnations bloomed. Maya sank back in her chair, wishing she could bottle this all up and take sips from it later, when she needed to remember that the world was bigger than Guatemala City.

She still hadn't gotten a text from Sebastian, but yesterday Lisbeth mentioned that she and the guys might go swimming at a hotel pool in Antigua for the day, and did she want to come? Antigua, the old capital, was only forty-five minutes away, but it felt like another world. *Of course* Maya wanted to go. But after telling Lisbeth she'd be away, Maya avoided texting her: she didn't want to hear about the fun she would be missing out on. She silenced her phone, then scanned the menu.

"Want to split something?" Maya asked her mother. "The hilachas sound good."

"Ooh, or the jocón de pollo!" Her mother sounded like a little kid. "But no, let's each get our own dish. And drinks."

"Really?" Maya peered at her over the menu.

"Really."

So *this* was Mama, not working. Her mother had always worked hard. When she was little, she picked up litter from outside storefronts to earn a few centavos. The tailor shops were her favorite, and soon the owners let her keep the scraps and, once they realized she already knew how to sew, even take on simple jobs.

Mama waved over the waitress, who took their order.

"So you seem to really like it here, mija?" Maya's mother leaned back in her chair.

"Yeah, I do." And she did, but . . . her mother's question . . . Where was this going?

"You know, it's changed since your father and I—"

"Mama? Why did we come here, *really*? Just tell me."

"Did you know back then the Mayas were turned away if they were dressed in their traditional trajes?"

"For real?" Maya actually really liked the traditional outfits, the variations in color tones from the dyes, the looseness or tightness of the wearing depending on the region. She wanted to incorporate some traditional textiles in one of her designs, in fact.

"Here's the truth: the Ladinos—my people—thought the Mayas were inferior because they were Indigenous."

Maya frowned at her. "They *what*?! That's totally messed up. *Papa* was Mayan!"

Her mother nodded. "And I admit," she continued, "I didn't know how your abuela would react when I introduced her to your father." Mama rested her chin on her palm. "But she loved him the moment she met him."

The waitress delivered a cold beer and a tall glass of horchata. Maya lifted the glass to her nose—she loved that first smell of vanilla that wafted up.

Mama took a long sip of her beer. Pulling the wrapper off the straw, Maya dunked it in her horchata and took a long sip as well, absorbing what her mother had just revealed. Whoa. She knew her father came from a village called La Reforma, that he was proud of their traditional Mayan dress, their culture, but it never occurred to her that people discriminated against him.

Her mother looked off into the distance. It was clear she was having a moment. Maya took the straw wrapper and curled it around her finger—first her pointer, then her middle, and finally her ring finger. Her mind drifted to Sebastian, and just as quickly she brushed the thought away. *Get a grip. Maya, you met him once!*

"It's funny," her mother continued at last. "He grew up in an area more remote than mine, but *he* took me to places I'd never been before. Fuentes Georginas hot springs. Volcán Chicabal . . ."

The sky had turned from lavender to a mosaic of orange and pink. Almost . . . almost like the patterning of the Mayan skirts! Across the street a few men and women advertised in singsong voices, "Tamales! Zapotes! Plátanos!" Maya's eyes wandered to the pastel stucco houses along the avenue, some with Bible verses in curly gold font painted on the sides. Wow, they were cute—like house cupcakes. Soon there was nothing left but ice at the bottom of her glass. She rattled the cubes, and only then did her mother blink back tears.

"When I left here for the capital with your father, I don't know who was sadder, me or your abuela."

"I bet."

"But she said something to me I'll never forget."

Maya perked up. She loved when her mother tucked in memories she'd forgotten about until the story called them up. "What?"

"She said, 'I'm always with you, mija. And you are always with me. Así es.'" Then, oddly, she raised her beer. In the distance the sound of a marimba band distracted Maya. "Raise your glass, mija." Then, even more oddly, she added, "To new beginnings."

Umm—Whaaaat? But Maya lifted her glass dutifully. And of course, the waitress arrived exactly then with their entrees! The warm comfort of the hilachas and jocón was an instant distraction—until her mother set her fork down.

"Mija . . . There's something I want to talk to you about."

Maya pushed a spoon into the creamy recado, her appetite

plummeting. She *knew* that voice. It was a voice that was going to try to convince her to do something she didn't want to do.

"Oh, don't make that face," her mother scolded. "Listen. I've been thinking about this. A lot. And we're going to move back here."

Maya's spoon slipped and the tomatoey sauce splashed across the table. "*Here?* To San Marcos?"

"You say it like it is the worst thing in the world. Like—" Mama's voice caught. "Like I didn't grow up here. Like it's not good enough . . ."

"No, Mama! That's not what I mean at all!" Maya said quickly, though not as quickly as her heart was racing. "It's just . . . where is all this coming from? It's, like, totally out of the blue!"

Mama picked up her napkin, began folding it into smaller and smaller squares. "Mira, things here are just . . . simpler. Safer."

Move *here*? The . . . the . . . contest! Lisbeth! Her school! And . . . Sebastian. She forced herself to stay calm. "But Mama"—Maya leaned in as the waitress cleared the plates— "when would you be thinking of moving? What about the fashion show? Plus, what about my school? Starting my own clothing line? With you? We've talked about it since, well, for-ever. Owning our own store someday?" Then Maya's face went pale. "Wait."

Her mother tilted her head.

"You don't think I can make it! That's what this is about!" Maya pressed her fingertips against the table edge to stop their trembling.

Her mother grasped her wrist. "No! Absolutely not."

"You don't think that I can actually do it!" Her voice was attracting stares from other tables, but she didn't care.

The waitress appeared. "Everything okay?"

Maya and her mother nodded.

"Look, Maya Luz. It was just an idea." Mama looked off at the square. A man had just set up his guitar and bass and had begun playing old corridos. "Here's the thing, mija. Sometimes the page is about to turn, and you'd better be prepared when it does."

"I don't understand." *Get to the point, Mama.*

"I mean, mija, that five years ago we didn't have to step over someone's blood on the street, or have our hearts stop when our daughters don't pick up their phones. Just this week the police questioned señora Pérez about her son for so long that she peed her own underwear, through her falda and everything."

Maya twisted her own paper napkin. "Is she . . . okay?"

"She was flustered, that's for sure. They think he's affiliated with one of the gangs."

"Oh my God." More like, *Oh, shit.* It was Maya's fault that poor señora Pérez peed through her skirt. If Maya hadn't told the police her address . . .

But still—*moving?* No joke, this would ruin her life. Maya cleared her throat. "Mama—listen to me. There is *no way* I can leave school right now. Promise me. Promise me we won't move."

"I'm ordering another beer."

"Mama?"

"Where is that waitress?"

"Mama. This is when you say, 'I promise.'"

Her mother reached across the table and squeezed Maya's forearm. "I can't promise, mija," she whispered. "I'm so sorry."

"I can't believe this," Maya said, pulling her arm away. She lifted her fork, put it down, lifted it again.

"There's one more thing, mija," her mother said.

What? What *else* could her mother possibly have to add to this misery mountain she'd just unloaded on Maya's lap? "What?" Maya mumbled.

"I want us to check out a house while we're here."

Maya dropped the fork again, appetite dying. "Mama? Seriously?"

"I've had my eye on it . . . you know, online. But I want us to see it in person. Tomorrow."

"Tomorrow!"

"Come on, mija. This is when you say, 'Mama, I'll go see it, for you. For us.'"

But Maya just slouched in her chair, said nothing. Appetite officially gone.

6

10 Days to Go

The following morning, utter panic woke Maya up. This town—it was nice to visit, but no way. No. Way. She hardly dared say a word to her mother in case her fury spilled out.

"Bueno," her mother said, toward the end of a silent breakfast. "You're mad. I get it."

Maya kept silent.

"But I still want you to see the house. It's a two-bedroom," her mother offered in a sugary-sweet voice, like she wasn't planning to uproot Maya from everything and everyone she knew. "And *afterward*," she said, putting an arm around Maya, "I was thinking we could stop at a textile cooperative I heard about. Local women run it—they sell fabrics, and offer training and even small loans to others who want to learn the trade. Vamos."

Maya considered. She knew exactly what her mother was

doing—bribing her. But they *were* already here. Might as well see it . . . "Fine," she said, her first word of the morning.

A ten-minute tuk-tuk ride brought them to a side street with a row of avocado trees casting glittery shadows on the perfectly paved sidewalk. Her mother paid the driver and practically jumped out of the vehicle, then took Maya's hand in hers. "Oh, the street looks even more beautiful in person," she exclaimed.

Maya didn't let go of her mother's hand. She'd never seen Mama so . . . happy.

"Mija! Look! There it is." She pointed at a pink stucco house with two large oval windows and gorgeous geometric designs on the stained glass that made the house look like it was wearing makeup. What a beauty . . . But Maya wasn't sold that easily. They were so *far* from home.

Still, she couldn't resist asking, "Can we go inside?"

"The real estate agent is away this weekend . . . but we should be able to very soon."

"Real estate agent? Wait—does this have to do with your early appointment the other morning?"

"Maybe," she said, all chipper. "Come on!" She pulled Maya toward the driveway. "We can still look."

The house *was* cute. There was a little driveway, and sunflowers had been planted along the side of it. From what Maya could see, there was a backyard with an old knobbly tree, and a hammock? Oh . . . she instantly pictured herself swaying on it, sketching designs in her book. Her mother busied herself by not-so-slyly taking pictures of the house.

"Don't you love it?" her mother asked, beaming.

"It's nice," Maya conceded.

"Mija, listen—and I mean, really listen."

Maya detected something in her mother's voice that was new. Something like genuine desperation. "I'm not asking you to move to another country." She was back to biting her bottom lip. "I just want you to know that—" Her voice caught. "I'm trying, mija."

"Mama!" Maya hugged her tight. "I know." She didn't like fighting with Mama. Besides, Mama *had* scoped out the textile cooperative.

Which was uh-mazing! *That* she couldn't deny. A swirl of colors and fabrics and spools of yarn and thread and more sizes of looms than she even knew existed! The artisans were selling their handwoven purses, belts, shirts, dresses, aprons, even shoes. Maya lifted a purple-and-magenta purse, admiring the zigzag design in the hand-stitching. She thought about buying it, just to support the women here, but Mama mouthed a polite *no*—the items here were meant for tourists, with their tourist wallets. Instead Maya purchased a bookmark, only five quetzales.

A woman in a long skirt knelt in front of a loom. The skirt's navy-and-turquoise pattern, with flashes of jade-colored threads, was so intricate that it seemed to glisten. She slid the weft back and forth with the grace of a dancer. What if Maya had been born in this part of the country? What if her father hadn't died? What if her parents raised her here, in San Marcos, and Maya grew up embracing her Mayan side? Would she have her own loom? Would she be as graceful with it as this woman was with hers?

Before they left, Maya's mother asked the co-op owner if they were hiring teenagers for part-time work. Was she serious?

What—were they going to move to San Marcos, like, *tomorrow*? The woman wrote down her information on a piece of notebook paper and handed it to Mama. It was sweet, but super-super obvious, what Mama was doing. Did she really think that getting Maya a job at a textile cooperative would make her want to move to San Marcos just like that?

On her way out, Maya picked a strand of bright purple thread off the ground. She massaged it between her fingers, stuck it in her pocket, and rushed to catch up with her mother.

Mama was now suggesting they visit San Simón.

"Who's that?"

She laughed. "The statue. The deity. You know, your father actually took me to visit San Simón when we were novios," her mother said matter-of-factly.

"He did?"

"There weren't malls to go to, you know. We had to come up with interesting things to do on dates."

"So he took you to see a Mayan god?"

"Yeah. Come on."

Along the edge of the hill, there were arrow-shaped signs pointing toward a small gray house. Wooden crosses were decorated with faded pink and yellow ribbons fluttering in the wind. A line had formed outside the house. One woman stood super close to a man, both their heads bowed. What was this place? As if reading her mind, her mother explained. "Mija, people travel hundreds of kilometers to come here. You can tell San Simón your problems." Her mother looked away. "Or ask questions." As they joined the back of the line, she added, "And then you pour a trago of rum down his throat."

"You *what*!"

"Or offer him a lit cigarette, or whatever you have. He likes these things; San Simón enjoys a good time."

Well, this was a different kind of saint, Maya thought.

"Or you can just light a candle for him," her mother added. "Say a prayer. Vamos."

As they inched their way forward, Maya saw inside. It was mostly dark save for the glow of dozens of candles on a table, and before she knew it, it was their turn. They crossed the threshold and moved toward a fake skeleton. (Or were they real bones? Yikes!)

"This is San Simón," Mama said, almost as if introducing him to Maya. She stepped backward as her mother stepped forward.

Was this weird to say about a saint? But San Simón looked . . . stylish. Maya kinda wanted to give him a thumbs-up for his fashion sense. A black cowboy hat, dark sunglasses, a red hand-kerchief tied over the bottom of his "face," and a jean jacket about five times too big for him. After all, he wasn't even skin and bones—he was just . . . bones.

Mama hesitated before saying, "Mija, why don't you meet me outside?"

"Oh—sorry. Right." Her mother wanted a moment alone with the Mayan god. Got it.

A few minutes later, Mama came out of the building, and her face looked pink and puffy. "What's wrong?" Maya asked.

"Nothing." Mama took her hand. "C'mon, time to get the bus."

On the ride back to Guatemala City, as her mother's head began to nod sleepily, Maya reached for her phone; she needed to fill Lisbeth in on *everything* from the last thirty-six hours. That was when she saw she'd missed five calls from Lisbeth. And a series of texts.

> Maya! Why don't u pick up?? Big news! BIG news! Directora announced that the prize for fashion show went up. BIG time.

Maya could barely read fast enough.

> More prize money. AND . . . the winner will get to sell their designs in LA FÁBRICA!!!!!!! I know, right?!?! OMG. You HAVE to win! SELL ur designs, Maya! This is major major. Like, you could really start ur label with this. I'm so happy for u. Now u have to win! Lol

> Call me when u get home
> Hope ur having fun in San Marcos
> xoxoxo

Maya's mouth filled with saliva, like she was going to throw up. She and Mama couldn't move now. They just couldn't. The detail about La Fábrica took her over the edge; it was the best fabric store in the whole capital! She crossed her arms and sank into the seat.

It was almost dark when they finally reached their street. A crowd of guys was hanging out at the corner, three houses down from theirs. Slicked-back hair, tattoos up and down their arms, and girls in high heels hanging on those tattooed arms. Drinking beer and smoking. One guy had a high ponytail, the sides of his head shaved. A gang sign tattooed on his skull. Mareros. Gang members. Maya thought immediately of Juliana. . . .

"Don't look at them," her mother yell-whispered. She gripped Maya's hand so tight Maya thought her fingers might snap. Mama fumbled with the keys. But just as they pushed open the green door to their home, Maya couldn't resist. She looked back. She could see him clearly underneath the full moon, with his spiked hair: Oscar, in a white tank top, revealing all the ink on his body she couldn't have seen when he wore long sleeves. His hands were raised, as if he were in the middle of telling a joke. And standing right beside him, offering a little wave, was Sebastian. Just days before, he had been standing on the roof, her roof, with his broad shoulders and dark eyelashes, taking out his phone and aiming it left, right, and center. And he did it again now.

And what she was seeing sank in fully. Oscar was in a gang. Did Lisbeth know? No . . . No way could she know—she'd never . . . And wait!! This also meant Sebastian was too! He knew where she lived. He had pictures of her roof. Was this why he'd taken so many photos, to show the other members? To claim their street in the turf wars? Mama had said the gangs were taking over their avenida. . . . Or . . . or, what else? *Flash.* Maya blinked. More pictures. *Flash.* Then Sebastian aimed right at Maya and her mother. *Flash.*

7

Maya, knees quivering, locked the door behind her, fingers so shaky it took three tries before she heard that satisfying *click*. She knew it was futile. If Oscar wanted to barge into the house, he could do so easily, with or without the flimsy lock.

"Maya?" Her mother's voice surfaced above the thrumming of her heart.

Maya turned hesitantly. Her face would tell the whole story. Her mother would read it and she'd know everything. How she had had Oscar and Sebastian up on the roof just days ago, and they would want to—demand to—hang out there again. She just *knew* it. Maya pictured the marero who had the sides of his head shaved, searching in Maya's refrigerator, helping himself, little Luna whimpering in the corner. No. No!

"Maya!" This time the word was like a slap to her daydreaming. More like daymare. Was that even a word? Nightmares didn't only happen at night.

Her mother touched her shoulder. "Mija, you've gone pale. ¿Qué te pasa?"

Think, Maya. Think! "Oh . . ." She searched for words that if strung together could make sense. But nothing made sense right now. Then, out came: "I just saw a rat—as I closed the door!" The lie came easily—Mama knew about Maya's rat phobia. The mere sight of one made her literally light-headed.

With that explanation, her mother muttered about *all* kinds of rats in this neighborhood now, and busied herself with unpacking and heating water for instant coffee.

"I'm going to take a shower, Mama."

"Vaya, pues. Put your dirty clothes in here," her mother said, handing her a plastic grocery bag. "We'll do the wash tomorrow."

"I will," Maya assured her. As she ran the water in the bathroom, she texted Lisbeth.

> we need to talk

No response.
And no response.
And no response.

The next morning Maya checked her phone before she even sat up in bed. Still nothing. Her mother had already left for work. The smell of a fried egg lingered in the air. She had to tell Lisbeth about Oscar! Would Lisbeth stop seeing him? *Could* Lisbeth stop seeing him? What if he wouldn't let her? Again, she thought of Juliana. Oh God. Maya's stomach lurched. She also needed to tell Lisbeth about the *major bomb* that Mama had dropped—moving. To San Marcos. Maya sent Lisbeth another text.

See you at school I guess . . .
I'm going in early

At her workstation, Maya cut scraps of denim fabric to layer onto the zipper dress, then draped them over the dummy. She worked right up until the first bell, checking her phone every few minutes. When there was still no word from Lisbeth, she half expected someone to run up to her with the news that she'd been kidnapped, or worse. Her head dipped low, Maya stepped into the hallway toward her locker. If anything happened, it would be on Maya. She had had a funny feeling about Oscar. She should've told Lisbeth to be careful. No. She should've *demanded* that Lisbeth be careful.

Then, a shriek.

The knot in Maya's throat tightened.

Then, laughter.

Lisbeth!

"Maya! There you are!"

Maya felt dizzy with relief. Lisbeth was barreling down the hallway toward her, wearing a new cheetah-print dress and black suede belt. A little much for a Monday, but Maya did dig the energy of the print. And she liked how Lisbeth paired the dress with white Converse.

"Lisbeth! You're alive!" Maya hugged her so tight that Lisbeth coughed.

"Yeah, so don't kill me, vos."

"Sorry . . . I just . . . Oye, Lisbeth . . ." She had to get a grip. "Lisbeth, we need to talk. For real."

"Vaya, pues. But why so intense? Are you okay?"

Just then, Manu strolled down the hallway, wearing a gorgeous green tulle skirt and navy-blue halter top, and paused in front of Maya. "Here," she said, handing Maya a little Post-it: *You got this.*

"Thanks, Manu," Maya said superfast, tucking the note into her jeans pocket as Manu approached others down the hall. Then she pulled Lisbeth by the elbow into a nook in the hallway. "Come here. Listen to me, okay? Este . . . Oscar . . ." How was she supposed to tell her? *Oscar is BAD NEWS. Oscar is a marero.*

"Oscar!" Lisbeth flashed a saucy smile. "Oscar bought me this outfit. Head to toe."

"He did?" Of course he did! He knew just how to get to her!

"Yeah, don't you love it?" She did a little twirl. Two girls walking down the hall looked in her direction, approval sealed in their smiles.

"Supercute. But listen—last night when my mom and I came home from San Marcos, we ran into Oscar and Sebastian."

"Really?" Lisbeth adjusted her belt.

"Yeah, they were hanging out with a bunch of . . ." Maya leaned in close and whispered, "Mareros. Lisbeth—they're in a gang. I saw Oscar's tattoos and everything." She lowered her voice even more. "Plus, Sebastian kept taking pictures of me and my mom. I'm kinda freaked out. . . ." She pulled back and let Lisbeth take in the information. It was a lot, Maya knew.

And she would be there for Lisbeth. They'd get through this, together.

Except, Lisbeth merely blinked, dug in her purse, pulled out lip gloss, of all things, and offered it to Maya. Was she freaking kidding?

Maya waved it away. "Did you hear what I said? Like holy shit. Juliana was *kidnapped* because of her marero boyfriend."

Lisbeth opened the jar and applied the sparkly pink gel to her lips, taking her sweet time. Only after she was done did she say, "I already know."

The bell rang. Within seconds they were the only ones left in the hall. But no chance Lisbeth was getting away with this three-word response. Maya pulled her deeper into the nook.

"Mira vos, calm down." Lisbeth gave her a *chill out* look. "He just happens to be in a gang. His brother's been in it for years, so it was just something they did together. It's not like they run around killing people, Maya. Remember I told you—they're good with computers. It's not always like it is on the news. Or like"—she lowered her voice to a whisper—"Juliana. For real, it's more like they all just like to hang together. Have each other's backs, you know? 'Cause of the *gang* gangs out there."

Maya leaned against the wall. What was she supposed to say? *Oh, okay then. He doesn't kill people, not like, daily. So he's a good guy.*

"*Please*, Maya. Just give him a chance? Oh, and Sebastian was asking questions about you all weekend. He kept wanting to know when you'd be back." Lisbeth nudged her knowingly.

"Really! But then why didn't he just text me?" Maya cocked her head.

"Maybe he was scared, vos."

"Of me?"

"Girls!" a voice interrupted—the school director, yikes! "Get to class *now*."

"Sí, señora," Maya and Lisbeth answered in unison.

As they hurried down the hall, Maya low-voiced, "Truth. I'm worried about you!"

"Don't be. You'll see. Come hang out with us after school."

"I can't. Mama and I are going to do the laundry."

"Tomorrow, then. Promise?"

"Girls!" the school director warned.

"Fine," Maya mouthed. "And hey—answer your texts!"

"Okay, *Mom*!" Lisbeth said, all light and airy, looking cute, like nothing had changed, like they'd just been discussing a movie they'd watched, before disappearing into a classroom.

Maya stared after her. She hadn't even told Lisbeth about Mama's major announcement. Maybe she wouldn't need to. Maybe Mama had just been all in her feelings in San Marcos. Tonight Maya would double down on working on her show pieces—Mama would surely see how important it was to her!

But in class, her thoughts kept swinging back to Oscar and Lisbeth. And shit yeah, Sebastian too. He hadn't *seemed* . . . How was she supposed to focus on the lecture, but never mind . . . But could Lisbeth be right? Maya supposed there *were* different types of gangs. Maybe not *all* of them were the kind that Juliana's boyfriend was in.

Class was a blur. The next class was too. After school, as Maya and her mother did the wash, all she could think about was the way Lisbeth had said so casually, "I already know."

Which made Maya think, what else did she already know?

8

8 Days to Go

As promised, Maya met up with Lisbeth at the bottom of the concrete steps after school the next day. As much as she'd sworn to herself that she'd sniff out more about Oscar—God, just thinking about it made her buzz with nerves—she also couldn't stop thinking about one other detail that Lisbeth had shared: Sebastian had been asking about her. How could these two feelings live beside one another—fear and curiosity? What did Sebastian want to know, exactly? And she couldn't stop smiling just thinking about it. Then got mad at herself for it.

And then there he was, with Oscar, leaning against a car, a red Audi with windows tinted dark as charcoal. A cigarette dangled from his lips as if it were a part of his body, another limb, loose and lazy. Could he really be tan malo? Like, he wanted to be a stand-up comedian! This spiky-haired dude with thin fingers and a bad sense of humor—was she being fair, judging him when she hardly knew him? She hated people who were so judgy—so llena de cosas. Maybe Oscar and Sebastian were in a gang because they liked being part of a group that protected one another. Everyone was in danger these days. They had each other's back. So could it be so bad? *Okay, Maya—give him a chance, for Lisbeth.*

That internal argument settled, Maya focused on Sebastian. His hands were in his pockets, his shoulders arched, just slightly, enough to give off the impression that maybe, *maybe*, he was . . . nervous too? To see Maya again? Her skin tingled. *Get a grip!*

"Hey!" Lisbeth broke away from Maya and practically flew into Oscar's arms. The cigarette plummeted to the ground, but Oscar didn't seem to mind. He instantly wrapped his arms around her, lifting her up as she giggled.

Maya took a deep breath. She could do this. And Sebastian was standing right in front of her and she had to say *something*.

"Hi," she managed brilliantly, while purposely avoiding Oscar's gaze.

Sebastian broke into a smile. "How was San Marcos?" he asked, running a hand through his hair.

"It was okay." Maya uncrossed her arms, tucking her hands into her pockets. She could smell Sebastian's cologne. Or maybe it was his deodorant. Or just him. No matter what it was, it smelled really good. Maya chose to overlook the fact that now he stared at his phone and not her, that he was scrolling as he listened—half listened?—to her.

"Oh yeah?" he asked, eyes on his screen.

"We went to this great restaurant. And then we visited a textile cooperative, actually. And this skeleton. San Simón."

At this Sebastian looked up.

"It's a long story," she said quickly.

Oscar and Lisbeth were all up on each other, not caring that other girls from school were eyeing them as they passed by, or that any moment a teacher might step out of the building. Not that hanging out with your boyfriend was against the law. But still. Maya *did* notice that Oscar had on another long-sleeved shirt.

"Here," Sebastian said in response. He handed his phone to Maya.

Maya paused—was it the picture he'd taken the other night? Perfect. Now she could ask him what was up with *that*.

Maya squinted down at the screen, angled the phone to get a better view. It was . . . a video? "What is this?"

Sebastian grinned. "Just watch."

A YouTube video. A fashion show. Women walked the runway, wearing looks Maya could only dream of designing—a massive fur coat draped over a model in a neon-green bikini, another, naked save for a thong and purple paint all over her body up to her neck, and finally, a male model wearing . . . was that a onesie? Like babies wore?

"Hey, this is cool." Maya could not stop looking at the screen. And she could not stop being hyperaware that Sebastian stood a breath away from her, and, yeah, wanting him *closer*.

He stood a little taller. "I thought you'd like it. It's this school in New York; it has some killer fashion shows. Lisbeth said that you're a finalist for the fashion show here, right?"

Maya couldn't help it; she blushed. "I am." He was still *so* close.

"That's cool. Maybe we can watch the whole thing some-time?" He lifted his phone. "You know, for inspiration?"

Thoughts jangled against each other—the most dominant being that she *had* to be wrong about him. This so wasn't a guy who caused trouble.... "Definitely." She blurted the word as she looked up, right at him. He held her stare. Tiny flecks of amber in his eyes. A trio of freckles on his right cheek. But Oscar—he was definitely in a gang. And Sebastian hung with him. Gah! She needed to know. Had to know. She dropped her voice to a whisper. "The other night . . ."

He flashed a smile. "What about it?"

Maya dug for meaning behind that smile but came up short. God, he was cute. *Focus, Maya.*

"Those guys you were with—are they like, well, who you hang with? Are they—are you . . . ?"

He tucked his phone back in his pocket, still kept looking her in the eye. "You can say it. A gang."

She glanced toward the school steps, as if the school director could hear her from deep inside the building.

Sebastian laughed. "You're so funny. What are you, like twelve?"

Ouch.

"Sorry—I didn't mean it that way," Sebastian added quickly, "it's just that, it's not a big deal. For real, almost every guy I know is in a gang or has a brother in a gang or is about to be recruited to a gang. You know this, right?"

"I don't have any brothers."

"Wow."

"No, I mean it. I guess I don't . . . totally get it."

"Get what?" Lisbeth asked. She and Oscar had finally come up for air.

"Nothing," Maya said quickly. "Fashion. We were talking about fashion."

Oscar placed his hand on Lisbeth's waist. "Whatever. Hey, let's go do something."

Lisbeth eyed Maya, the question in her expression bright as lights.

"Okay, sure," Maya agreed, then turned toward Sebastian. "But, a question: Why were you taking pictures of my mom and me?"

He blushed. He actually blushed. "I was taking pictures of you. Just you. But I had to make it look like I was taking pictures of both of you. Otherwise, the guys . . ."

Of *her*? Just *her*? Her breath caught. Recover! Say something, Maya! "So, that fashion show," she spouted, gesturing at the pocket holding his phone. "How 'bout we see the rest?"

From the open window in the back of the Audi—the guys were in front—Maya could see Ana Mendez walking down the sidewalk. Ana's mouth fell open. Her expression said, *Huh*. Maya had never hung out with a guy around school like other girls did. But Sebastian—she could already tell—wasn't just any guy. She thought about what he'd said about the gang. *It's not a big deal*. And yeah, all right, it had to be almost impossible not to touch the web of mareros in the city. Everyone *did* have a brother or a cousin or an uncle . . . and yeah, tons of them were in gangs. Or working for gangs. She thought about it—it must suck to be a guy. Like, what if you weren't in a gang but they still gave you a hard time—what then? She could see how joining one could be kind of the safer option. Still, Maya decided she should stay shadow-close to Lisbeth.

Oscar turned up the music—Bad Bunny—and the stereo system seemed to be coming from somewhere inside Maya. She could feel the bass in her thighs, between her legs, in her heart. Lisbeth nudged her. Maya nudged back. As they drove around the capital, Maya didn't care where they were going. She wanted to stay in this cocoon of a moment, let the music reach up to her throat and tingle her ears and forehead, forget for a moment that her mother was thinking of yanking her out of the capital to move to San Marcos because of "the situation" at home. She refused to dwell on what her mother would say if she could see Maya right now.

They pulled into a gas station, Sebastian getting out to pump gas while Oscar went inside to pay. Through the tinted window Sebastian checked out his reflection, and then lingered, as if he could tell Maya was watching him. Which, of course, she was.

Lisbeth clicked her tongue. "I knew it—you like him!"

"No, I don't!" Maya protested like a little kid. She remembered what Sebastian had said about her acting like she was twelve years old. It stung.

"Yes. You do. Maya, I can tell when you're frustrated with a design, when it's that time of the month, and when you have a crush. Remember Eric Coronado?"

"Ha! I can't believe you remember that. That was like, three years ago! And he gave me his old Carlos Ruiz fútbol jersey. How could I *not* crush on him?"

"Well, if his family hadn't moved north . . . I'm just saying."
She winked.

Maya's ears burned. Eric was the first boy whose hand she'd
held. If they'd stayed together, maybe, eventually, they would
have kissed. Maya had never kissed a boy. Yes, she was sixteen.
No, it wasn't a point of pride. But maybe . . . maybe that would
change soon.

When Sebastian hung up the gas pump and swung open the
front passenger door, he didn't get into the car. "Hey," he said
to Lisbeth. "Trade spots with me."

Maya couldn't keep from blushing.

"I knew it," Lisbeth mouthed as she swapped places.

Sebastian climbed into the back, his right knee almost touching Maya's left one. His scent was . . . everything. She adjusted
her seat belt, and as she did, tried to nonchalantly inch to the
left, a bit closer. When Oscar came back from paying for the
gas, tucking a fresh pack of cigarettes into his jeans, he broke
into a rarely seen grin.

"Ha! ¡Cabrón!" he said as he slid into the driver's seat. Then
he handed Lisbeth a package of coconut candies—her favorite. She squealed in delight. *Huh*, Maya thought. He blasted
music. Maya felt like she was floating and floating and floating.
Besides, she'd talk to Oscar eventually. Ask him about how
involved he was in the gang, for real. She'd get to it all later.
But right now, all that mattered was . . . right now. And when
Sebastian reached out his hand and placed it over hers, right
now mattered even more.

9

Way too soon, Oscar was parking on a side street a few blocks from Maya's house. She went from floating to landing with a thud. Her neighbors couldn't see her crawling out of a car with two guys! Like those old-fashioned operator systems, the news would travel fast as lightning right back to Maya's mother. But actually, the street—really more like an alley—was empty. It certainly smelled like an alley—a whiff of garbage and urine lingered in the air. She'd never noticed this tiny street before. She looked over her shoulder as Oscar tucked the car keys into his back pocket and then used another set from his front pocket to unlock a gate.

Go in.

Don't go in.

Maybe it wasn't too late to turn back. Maya tried to catch Lisbeth's eye, but she was too busy adjusting a false eyelash with her pinky. Maya could leave right now, say something about an errand she had to run before her mother came home from work. . . . But then she spotted Sebastian trying to pat flat a stubborn piece of hair on the side of his head, and she realized he actually *was* . . . nervous. It was sweet. He wasn't acting like a player, that was for sure. So she took a deep breath and walked through the gate.

Oscar gave a quick look, left, then right, then knocked on an iron door three times, paused, then knocked four times, paused, and finally, five times. A secret signal. Maya looped her arm into Lisbeth's uneasily. What if this was how it'd started with Juliana? Simply hanging out after school one day, before . . . *Stop*, she willed herself. *Get out of your head. Porfa.*

A guy dressed in a gray hoodie—even though, yeah, it was burning hot out—answered the door. He and Oscar shared a complicated handshake, and then he repeated the same with Sebastian. To Lisbeth and Maya, he simply lifted his chin.

"They're cool," Oscar said, pushing his way inside. "Come on."

Maya couldn't help it. She looked behind her—the gate she'd just walked through was already locked, and soon the door would be too. The irony was that she was so close to home. If something happened to her and she screamed, maybe señora Pérez would hear her. But people in the colonia had a way of not hearing what was none of their business.

"Quit being paranoid," Lisbeth whispered to Maya.

"I'm not!"

Inside, Oscar led them through a maze of stucco-walled hallways, all painted a sea green, all dark except for a few barred windows, granny-style lace curtains dangling crooked from long rods. What was this place? Down another hallway and through a door and boom—they entered a big garage that had been converted to . . . a lounge? A row of desktop computers sat on top of three folding tables pushed against one wall. Bean-bags and a sofa and a couple of recliners (which had seen better days) formed an L shape in the middle of the space, facing a massive flat-screen TV. Christmas lights lined the perimeter of the ceiling. When Oscar flipped a switch, they sparkled in green, red, blue, and yellow, and the whole garage transformed into something almost magical.

"Qué cool," Lisbeth said, and pulled his arm. "See?"

"It was a great idea," Oscar admitted, and gave her a light slap on the butt.

Sooooo—the Christmas lights were Lisbeth's idea? How many times had she been here? And could he *stop* with the slapping-her-on-the-butt thing?

Sebastian offered Maya a cold bottle of Coca-Cola. "Want one?"

"Definitely." As she took it, their hands brushed past each other. Sebastian motioned for her to sit on one of the couches. The flannel pattern was hideous—yellow and maroon—but it wasn't like she was going to *wear* it, so she sat down, hoping Sebastian would do the same, like in the car. Instead he settled into an armchair perpendicular to her. At least this way she could look at him without sneaking glances, take in his tan face and dark hair and again—those eyes. Already she had it bad, dang. Oscar and Lisbeth had abruptly vanished—probably to some other room. Talk about having it bad.

Sebastian leaned forward. "So, your designs. How do you come up with your ideas?"

Maya crossed her legs, uncrossed them. She needed to answer! But she couldn't help it, she needed to ask more about the other night. "Oh, you know. Life, my neighborhood. So— you and Oscar—you guys are pretty close, huh?"

"Yeah, I even designed half his tattoos," he said, scootching closer to her. "Nice way to change the subject, by the way. Real subtle."

"Ha!" She took a sip of soda. He was *so* close! Be cool, be cool. Her gaze then wandered to the one poster, of a red Ferrari, on the otherwise bare walls. And then to the mini fridge in the corner. How long had he and Oscar been hanging out here? Who did this place belong to? Was this Oscar's house? Where were his parents? Did he even have parents?

Sebastian leaned in even closer. What she would give for a piece of gum. She took another sip of Coke, the taste of cold sugar spreading on her tongue. "So, do you, like, live here? And do— other people?" She looked down at her cuticles, so dry. Sewing did that, as well as leave little nicks everywhere on her fingers.

He pointed toward the ceiling. "I live with Oscar and his parents, upstairs."

Parents? Maya hadn't expected that. She pinned them as orphans, living off takeout in Styrofoam containers. She'd seen on the news how lots of mareros just took over houses and then threatened landowners or government officials if they tried to make them leave or punish them.

"Yeah. What did you think? Oscar was born from mules?"

She laughed.

"Look, I know he seems rough," Sebastian went on, "but don't be so hard on him. He hasn't had an easy life."

"I didn't think—I mean—"

"Don't tell him I told you, but . . ." He dropped his voice so low Maya had to move even closer. "His father doesn't actually live here anymore. He's in prison. Don't ask me for what. And his mother could barely survive without the father's income, so Oscar and his brother, Martín, joined a low-key gang to help out, you know? And then after I was deported, they took me in. Even though they can barely make ends meet. But, family."

"Claro," Maya said. Suddenly the maroon-and-yellow couch looked . . . different. She wanted to reach out and touch the fabric, as if apologizing for judging how ugly it was.

"Yeah, his father and my mother are brother and sister. I mean, were."

Sebastian said *were*. *Ask him about it? Don't ask him?* Luckily, he kept talking.

"But, honestly, Oscar's mom went to a bad place when my tío was taken away—basically, she lost it. Some days she barely leaves her room. Just watches TV all day. She'd barely eat if Oscar and his brother didn't bring her food."

"That's—" Maya was going to say, *That's not what I pictured.*

"Yeah, I know. That's not what you pictured, huh?"

Maya scrunched her nose. It was like he was in her head. In a good way. "Sorry?"

"I get it. But the thing is, we're not all like the mareros you see on TV. Honestly, we help out the more hard-core guys with computer stuff. And we let them use this garage for, let's say, business deals."

"Business deals?" She told herself to stay chill, but this didn't sound good. These "deals" could be about drugs or guns or . . . worse—and now her brain went into overdrive!—women being sold into sex slavery! She wanted to get the hell out of there. But which door? She came in from the left, but what if she couldn't get out fast enough? And what about Lisbeth? She took a deep breath. Maybe the "business deals" were more like computer and finance stuff. Maya was for sure going to ask him, but not when she was trapped inside their garage.

"Are you going to repeat everything I say?"

Maya dipped her head. He couldn't tell what she'd been thinking this time. Good, good. But she needed an excuse to leave. With Lisbeth.

But then he said, "It's okay. It's cute."

So she asked, "Tell me about the tattoos."

"Oh yeah. So, back when I was in San Jose, I'd send Oscar designs and he would bring them to his tattoo artist."

"How do *you* come up with *your* designs?" Maya asked, focusing on his face, especially his eyes, instead of "business deals."

Sebastian bolted up, a flash of happy in those eyes. He left the room, was back a minute later with a sketchbook.

"Let me show you." He plunked down beside her. Previously well-mannered tingles now fired throughout Maya's body. She put the bottle of soda on the floor as he opened to the first page.

It was a color explosion, every drawing oozing, almost alive, as he flipped from page to page. A one-eyed gorilla spewing glittery fumes from his nostrils. A man in a gold top hat playing three saxophones at once. A pink tree with glistening green mangoes that looked to be on the verge of dropping to the ground.

"How did you do *that?*" she asked, pointing at that one. "Make them look . . . heavy and swollen, like they're actually about to fall?" Damn. He was every bit as good as the best artists at school.

"I don't really know. My hand just . . . draws." He leaned in even closer. Air. She needed air. No, she didn't. She needed this moment to freeze in time, like the drawings themselves. He was *so* close to her now that if she turned a centimeter to the left . . .

As if reading her mind, he shifted his head toward her. But he wouldn't kiss her. It was obvious he wanted her to meet him halfway. Ah! She didn't know what to do. How to do it. Too much thinking, but she couldn't help herself. It wasn't like—

She stopped, turned, and their lips touched. And she felt like that green mango, on the verge of falling, but locked in that sweet place just before the crash.

10

An hour later she was in her kitchen, apologizing to Luna for not coming home sooner. As she took the dog for a walk, all she could do was touch her lips and smile as shimmers of the last hour surfaced and resurfaced. From Sebastian's tattoo drawings to that first kiss that led to so many more, to Lisbeth and Oscar interrupting them, Oscar whistling like a maniac, to Maya and Lisbeth walking back, Lisbeth wanting to know every last detail. *Now* who wanted every drop of the story? They were going to meet again after school tomorrow. Sebastian wanted Maya to bring *her* sketchbook. But first, tonight, she had to stitch the exposed zipper onto the jean dress.

Maya's head was so in the clouds that she didn't notice señora Pérez—clutching her rosary, crying—standing right in front of her on the sidewalk.

"¿Señora?" Maya pulled the leash to stop Luna.

"Ay, mija," señora Pérez moaned.

"What is it? What happened? How can I help?"

Señora Pérez shook her head. It was then that Maya noticed she was dressed head to toe in black. Even wearing her black chanclas.

A car with tinted windows pulled up to the curb, practically running over Luna.

"What the hell?" Maya scooped her pup up.

The driver, wearing silver sunglasses, rolled down the window just enough for señora Pérez to hand him an envelope. Through the reflection of his sunglasses Maya could see her neighbor's hand quaking, barely able to slip the envelope into the car as if it were an ATM. The man said nothing, simply rolled the window back up and took off, leaving Maya and the señora coughing from the fumes.

"Ay, mijita," she said. "The world is coming to an end. Go home. Hug your mother."

Maya rubbed the leash between her fingers, avoiding señora's gaze.

"And whatever you do, niña, stay away from those pinche mareros."

Quickly, to change the subject, Maya offered to walk her home. "I'll make you some tea."

She shooed away Maya's hand. "No! Go home, mijita. No. Better yet, go away. Far away. Move if you can. I'm too old. I don't have the money to move. But you and your mother. She's smart. I know she's been planning for this day. God bless her. Go. Go. Anda."

11

Maya unhooked Luna's leash, and the dog skipped toward her bowl of water, licked three times, then moved to her little bed, tan like her, and circled a few times before she finally curled up into a ball. Within seconds she'd be snoring.

Thinking all the while, Maya washed her hands, then dried them on the stiff towel (her mother insisted on drying towels on the roof). The image of the man in sunglasses taking the envelope from señora Pérez resurfaced stubbornly. Maybe he was just . . . collecting rent. Maybe he . . . But even in the hypothetical she couldn't find a satisfying end to the sentence, given señora Pérez's distraught state, especially given the warning she left Maya with.

But Maya couldn't let this distract her, not right now. She had work to do. So much work! The fashion show! She checked on the corn husks, which were finally dry, but La Betty called to her. She turned on the sewing machine and pulled out the jean fabric and zipper from her backpack. Zippers were always challenging, so she gave La Betty a little tap. "Let's do this, girl." When she was done, she took in her work. The exposed zipper needed to be bigger than this one to make a statement. Hmm . . . Where could she get one? Or could she make one? Wait—she'd seen these super-oversized zippers for sale at a store by the farmacia. They opened super early. She'd pick one up tomorrow. Now, on to the quince dress. She pulled out her sketchbook once again, but as she sketched out ideas for a petticoat, the pit in her stomach kept growing. Her fingers fumbled the pencil. The picture in her mind kept moving from Sebastian's sweet face, the trio of freckles on his cheek, his lips . . . to the envelope slipping into the driver's-side window, señora Pérez in tears. Maya cleared her throat. Her phone practically blinked at her, willing her to call Sebastian. She wanted to hear his voice. Then, miraculously, it rang. Sebastian!

"Hey," he said, his voice all cheery. "I think you forgot something here. So you have to come back."

"Ha. Can't. I'm working on my designs."

"Oh, bummer."

She paced the small kitchen, growing quiet.

"Hey. What's wrong?"

"Nothing . . ." She couldn't mention señora Pérez—no, she couldn't. "I'm stuck with this design. I need a big zipper for this dress, like really big. And then there's this other dress I can't figure out."

"You sound totally confident," he said in his signature dead-pan voice.

"It's just . . . I can't figure out how to make this quince dress bigger—it's made from pink plastic tablecloths."

"Tablecloths? That sounds so cool."

"Thanks . . . But, yeah, I've tried different materials for the hoop, what goes under the fabric to make it look puffy or whatever. But the problem is that whatever I use just puckers the fabric—the plastic. So it just looks terrible."

She could hear him breathing, thinking. Then she heard it. A clicking at first. Then rustling. But it wasn't coming from the phone. Luna's ears pricked up high. Pounding on the door. Someone was trying to break in! Luna growled.

"Maya? You there?" Sebastian was asking.

She looked around for something, anything. Her scissors. She gripped them and braced herself. Now someone was pounding harder. Luna began to bark furiously.

"Maya? What's going on?"

"I think someone's—trying to get in—" She fumbled the phone, dropped it.

More banging. Her thoughts flashed to her mother—she'd come home and find Maya and poor, quivering Luna on the floor. What could burglars want from *her* house? Wait—the guys who took the envelope from señora Pérez—

She . . . was a witness!

Then, "Ay! This stupid key."

"Mama!" Maya bolted up, scooped Luna to her chest like a baby.

In the doorway stood her mother, heavy-looking white plastic bags hanging from her wrists, as she finally successfully undid the lock. "Maya!"

"What are you doing!" each exclaimed to the other.

Her mother motioned for Maya to help her with the bags, but Maya literally couldn't move.

"The lock, was it stuck? Why didn't you just knock? You scared us." Luna burrowed into Maya's armpit.

"*Me? You* scared *me*. It's Tuesday. You stay late at school for open studio, no?"

"Ay, no! I totally forgot!"

"You *forgot?* What do you mean, you *forgot?* Maya, you look forward to it every single week. And with the fashion show coming up . . . What's going on with you?" She dropped the bags at her feet.

"Nothing . . . I . . . I really just forgot. I—was thinking about getting home to work on my projects—and I forgot!"

"Maya." Mama crossed her arms.

"Why didn't you just use your key, Mama?"

Her mother gave her an *are you kidding* look. "I had my hands full. It's hard to undo the lock when your hands are full of groceries, mija. Besides, you didn't answer me. I mean it, Maya. You know we don't keep secrets from one another."

"Are you sure?"

"Maya Luz."

Maya knew she was pushing it. But how could Mama have the nerve to say that they didn't keep secrets from one another? What about her plotting a move to San Marcos?

Begin stare off. They were good at this game. Suddenly a shadow caught Maya's attention. Shoot. Shoot! There was Sebastian, panting, suddenly inside her house, a small knife in his hand, glinting in the final light of the day.

"¡Ay, Dios santo!" Mama fell to her knees, pulling Maya with her. Just like in the telenovelas. Only, this was not a soap opera. And this was not a murderer. It was Sebastian.

"Mama! It's okay!" Maya cried out, pushing herself up.

Mama was scooching back toward the wall, her expression wild. "Please, no! Don't!"

"Mama! I know him! It's okay!"

Sebastian looked confused. "I thought someone was trying to break in. Are you all right?" He stepped toward her. Mama screamed.

"Get away from her! Don't take another step. Madre de Dios."

"Maybe put down the knife?" Maya suggested.

"Oh. Right." He did. "But I thought . . . Are you all right?" he asked again.

Okay, this whole thing was unreal! But at the same time, all she could think was that he'd run all the way over to her house—with a knife, no less!—because he was worried about her, even if he was scaring the hell out of her mother.

"Mama . . . it's fine. It's fine. This is Sebastian. I know him! He's a . . . friend of mine. He thought something was wrong— that's why he came over; he was worried!"

Her mother went from looking terrified to puzzled, to the starting simmer of anger. "Bueno," she said, slowly getting up. Sebastian reached out a hand, but she did not accept it. She brushed her hair out of her face and wiped her hands on her pants, evil-eyeing Sebastian, then Maya, then Sebastian again.

"Mama, he came to help! He thought we were in trouble!"

"Buenas tardes," her mother said, nostrils flaring, voice stone cold.

"He's just a friend, Mama." Right after she said it, Maya wished she could take back the words. *Just a friend*. She didn't dare look at Sebastian, but she could feel his stare like she could feel her mother glaring daggers. Maya sensed the questions about to fly at her.

"A 'friend.' Really? And how did you meet your 'friend'?" Mama rubbed her hands together, a thing she sometimes did before going in for a long argument. *We could be here for a while,* Maya thought, biting the inside of her cheek.

What was she supposed to say? She'd invited him over with Lisbeth's new boyfriend, and oh, by the way, they're both in a gang? *Nice to meet you, too,* her mother might say. Yeah, right.

But Sebastian knew exactly what to say. "I'm new to the neighborhood," he began smoothly. "I just moved in with my cousin. I was . . . I was recently deported from the States."

"Oh?" Her mother's face suddenly softened. "I'm so sorry."

Sebastian brushed his own hair back, meeting Mama's eyes. "It's okay. I mean, at least I have family here. Maya and I met through Lisbeth. My cousin is her . . . I guess you could say they're dating."

"Oh." Her mother sat down on the arm of the sofa but didn't offer for Sebastian to sit. She looked overcome by all this new information. "Well," she said. "I'm learning lots today about my daughter that I didn't know. Sebastian?"

"¿Sí, señora?"

"You can go now."

"Sí, señora. Mucho gusto."

Sebastian exchanged a look with Maya and picked up his knife. Maya mouthed, "I'll text you" before closing the door behind him. The room was suddenly black. She turned on the lamp in the corner, but it only helped so much.

"No secrets, hmm?" her mother said, shooting Maya a look of such disappointment that now Maya felt like sinking to her knees, before stepping into the bathroom and locking the door behind her.

12

Her mother was in the bathroom for so long that Maya eventually knocked. "Mama? Do you want me to make some dinner?"

"No."

"Mama . . . I'm sorry. I told you, he's just a friend. Like he said, we met through Lisbeth. I can make some coffee. We still have pan dulce from yesterday."

Silence.

"Mama? Please. This is when you say, 'Okay, Maya. I'll let you explain.'"

"How does he know where we live, Maya?"

More secrets. They were like fruit flies. She didn't want to lie to her mother again. It would just create more lies. "Okay," she said. "I'll tell you everything. But please come out of the bathroom. You should eat something."

Finally, after a few thick seconds passed, a click of the doorknob made Maya's heart flutter with relief.

And she did tell her mother everything. Well, *almost* everything.

"Promise me, promise me," her mother begged when Maya was finished. "You will *never* have them over again, Maya. I mean it. On your father. Swear it."

"Mama! Why do you have to bring my father into this?"

"Because I need you to mean it. You don't know who this patojo is. He seems nice, sure. But you don't know his family or his friends or what trouble they might bring."

Maya struggled to keep her voice calm, even. "Why do you assume he'll bring trouble?"

"Ay, you need to open your eyes, grow up, mijita. Every young man in the colonia gets tangled up in something before long. And I'm not just talking about gangs."

Maya's heart stopped.

"It's a larger network than you think. Sometimes they have innocent-looking boys, or even girls, do the dirty work. They're sneaky. Their tentacles are long. You have to be careful. Dios nos guarde. This is why—"

"What is it?"

"This is why . . . we *have* to move, Maya. Start packing."

"No!" Maya jumped up.

Her mother reached under the couch and pulled out a half-dozen flattened cardboard boxes.

Maya gaped at the boxes, instantly nauseous. When had she gotten *those*?! Oh my God. Oh my God. Oh my God. No! This wasn't actually happening. This *couldn't* be happening. She couldn't leave her friends, her school, and the fashion show! She jumped up, away from her mother.

"Mija, I wish the situation were different. Doña Pérez . . ." Now her mother could barely get the words out.

"I just saw her this afternoon—"

"You *did*? Where?"

"I was walking Luna. A car pulled up and she handed them an envelope. She was crying—"

"Ay, Dios santo! Did they see you? Maya—" Her mother grabbed her by the shoulders, gripped so tight that her nails dug in.

"Ow!" Maya tried to squirm away.

"Did they see you? Yes or no?"

"No . . . jeez. I mean, I was with Luna. I didn't even see the guy. He had sunglasses on and—why was señora Pérez wearing all black?"

Her mother drew a deep, strangled breath. "Maya. They . . . the gang . . . took her son."

"Daniel? But why?" Daniel was only twenty, but he seemed *much* older.

"Just listen." Her mother, who hadn't even sat down yet, made a quick cross over her chest. "Daniel. He was giving information to the police. But *they* just work with the mareros and take bribes anyway, so it got back to the mareros. And now . . . they have Daniel. Ay, Dios mío. Doña Pérez has to pay them five hundred quetzales each day to keep him alive, until she comes up with some massive amount they are demanding."

Maya stepped backward, reeling. "I need some air."

"Oh, no you don't. You're not going anywhere."

"I was just going to the roof. Jeez!"

Her mother shut her eyes, muttered a prayer under her breath. Her beautiful mother, who was frightened to death.

"Mama . . . it's horrible that they took Daniel. It really is.

Poor señora Pérez. But . . . we don't have anything to do with him, like, directly. Why should we—I mean, you'll see, Mama. The fashion show—it's barely a week away! I'll win and get the cash prize and then they'll let me sell my designs in La Fábrica! I'll be able to start my own line, just like *we* always wanted. *Then* we can talk about San Marcos. But for now, please. This is something I've worked for forever. *You* know. You've been there beside me all along. Please don't make me quit now. Please!"

Her mother stayed silent. But silent wasn't "no." Maya willed herself to stay quiet too, not to explode in frustration, give her mother time to consider.

"Vaya pues," she said at last. Really? *Really?* Maya could hardly believe it!

"Gracias, Mama. You won't be sorry." She reached for Mama, squeezed tight, tighter. She would win. She would. And she would change her mother's mind, even if it was one stitch at a time.

"But you have to promise me something, then."

"Anything!"

"You focus on the fashion show. That's it. No distractions, and no new 'friends.' No boys. We're moving. Right after the show. I'm serious, Maya. The sooner you accept it, the better. ¿Entiendes?"

How could she agree to that? The memory of Sebastian's mouth on hers was still so fresh. Maya hadn't even had the chance to replay it a dozen times. She knew she would. Oh yes, she would. But Mama wasn't messing around. The moving boxes were already under the couch!

"Okay, Mama." There was no other acceptable answer that wouldn't send them 250 kilometers away that very night.

After her mother finally unpacked the groceries and Maya petted Luna until her hand was numb, after her mother announced that she wasn't hungry and was going to take a long shower, Maya grabbed a couple of pieces of pan dulce and a bottle of water and finally headed to the roof. She sat in a beach chair and gazed at the few stars that had pushed through the smog. They blinked while Maya chewed the sweet bread and stared at the grid of streets, the only ones she'd known her entire life. Guatemala City, divided by zones, twenty-one numbers that determined whether you were rich and lived on a nice street like in Zone 10, or poor and lived in a red zone, like Maya. She thought about what was beyond the grid, about Guatemala, the country. It was a beautiful country. Volcanoes. Mountains. Beaches on the Pacific and the Caribbean sides. Hmm—wait!

She had an idea for a dress!

A volcano!

A volcano dress! She could create a neckline of ruffled fabric in red and orange. Okay, she'd better make note of this idea in her phone before she forgot it. She had a week. If she totally focused, she could do it. She could! As she typed *volcano dress* and *fire fabric neck* into her phone, however, she felt sadness settle like mud. Why did dreaming of becoming a fashion designer suddenly seem so . . . radical? Maybe that wasn't the word. Unrealistic? Futile? Mama was so set on moving to San Marcos. Even if Maya was lucky, lucky, lucky and *won* the fashion show, would that really change Mama's mind?

Then another thought struck her. The prize money would be enough to let them move to another zone. A *safer* zone. Yes! That was it! They could move somewhere safer!

The streetlights were beginning to flicker off one by one. The city had to sleep. Get her beauty rest, because in the early morning the men would collect trash and the shop owners would open the cranky iron gates. Women would call out in their singsong voices the prices of tamales and hot atole de elote. Cars would honk and buses would purr. Life would move on, and all the while the cardboard boxes underneath the sofa would sit like an alarm clock.

Her phone buzzed. Incoming call. Sebastian! What was she going to say to him? *It was so great hanging out with you, but um, I'm moving soon so, I'll probably never see you again.* Not. She picked up.

"Hey! Sorry my mom was like, super intense."

"No prob. I get it. Moms are like that."

"Yours too?"

"My mom—she died when I was a baby." He said it easily, stating a fact.

"I'm sorry. I—"

"No, it's cool. Your mom kinda reminded me of my aunt, though. In San Jose. She's like a mom to me. She's super protective too, but also sweet."

Maya forced a little laugh. "Yeah. I guess that's like their job. To be overprotective."

"I said super protective, not *overprotective.*"

"Well, she was! She doesn't even know you. Or your art or anything else . . ." Her mind trailed to his lips. Kissing his lips.

"Yeah. And I carry a knife and I scared the hell out of her—"

She laughed again, maybe a little too loud. From downstairs her mother yelled, "Maya! Are you still up there? Come down! It's late."

"¡Ya voy, Mama!" Then she whispered into her glowing phone, "I have to go."

"See you tomorrow?" he asked, the question enveloping her.

Maya looked up once more, searching for the stars that had been there just moments ago, but the night sky had swallowed them up. She wanted to do the right thing, but all reason had evaporated, like the stars themselves.

"Maybe," she said.

He was quiet.

She wanted to add, *I really want to, but my mom . . . but maybe we can, but*—when he cleared his throat and said, "Oh—I thought of something you could use. For your quinceañera dress design."

"Oh?" She sat up.

"You could blow up little balloons and somehow tie them underneath the plastic tablecloth fabric. This would create that volume effect, you know?"

"That's brilliant!" she practically yelled.

"Maya Luz?" her mother called again.

"I have to go—but thank you! Thank you!"

"You got it."

She hung up, the phone warm in her palm, and stared up at the stars once more. She couldn't see them, but she knew they were there. Maya had so much to tell Lisbeth tomorrow. They had agreed to meet at Lisbeth's locker before first period. Until then, it was back to working with La Betty on the zipper dress.

13

7 Days to Go

And there was Lisbeth, hand on her hip, waiting for Maya before first bell. Maya had already been at school for an hour, sewing the oversized zipper onto the jean dress. She'd stopped to buy it this morning. No time to waste. "Este, Sebastian gave these to Oscar to give to me to give to you, so here." She handed Maya a packet of small balloons. Maya stared at it, hardly believing it. When had—he must've gone to a corner tienda last night.

"Hello? Maya? They're balloons, not diamonds."

Maya laughed. "Right." She took the package and carefully tucked it in her backpack. She hadn't told Lisbeth about the move, or about the cardboard boxes, or Sebastian busting into the house holding a knife. She only told her about the kiss. Anyway, she had to go. Class was starting. Studio.

Her favorite. Maya *still* couldn't get over that the school provided so many mannequins to try the designs on. She'd asked for one for Christmas last year, but Mama had pointed out that the cost equaled half a month's rent. Now Maya lifted one toward her workstation, careful to balance it on her hip and not drag it against the floor. Then she got a second one. Finally she got to work. She spent a good hour blowing up the little balloons and positioning them under the quinceañera dress. Then she stood back and admired the silhouette. Sebastian's idea worked perfectly!

Next she sketched her volcano design idea and even included a ruffled neck. This just might work as her third look. She had the quince dress, the zipper dress, and now the volcano dress. Unless she kept the chuchito corset . . . Ay! She would have to see, and soon. The other ten or so girls in the room were also in their own bubbles. That was something else she liked about studio. No one had to say anything or even acknowledge one another. Everyone just knew. They were there for the art.

After adjusting the neckline in the drawing to make it more dramatic, Maya headed for the fabric storage closet. The pickings weren't *amazing*, but they were free, and so Maya went "shopping" in the closet instead of the expensive stores like in the underground mall in Zone 10.

Inside the closet, which, *seriously*, was about as big as her house, bolts of fabric—thick rolls, skinny rolls, short rolls, tall rolls—were lined up against the right wall. On the left, a stack of crates held shoeboxes full of different sizes and colors of thread, tape measures, styling tape, and tailor's chalk. Beside the crates sat even smaller boxes full of every kind of pin imaginable—from pearl head, to pear-shaped, to T-pins. And of course, safety pins. In every size. Maya grabbed a fabric-lined basket at the front of the closet and began making her way around the perimeter, collecting materials.

As she did, she imagined herself in a studio of her own someday. She's taking tailor's chalk to a gorgeous velvet fabric. She's using fabric shears to cut along the lines. She's draping the fabric over the dressmaker dummy (her own) and stepping back, squinting, rocking her head slightly. She's clicking her tongue against the roof of her mouth, thinking, thinking, when suddenly she has an aha moment! And then her assistant interrupts her to say there is a special delivery at the door that señorita must sign for herself. *Oh, just sign for me*, Maya says, waving her assistant away. Who returns a minute later with a brown box in her arms, the label in English. Maya takes the pin from her mouth and pushes it into the cushion on her wrist. Inside the box is the latest model of the mini sewing machine from a company in the States that's been courting her, wanting to partner with her on a new marketing campaign. She's carefully pulling out the machine, although it's much lighter in her arms than she'd imagined—the technology has become so advanced. *Shh*, she says, and holds it in her arms like a baby.

The day flew by after studio. It always did. She and Lisbeth planned to meet on the front steps before heading home. Maya had lots more to do on the volcano dress. Only, today Sebastian stood inside the school entryway, the same place Lisbeth had announced the finalists for the fashion show a week ago. Time. It was so bizarre. Maya hadn't yet met

Sebastian then. And now, here he was . . . holding iced coffees topped with whipped cream and chocolate sprinkles secured in a cardboard tray.

"Hey," he said. "I thought you might want one."

Girls gathered in clusters and whispered behind hands. Maya felt a little jolt of electricity. She'd never been the girl at the center in this way. It was *not* a bad feeling, she had to admit.

"Hey yourself, and thank you! That's so . . . sweet." She locked eyes with him, adrenaline rushing through her.

Sebastian smirked. "Ha. *Sweet?* Good one."

"So, now you're a comedian too?"

"Well, I'm not quite at Oscar's level of funny, but . . ."

"Where is he? Where's Lisbeth?" Maya looked around as if they'd pop up right behind him.

"Oh . . . they just left. I thought today you and I could go somewhere different. That doesn't involve a smelly garage, for example. There's a park around the corner."

"For *example*." Maya hesitated, adjusted the backpack strap on her shoulder. A park was a public place, and if they both happened to be there at the same time, it wasn't like she was *totally* disobeying her mother, right? Right! "Let me go put this in my locker—it weighs a ton," she said. "I'll be right back. Oh—" She pivoted. "And thanks for the balloons! *That* was really sweet. And you are a genius—they worked perfectly."

"For sure." Sebastian leaned against the doorway, smiling shyly, girls buzzing around him. From the corner of her eye she saw Ana approach. Maya pivoted once more.

"You know what? Why don't you wait for me over there?" She pointed to the side of the building.

∧∨∧

"Your school is incredible," Sebastian said once Maya had exited out the side doors and onto the spacious Zone 10 sidewalks that led to the park.

"How do you mean? You were here yesterday," she said with a laugh.

"I know, but I got a better look today. It's like a school in—" He stopped himself. But Maya knew what he was going to say.

"Like a school in the United States?" She took a sip of her coffee. Wow, it was delicious.

"Well, yeah." He took her hand in his.

She squeezed his hand, hoping—well, more like praying—that no one who knew her or her mother would see them. "I know what you mean," she said. "I feel really lucky to be able to go there. Makes me wonder what those schools in New York, like Parsons, must be like!"

Sebastian full-on stopped. "You've heard of Parsons?"

She raised an eyebrow. "Sure. I mean, I *have* watched almost every episode of *Project Runway*."

"Ha. Well, for what it's worth, I have a feeling you're better than all the designers on *Project Runway*, or any other show."

Her heart raced, so amped was she by his comment. Sipping this sweet coffee drink, taking in the smells of the warm afternoon, the marigolds for sale in bunches, tamalitos, jugos, and helados, while leaves on the trees created sparkly designs on the sidewalk and she held Sebastian's hand—her mother wanted to rip this all from her life. How could she? Right when *everything* was clicking into place? A flash of devastation crossed her face. Sebastian noticed.

"Hey," he said. "What's wrong? And don't say nothing."

She blinked the tears back and met his eyes, the hazel bits even brighter in the daylight. They were full of concern . . . for her. And the need to be with him, now, overtook the worry about being somewhere else, later. She didn't care about anyone watching. She had to stand on her toes. He lowered his head to meet hers. When she pulled away at last, she only wanted to lean in and kiss him more. She would do whatever it took, but she wasn't moving to San Marcos. Or anywhere.

She realized she had to get a grip. Guatemala City was huge, but it was also a place where news traveled like wildfire. "So, the park?" Maya asked with a smile.

"I have another idea," he said, reaching again for her hand and kissing her on her forehead, her lips, and her neck. Maya suddenly thought, *Wait. Oh no.* Did he think she was going all the way with him? She definitely wasn't ready for *that*. And even if she was, she never imagined it happening in, you know, a garage. Or some random dark room down the hallway from a garage. She didn't know what she pictured. Rose petals on a bed in a hotel room? Man, she'd watched too many romantic comedies. Truthfully, she'd never actually pictured *it* really, truly. It was something that would happen in the capital *F* Future, where other things lived, like starting her own fashion label, and Lisbeth and Maya posing for pictures on graduation day, and Mama buying their first car.

"Maya?" Sebastian squeezed her hand tighter, his coffee long gone. "I was thinking you could show me some of *your* designs—it's your turn!"

Ohhhh. Okay. Okay then. That was where this was going.

And it wasn't that she didn't want it to go the other way, eventually. . . .

"You gotta show me how those balloons worked out!"

Huh? "But we just left—"

"Yeah, but most teachers should be gone by now, right? You can show me your work space. I'd really like to see your stuff."

"Oh." Maya *did* want to show Sebastian her designs, but this was technically breaking a rule. What if . . . her scholarship, or the contest . . .

He gave a confused frown. "I thought you'd be psyched. . . ." Then, under his breath, "Girls are so confusing."

She couldn't help but laugh, relieved, to be honest. "It *is* a good thing."

"Tell you what," Sebastian said, grinning at her. "Let's go to the park after all. I'm sure some kids will be playing ball. I'll ask to make three shots. If I get all three, we go to your school. If not, we'll stay at the park."

"Ha! Okay, deal."

Sure enough, a group of patojos were playing basketball. Sebastian approached them and was all smiles, pointing back at Maya. The boys squinted at her, then him, nodding like crazy.

Maya stood courtside, hoping he'd make the shots, but also not. . . .

Shot one. Swish.

The group of boys clapped. One playfully shoved the other in the shoulder.

Shot two. Swish.

The boys cheered. Sebastian flexed. Maya cracked up. "You're crazy!" she yelled to him.

Shot three. He passed the ball from one hand to the other as something in his expression shifted. Like when a cloud covers the sun. What was wrong? He dribbled the ball, held it up to cover his face for a few long seconds. The guys quieted down. Maya took a sip of her iced coffee. Sebastian at last raised the ball in the air and clumsily tossed it toward the basket. It hit the backboard, circled the rim once, twice. And it didn't go in.

One of the kids yelled, "Aw! Three out of five! Three out of five!"

But Sebastian bounced the ball to them and walked over to Maya, looking, somehow, shaken.

"Hey," she said, reaching for him. "What happened there?"

"Nothing. I'm good," he said, stretching his arms to the right, left.

"Sebastian." Maya touched his arm.

"It's just . . ." He looked past her. "Memories, ya know? I was playing ball when . . . ICE came up on the court. Out of nowhere . . . A big dude demanding to see our papeles. Next thing I know . . ."

"Oh my God—I'm sorry!" Maya hugged him tight. "Next thing you know . . . you're here."

"Yeah," he said.

"Hey," Maya said. She couldn't believe she was saying it, but out it came. "Let me show you my stuff. Two out of three ain't bad."

"For real?"

They'd be in and out in five minutes, she figured. "Let's go."

∧∨∧

After tossing her empty coffee cup in the trash, Maya led Sebastian directly to her work space. She couldn't risk a teacher or a janitor or anyone working late seeing her, and with a boy no less. It *was* an all girls' school. Halfway there, she brought a finger to her lips and he nodded. Earlier, she'd been in this very space, perfecting the volcano dress, never dreaming she'd be sneaking in here with Sebastian only hours later. It crossed her mind that life was so strange like that lately. She didn't know what to plan for, what to expect, what surprises lay within arm's reach.

Sebastian was looking everywhere at once, seeming dazzled by it all. Maya was happy to see him *back*, back to the Sebastian she knew, after the basketball court and all. Mannequins were positioned all over, all dressed in various stages of design in progress. That was one great thing about this school. Girls respected each other's materials and designs, even if they were catty about other things. And when she said, "Ta-da!" and waved her arm in front of the mannequin that had balloons just below the hem of the pink plastic for the quinceañera dress—the balloons serving as tulle—then at the mannequin that still had her volcano dress draped over it, including the beginnings of a ruffled red neck, his mouth fell open. He looked from them, to her, to the mannequins again.

"What do you think? Tell me honestly. I just came up with the idea last night."

Sebastian circled them both. He touched the velvet fabric of the volcano dress with his thumb. Stared at the "fire neck" for a long time. Finally he stepped back and actually started clapping.

"Are you for real?" Maya blew a piece of hair out of her eyes. "Or are you just being nice?"

"No. Seriously." He stopped clapping and, taking her by surprise, pulled her into a huge bear hug. "Maya! This is incredible. The neck? Come on. *This is fire.*"

"Good one."

"See what I did there? Fire . . . 'cause the neck."

"Ha ha. Hey, want to see more?"

"Claro," he said, and she could hardly remember ever feeling happier.

She scrolled through images on her phone until she found the ones of the tube top constructed from chip wrappers, and the collection of ties she'd assembled—one using only saran wrap, another tree bark, and then one made from cupcake liners.

"Maya," he said, his voice low. "You are crazy talented, you know that?"

"Thanks. Really—thanks." She tried to keep her voice cool, but truth? She was on the highest high.

"You know, there are some amazing fashion schools in the States that you should totally apply for. In New York, and L.A. And you know what, I bet you could even get a scholarship."

And . . . then, cue the record scratch.

"Yeah, right. That's crazy talk. Anyway, this is a pretty great school too," she said, her voice laced with the thinnest layer of defensiveness.

"I meant *colleges*," he said, scrolling through the designs on her phone again. Wow, she was an idiot! She had to get a grip.

"Ohhhh." She peeked at the image he'd paused at. "The

rest are just sketches. Stuff I'd get to if I had the materials. You know how it is."

He handed back her phone. "Well, I want to see them all. Every last one."

"Really?"

"Really."

"Okay. There are more in my sketchbook. But it's in my locker. I'll go get it; hang on."

"Can I use a bathroom?" He shrugged. "The coffee and all."

"Oh. Hmm, the restrooms on this floor are girls only, but I think it's okay."

"It, um, is gonna have to be." He did a little dance and she laughed.

"Got it. Follow me." She pointed out a bathroom and hurried to her locker.

"Maya?"

Oh shit, shit, shit. It was la directora. Maya turned around, summoning all the calm she could muster.

"¿Sí, señora?"

"What are you doing here so late?" Suspicion clouded her angular face.

Think. *Think!* "I . . . I was just . . . working on my designs." It wasn't a lie. Not technically. "I had a new idea for the fashion show"—not a lie!—"and I don't really have a lot of materials at home, so . . ."

"Are you here alone?"

"Mm-hmm."

"Okay. I wasn't sure if Lisbeth might be here too. I'm about to lock up the building, so just be sure to leave out the back doors. Note that once you leave, you won't be able to enter again."

"Of course. Thank you."

"And one more thing, Maya?"

She curled her toes, willing the powers that be that Sebastian wouldn't come looking for her. "¿Sí, señora?"

"Next time, please let me know if you plan on staying late. ¿Entiendes?"

"Sí, señora."

"Bueno. Have a good night." Although the cloud of suspicion had mostly lifted from her face, wisps still lingered.

"Buenas tardes, señora."

Maya speed-walked to her locker, snatched out her bag, and speed-walked back to the workroom. As she entered, Sebastian reached out from behind a dress mannequin and grabbed her playfully. She gave a shriek, which startled Sebastian, who knocked into the mannequin, which toppled over, hitting him in the cheek. The clang was so noisy, la directora had to have heard it.

"Let's go! We have to go right *now*." She reached for Sebastian's arm, but he was wincing, cupping his face. The right side was smeared in blood. There must have been a pin in the mannequin! "Oh no! Are you okay?"

He dabbed his cheek with the corner of his shirt, but the bleeding didn't stop. "It probably looks worse than it is," he tried to assure her.

"Let me get a paper towel." Maya ran to the sink and let water run over a wad of them. "Here!" she said, bringing it to his cheek.

"It's really fine. I'm good. I just didn't know fashion could be so . . . violent."

She couldn't help it. She laughed. Maybe it was relief or fear or something like love, but it was all boiling up in her and she let it out. Too loudly. Behind the laugh came a rough cough.

La directora stood in the doorway. Hands on hips. The cloud of suspicion was now a storm of fury.

Shit, shit, shit, shit, SHIT.

"Maya! Who is this? You said you were alone! You know the rules! I'm calling—! I expect—! Maya!"

Bad. Very bad. La directora couldn't even string two words together. Of all the words, though, Maya focused only on *I'm calling*.

"Please, señora. My friend—he was just helping me carry my . . . bag."

"What is this blood? Ay, Dios mío. I'm calling security."

"No!" Maya and Sebastian said simultaneously.

"He just got cut on one of the pins. He's fine," Maya said quickly.

"I'm fine," Sebastian echoed in that deadpan voice. Maya could not start laughing now. No. No . . . Still, a smile formed at the corners of her mouth.

"You think this is funny, Maya?"

"No, señora."

"Honestly, I expect more from you. And the fashion show . . ." She shook her head ominously.

Maya stood up straight. "What about the show? Señora, this won't happen again. I swear. I mean, I promise. I am serious."

She pursed her lips. "I'm calling your mother."

"No! Please, please—you don't need to call—"

But la directora cut her off. "Sí. Now, go. Both of you. But first, clean up this mess. Ahora mismo. I'll be waiting in the hall."

Maya was so stunned she could hardly think. Sebastian lifted the mannequin with his free hand. At last Maya summoned the wherewithal to collect her bag and move the mannequin to exactly where it had been when they'd arrived. Sebastian glanced at her, biting his lower lip. He got how bad this was, she could tell.

From the hallway Maya could hear la directora talking on the phone. Yep. To her mother. She could hear snippets.

Buenas tardes, señora Silva.

Maya . . . con un muchacho . . .

Sí, sí, sí . . .

Lo siento . . .

Exactamente.

Buenas tardes.

Maya knew that her own phone would ring within minutes. But she was wrong. It wasn't minutes. It was seconds.

14

When Maya opened the front door half an hour later, her mother wouldn't even look at her. The sound of packing tape ripped through Maya's ears. Framed photos, kitchen appliances, all ready to be wrapped in pillowcases and T-shirts, sat beside now unflattened cardboard boxes piled everywhere. The bare walls only added insult to injury. Yes, Maya had disobeyed her mother. But she still longed for a room of her own to storm into, a door to slam like the North American girls on TV, a window she could crawl out of and escape this hellish existence. Too much? Not enough. Her mother was ruining her life. *Rrrriiip.* The sound of the tape was excruciating.

"Mama! I'm sorry. I'm really, really sorry! I am. But don't you think . . . maybe . . . you're overreacting just a *bit*?"

Mama rolled a T-shirt and positioned it between a blender and a mug. She moved like she was in a packing competition. Once they'd watched a man eat fifty-five hot dogs in ten minutes and win ten thousand dollars. But this was not a contest and there would be no prize.

"Mama! *Please*. Talk to me!" she begged as disbelief and guilt wrestled one another in her voice.

Her mother looked up, holding a mug with the words IN DOG YEARS I'M DEAD. Not exactly a good sign. "You disobeyed me," she said, not an ounce of melodrama in any of the three words. "You couldn't be trusted for one *single day*."

What could Maya say? Her eyes darted around the room. One box was already filled and sealed shut.

"Mama—please!"

"¡Escucha!" her mother yelled. Her mother *never* yelled. "I spoke to la directora and she told me everything." She raised her chin, glowering, her beautiful, dark-as-coffee eyes narrowed as if the very sight of Maya disgusted her. Maya honestly felt bad that she'd disobeyed her mother. But she didn't regret what she'd done. She just didn't. Was that horrible? She opened her mouth to respond, but her mother held out a hand to stop her.

"Mija, we're moving this weekend." She squared her thin shoulders.

No.

"La directora said you can still rep your designs in the show."

No.

"We'll come back for it."

No.

"We can stay in a rooming house until we find a permanent place."

No.

"I can't get the tuition back for the rest of the year, but así es."

"Noooooooo!" Maya felt every molecule in her body convulsing. There was nowhere to run. If she went up to the roof, she was afraid she'd jump off it. Luna barked from her bed in the corner.

"Why don't you take a hot shower, Maya, and calm yourself? The sooner you accept this is what's happening, the better. Anda."

Maya ripped the mug from her mother's hand and smashed it on the floor. Shards flew in every direction, scaring Luna so that she peed.

"Maya Luz!" Her mother gaped, astonished. "What's come over you? I understand that you're upset, but this is too much. You've brought this upon yourself. Go take a shower. Go!"

Her hands balled into fists, Maya stormed into the bathroom, if only to get away from her mother. Inside, she tore off her clothes and let the water run as hot as she could bear it.

Think. *Think*. She needed a plan. A way to convince her mother that this wasn't the right thing for them. That Sebastian was a good guy, a *really* good guy. That he and Oscar, although *technically* part of a gang, weren't *bad guys*. But *how*? *How*? The water was so hot that it made her skin pink, then red. Not hot enough. She turned the knob. Hot. Hotter.

Later, because there was literally nowhere else to go, and the roof seemed so far away now that she was in her pajamas and her hair wrapped in a towel, she sat on the couch and sketched ways to make the ruffle for the neck of the volcano dress stand out more, while watching whatever was on TV. But

she would *not* help her mother pack. No way. Her mother—
who had cleaned up the shattered mug—sat on the floor once
again, folding towels and clothes and placing them in still more
boxes, ripping packing tape with her teeth. Was she going to
grab the towel off Maya's head and pack that, too?

On the television a newscaster announced another death in a
gang war. *Perfect.* Of all the channels to have on. Their trolling
for ratings was so obvious that it was pathetic. Wasn't there any
other news in the entire city? In the country? In the world?

Maya changed the channel and leaned back with a huff.

"Bueno. You're mad. But, Maya Luz . . ." Her mother's tone
had shifted. Grown softer. Okay, Maya felt bad. She did. She
wanted to reach for Mama, to rush to the part where they
made up and painted each other's nails, but her mother simply
sighed. Maybe she could convince her to stay at least until the
fashion show. What was one more week?

"You know, mija, the moment your father and I found out
we were pregnant with you," she began, "we wanted to protect
you, no matter what. Your father . . . He wouldn't have wanted
us to live this way . . . with such worry."

"Mama . . ." She placed her hand on top of her mother's.

"You know, the day we met he was handing out flyers for
some protest at the university. I could feel he really wanted to
change things, you know? Not just for himself, but for others.
To be honest, I had never really met anyone like that until
then. But, mija . . . after your father . . . I made a promise to him
in heaven that I would do whatever it takes to protect you. His
principles cost him his life, but I can't bear to lose you, too. I
would—" Her voice caught.

"You won't, Mama. You won't!" Maya hugged her tight. This was all so . . . heavy. She knew things were . . . not ideal. But did they have to up and *move*? It just felt so extreme. Was everyone on every block in the colonia going to leave too? There had to be another way.

"The gangs, mija. These men are ruthless. And to think they are just boys, really. If there were more jobs, more schools, opportunities . . . Ay, mija. Maybe it wouldn't be like this for them . . . I just don't know anymore. The situation . . ."

Maya nodded. Enough for tonight, though. She didn't know how much more she could take. So she got up, poured corn-flakes and milk into one of the last unpacked mugs. A few flakes spilled onto the counter. As she cleaned them up, she briefly considered using cereal on one of her designs . . . but how? She was so distracted that at first, she didn't hear the knock on the door. When she did, she glanced at her mother, expecting her to be jumping out of her skin. Instead she stood up, stretched her back, and peeked from the curtain. Then she unlocked the door like it was the most normal thing in the world to have company over at eight o'clock at night.

"Buenas noches," she heard her mother say. "Come in, come in."

Come *in*? Maya was in her pajamas! She put down the mug of cereal. Who was it? Señora Pérez? Oh no—had something more happened to Daniel?

"Buenas noches," Maya said as señora Pérez, still dressed in black, still clutching the rosary, entered.

"Hola, mija."

Her mother motioned for señora Pérez to sit down. She did.

"Bueno," señora Pérez said. "This will work out for both of us, then."

What will work out? Maya felt like she'd walked into the middle of a conversation. She eyed her mother.

"Sí, sí," her mother said, ignoring Maya.

What the hell? "Mama? What's going on?" she had to ask.

"Maya," her mother said in a tone reserved for preschool kids. "Señora Pérez is going to come here every afternoon, until I get home from work. You are to stay with her at all times. Don't even go to the tienda, understand?"

Maya actually gagged. She at last managed, "Umm . . . Is she—are you . . . my babysitter?"

Señora Pérez lowered the rosary to her lap, looking stricken. "Mijita, I'm not so bad."

"I didn't mean it like that! It's just—"

"She will be here with you from when you get home from school until I get home from work and that's that," Maya's mother said in her flat *do not argue with me* voice.

"And I need to make extra money, for my trip," señora Pérez said matter-of-factly.

Maya was dumbfounded. "So . . . let me get this straight. You're paying her, like actual money, to *watch* me? That's a babysitter. Mom! I'm sixteen! This is pathetic."

"Quiet, Maya. I've had enough. We're trying to *stay alive*."

"Mama. Seriously?"

Señora Pérez massaged the rosary between her thumb and forefinger.

"Just until the weekend," her mother said. "Then we go to San Marcos."

"What trip?" Maya said to señora Pérez, refusing to acknowledge what her mother had just said.

Señora Pérez glanced warily at Maya's mother, but continued. "Bueno. As soon as those evil mareros let Daniel free, we're going north. Crossing the border. I've used almost all my life savings to keep him alive this far, but after I get him back, nos vamos. I will spend the rest of my life paying back debts, but I don't care. We have to go. It's not safe for him here. Or me. Or you! Your mother is right to be moving to San Marcos. Someday you'll understand, and you'll thank her. I promise you this."

Maya looked down at her mug, the flakes crackling, starting to sink.

Her mother, however, was now looking at her friend in alarm. "You're going to cross? Are you sure it's safe?" She dug out the spare key and a wad of quetzales from her purse. "It's my only spare," she said, as she handed both to señora Pérez quicker than quick.

"Vaya pues, I won't lose it."

"You know . . . ," Maya's mother said, her voice hesitant. "I have . . . a friend . . . who used to cross people. But he doesn't do it anymore. Too dangerous."

"Dangerous? ¡Por supuesto! But it's not safe here, either. Besides, I have faith in God that a good coyote will get us across."

"Sí, sí. But . . . I've been watching the news. They're saying no one gets asylum in America anymore—it's close to impossible."

"I have faith in God," the señora repeated.

Mama nodded. "And for Maya . . . gracias, oye?"

"Of course," señora Pérez said. "That's what neighbors are for, no? I should get going, though. It's late."

"Bueno. I'll watch to make sure you get home safely."

"It's just two houses down, but gracias, Carmen." She turned to Maya. "Hasta mañana, mija."

Maya forced a tight smile, hardly believing what was happening.

After her mother locked the door, Maya made up the bed in the living room, turned off most of the lights, and curled herself into an angry ball. It was the first time in all her life that she'd gone to bed without saying good night to her mother. Her heart felt so heavy, too heavy.

Just as she closed her eyes, closed *everything* out, her phone buzzed.

"Here," her mother said. "Give it to me."

Now was she going to take away her phone, too? How much worse could her life possibly get?

"It's just Lisbeth."

"Text her that it's late. Go ahead. Then I'll plug it in for you."

Maya did. *Talk tomorrow.* She handed her mother the phone with a stone face.

As her mother plugged it in, Maya's eyes caught the calendar on the wall, the date for the fashion show circled in bright red. What even was the point anymore? Her mother should've packed that, too.

15

6 Days to Go

"That really sucks," Lisbeth sympathized after Maya explained everything. "I'm really, really sorry." She reached across the table and held her hand, tight. They were sitting inside bustling San Martín—every table packed, the smell of espresso and pan dulce in the air—finally celebrating Maya making it to the finals in the fashion show. Lisbeth ordered an egg and avocado croissant sandwich, Maya a huge cinnamon roll. But they each only picked at their food. "What are you going to do?"

Maya used her fork to spread the glazed sugar on top of the roll. "What *can* I do? My mom was literally ripping packing tape with her teeth. She means business."

Lisbeth winced. "Damn, vos." Then she narrowed her eyes. "Un momento, pueblo. I have an idea—"

"What? Anything."

"What if . . . I mean, it's kind of sneaky, but it might work."

Maya let go of Lisbeth's hand. "Tell me, vos!"

"What if you told her the prize money increased to like, a million quetzales?" She waved her hands in the air with a flourish.

Maya dropped her head into her hands. "No, that wouldn't work."

"Why not?"

"Because my mom already said we could come back to show my designs. That one night isn't the problem. It's all the other nights before and after. You know, like, otherwise known as *my life*."

"Oh. Yeah. You have a point there." Lisbeth frowned in solidarity. "Have you told Sebastian about the move yet?"

"No." And Maya burst into tears.

"Oye, it's going to be okay, vos. It will." Lisbeth handed her a paper napkin.

"It's not just that—" Maya wiped her nose. "It's that I feel like my dreams are slipping away, ya know? What if I'm not actually going to be a *designer*? With no more school, no connections—"

"No, Maya! No. Don't spiral. You are the most talented designer in this whole damn school, and seriously, this is just a bump in the road. Or a wrinkle in the fabric. Or—"

"Or chuchito wrappers?" Maya forced a smile. "I woke up extra early today to work on this design, but what is the point . . . Anyway, thanks, amiga." She used the side of her fork to slice off a piece of the cinnamon roll. She managed a bite, but tasted nothing.

"What else is up with you, Maya? Come on. I know you."
Lisbeth took her own fork to Maya's cinnamon roll. Ate a bite.
"Damn! This is good, vos." She reached for more.

"Well . . . it's dumb, I guess. But . . ."

"*¡Tleme!*" Lisbeth said, mouth full.

"Okay, so, well, I've always had this secret wish . . . to study
design in college—"

"Um, *duh*," Lisbeth interrupted. "How long have I known
you?"

"In *New York*."

Lisbeth's mouth fell open. Brown mush *actually* fell onto
the table. Now Maya couldn't help it. She laughed, and then
Lisbeth laughed, and then they were laughing so hard people
were staring. Maya didn't care. It felt so, *so* good.

"Stop," Lisbeth groaned, and wiped the mess with a napkin.
"Maya, if anyone can do it, it's you. And obviously, I'll visit you.
Like, constantly."

"Gracias, oye. It's just . . . I feel like I'm moving backward by
going to San Marcos. There isn't even a design school there.
I'll be that much further away from my dream, ya know?"

"Yeah, but you can still take what you've learned at Salomé
and work on your designs. You can still apply to schools in los
Estados."

Maya sighed, nodding. She glanced at her phone. Speaking
of Salomé, first period would start soon, and she was already in
hot water with la directora. "We'd better go." Lisbeth tossed
her half-eaten croissant in the trash, but Maya wrapped what
was left of her cinnamon roll in a napkin and tucked it into her
bag.

∧∨∧

After school she took the back exit and jumped on the first bus she could find, even if it meant having to take a different route home. She couldn't bear seeing Sebastian and Oscar waiting for Lisbeth and her, and having to explain to Sebastian why she had to go straight home. She sent him a text saying that she had a doctor's appointment. Included a kissy-face emoji, hoping that would be something. It wasn't. He called her, but she didn't pick up.

Hey. Pick up.

Can't. on bus.

Lisbeth told me everything

!!! That was fast

Maya . . . can u talk?

Will call u when I get off bus

Promise?

Promise

And wow. Lisbeth took all of five seconds to dish the dirt. She couldn't blame her, Maya supposed. Besides, she was secretly glad she didn't have to tell Sebastian the real reason she couldn't meet him after school. Maya tried to put them all out of her mind. She popped in her headphones and played a trap Spotify station as the bus chugged along through traffic. They passed the Starbucks on Ciudad Cayala, one of a handful in the capital. Only rich people or tourists went there, and there were actual guards in front of the shop. The irony? Local Guatemalans couldn't afford the coffee there, even though the best beans came from Guatemala.

Maya's mind drifted to the fashion show—now less than a week away! She had to find a way to make the fire neck on the volcano dress *pop*. And she needed a model to try on the chuchito corset before she made adjustments, assuming she would swap out that look for the zipper dress. She wished she could have four looks! Well, maybe . . . Oh, who was she kidding? It was all pointless. She stared stonily out the window as the bus stopped at a red light. Maya fixated on the painting of papayas, limes, and strawberries above the storefront. *Pft.* Sebastian could do a better job. She pulled out her phone. No more texts from him. Her thumb hovered over his name. Missed call. What else was she missing—what were he, Lisbeth, and Oscar doing? What else would she miss after she and her mother moved to San Marcos? *Pretty much everything.*

The bus started to move again. Then she saw it. Had it always been there? She pressed her body against the window, bumping into the woman beside her, who sucked her teeth with annoyance. "Nena," she snapped. "Watch it."

"Sorry," Maya mumbled. Outside, along the sidewalk, a giant utility box had been painted in the most stunning graffiti art. A woman's profile alongside a mountain. Her nose looked like one of the peaks. Her mouth, another. It was beautiful. Above it, the words: *Que tus sueños te lleven a la vida que te haga feliz.* May your dreams lead you to the life that makes you happy. This time, Maya pulled out her phone and snapped a photo for Sebastian. The words "the life that makes you happy" throbbed in her mind. Mama would kill her. . . .

The woman glared at her. "Nena! Your bag!" It was in the woman's face.

Maya said, again, "Sorry!" Only this time she ran to the front of the bus and told the driver she needed to get off.

"Next stop is Mercado San Jose," he said without so much as glancing at her.

"I have to get off *now*," she demanded.

He didn't respond, kept his hands on the big wheel, and stared straight ahead. Her heart was racing. "Señor. Unless you want me to have an accident right here on the bus, I need to get off right now." She crossed her legs.

His eyes bulged. "Ay," he sputtered. He put on his blinker and pulled over. A few people complained, but Maya didn't look back. She practically flew down the steps and ran onto the sidewalk. When she caught her breath, she texted Sebastian.

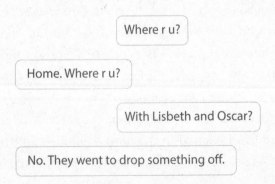

> Where r u?

> Home. Where r u?

> With Lisbeth and Oscar?

> No. They went to drop something off.

Why didn't u go?

Felt like drawing.

Can I come over?

With that, he called her. This time she picked up.

"I thought you had to get home to be with that lady, señora what's her name."

"I do. I mean . . ."

"Take a taxi. I'll pay for it."

Maya's mind was a swirl. Her mother. The boxes. Rules upon rules. Señora Pérez. Sebastian's drawings and his voice and his lips and . . . She knew her mother would kill her. But if Maya truly only had a couple more days living in the capital . . . And if they were going to move this weekend anyway . . . In two days! She could . . . she could . . . *Think, Maya!* She could tell señora Pérez she had a last-minute after-school thing, something to prep for the show.

"Maya?"

"Okay," she said. "See you soon."

The drive over to Sebastian's place felt like an entire year. The taxi hit every red light, every traffic jam, every old lady crossing the street with a giant basket on her head, taking her sweet time despite the honks. She messaged señora Pérez, telling her not to worry, that she needed to go to a mandatory meeting about the fashion show. She'd be back in an hour. Finally Maya arrived at Sebastian's. She texted him so he'd know she was outside. She didn't really understand where the front door was; it was all a maze. He met her in the small alleyway and paid the taxi driver. Then he hugged her tight, tighter. She inhaled his smell—never did find out if it was cologne or deodorant or what, but it was *him*.

"Here, come on in," he said, holding on to her. For the first time in twenty-four hours, she felt like she could actually breathe.

"You have to let me go first," she said, smirking.

"Nunca," he said. Never.

She knew she was in deep. Playing with fire. All the things. Just like she knew it was señora Pérez who was this very second blowing up her phone with text after text saying, *Maya, Mamita—I got your message. But come home the minute it's over. I don't want to have to call your mother.* Maya ignored each ping. She knew she'd get in major trouble. But she didn't care. Did. Not. Care. She let Sebastian take her by the hand and lead her inside, not to the garage where they'd hung out before, but into the dark hallway, where he kept looking back to make sure she was okay with it, and each time he did she nodded, until he eventually led her inside his room, and clicked the door shut behind them.

16

The walls were painted that same sea-green as the hallways. A poster of Messi hung on one. A rusted mirror hung on another. A single window let in light, but not too much. Maya tried to picture Sebastian here alone. As if reading her mind, he said, "Honestly, I just sleep in here. The rest of the time we're in the garage."

"Right," Maya said. "Well, at least you have your own room."

"It's all I need. *We* need," he said, and pulled her toward him.

And then they were sitting on his bed, kissing and holding and taking off his shirt, then hers. He reached for her and their bodies fell back. After every hard kiss and soft bite, they sank deeper. She lay on top of him and her hair spread into his face like ink. He took a strand and put it in his mouth. Her fingertip grazed his cheek where the pin from the mannequin had cut him. "You think it'll leave a mark forever?" she asked.

"I hope so," he whispered, and kissed her again, her lips, her neck, then lower still.

The world beyond that small room evaporated. Lisbeth never talked about it feeling this way. Like being underwater, like being in another room inside your own body.

"Stop thinking so much," he said, nibbling her ear. He reached for her waist, playing with the button on her jeans. "Close your eyes," he said.

Maya relaxed. A little. Then, a lot.

He shimmied her jeans down, just below her hips. With his fingertip he traced the curve of her underwear, that elastic lining with a crisscross pattern she'd never really given thought to, until now. She took a deep breath and circled her own fingertip around his belly button. A little groan escaped his lips. She wasn't sure what she was doing, but she continued anyway. She traced the tattoos on his chest, words in English, except for *San Jose*, which spread across his torso in block letters. Why did people get tattoos? she thought hazily. They weren't like outfits you could change; they were permanent. Sebastian kissed her bare shoulder. And she, his. Tattoo thoughts evaporated. His whole body beside hers. They could do so much more, to each other, and together. This much she knew. He knew it too. There wasn't much time, not today or tomorrow or the next day. She was moving this weekend. So why not? Everything told her to say *yes*. Head to toe, her body felt like a million butterflies had landed on her skin.

"No," he whispered. "I can't believe I'm really saying this, but—"

She pressed her thumb against his lips. They were so, so soft. Neither of them moved for a long time.

Finally he took her hand and lowered it. He sighed. Stretched his arms above his head, and made a pillow out of them. Maya rested her head on his chest. He kissed the top of her head so lightly it could have been her imagination, or the wind moving through the window, reminding her of the outside world that awaited her, whether she liked it or not.

"Just one more minute," she begged playfully.

He kissed the top of her head again. It all felt too real to be wrong.

When they got up and dressed, Maya spotted his backpack in the corner. "Is that the same backpack you had in California?"

He smoothed the bed comforter. "Yeah. They took it from me when I was detained. But then gave it back when I was released."

She stood there, fixated on the backpack, like she'd only just realized he'd had another whole life in the United States. What grade was he in? He hadn't been able to say goodbye to his friends. He said he'd been playing basketball with them one day and the next, he was on a government plane on its way to Guatemala, a place he had no memory of because he was a baby when he and his parents crossed. Maya wondered if that was how his mother had died. She also wondered if he had an old binder in the backpack, old homework or assignments, drawings he'd begun sketching in his previous life, never guessing that the images he'd make in the book's final pages would be made in an entirely different country.

"You're doing it again," he said. "You're thinking."

"Sue me."

He laughed. "What were you thinking about anyway?"

"Honestly . . . I was wondering about your life in California. It must mean enough to you to have it tattooed on your chest. What were your friends like there? Do you still talk to them on WhatsApp or anything? Can you still graduate high school?"

He ran a finger along her arm, came closer, and leaned in to kiss her.

"Let's not start again," she said with a grin. "I don't want to give señora Pérez a total heart attack. If I don't come home soon, she'll think I've been kidnapped." Ooh, bad joke.

"Well . . . you have? Kinda?"

Maya tied her shoe. "Or maybe I kidnapped *you*."

"Hey, how do you know señora Pérez?"

"What do you mean?" Maya tied her other shoe. "She's the lady Lisbeth told you about. The one my mom basically hired to be my babysitter."

Sebastian's face flushed. "You—you never said her name—" He squinted out the window, his jaw clenching.

"Hey." She touched his arm. "What's wrong?"

"Nothing. Let's go."

"Seb—"

"I said nothing. I'll walk you home."

"I'm sorry," she said, confused. Shoot. She shouldn't have mentioned California. Stupid, stupid! "I didn't mean to bring up old stuff. I'm really sorry. I shouldn't have said anything about your old life."

"It's not my *old* life," he snapped. But then he gave her hand a gentle squeeze. "Sorry. I mean, that life is still me. This is my life." Still, note to self, Maya thought: *Don't bring up California and don't refer to it as his old life.*

On their way out of the maze—so many dark hallways and random rooms; honestly, the place felt more like a hotel—Maya heard Oscar's voice. Maybe Lisbeth was still with him? Only, as Oscar's voice grew clearer, it was obvious he wasn't talking to her.

"I said *soon*, pendejo! I'm tired of fucking waiting. They're on my ass, which means I'm on your ass, which means you better fucking hurry this shit up. I'm not playing with you." Wait. *Was* that Oscar? Or someone else?

"I know. I told you. It's taking more time. But I'm on it." *That* was Oscar. Definitely Oscar. So who was he talking to?

"You're such a piece of shit, you know that? I shouldn't have brought you into it. I knew this would happen. You can't do anything right. You're the dumbest pendejo in the whole clique, telling your stupid-ass jokes all the time."

Maya's knees froze. Sebastian went stiff as well, but he clutched her hand, hard, and with his eyes, urged her to be quiet.

"I knew you wouldn't be up to it," the first not-Oscar guy said. "I had this feeling. I told myself, your little brother is too stupid. Oscar is too weak. Too soft. Always telling jokes and shit. The 'comedian' is a *joke*. Now we have to fucking pay. Do you know what that means?"

The sound of a slap, hard, against a cheek.

"Stop, okay?" Oscar pleaded.

"You'd better get it done. Or they'll slice you apart bit by bit, starting with your ear, then—"

"I said I would do it!"

Maya didn't hear the rest as Sebastian was pulling her back down the hallway and toward another one. It wasn't until they were outside, the sun on their faces, that Maya took in a huge, shaky breath. She couldn't stop trembling. Sebastian wrapped an arm around her. "Just keep walking."

The late afternoon sun beat down on the side of her head that Sebastian had kissed just minutes ago, the glare making her squint. Her ears were ringing with what she'd just heard. She finally understood sensory overload.

"You want my sunglasses?" Sebastian offered.

"No, thanks."

"You sure?"

"Yeah. I'm fine, thank you." But she was aware of how their voices were more starched than usual, their words on display for one another. We're okay. This is okay. Everything is *okay*. She was also aware that they'd avoided looking at each other since they left. Ahead, a man pushed an ice-cream cart along the sidewalk, the bell jingling, taunting little kids in this heat. Maya had always vowed that if she made it big, if her designs made her rich, she'd come back once a week to her old colonia and buy ice cream for every single kid there.

"¡Helado! ¡Helado!" the old man sang half-heartedly.

"No, gracias, señor," Sebastian said to the old man.

Up the block, in front of the taquería, two boys on bikes

offered rides to other kids for a quetzal each. Everything was a
business opportunity here. That was how, she knew, the mareros saw *everything*. The job market sucked. Mama said there was
corruption everywhere. Even the police couldn't be trusted. So
what did you do when you were desperate? Maya shook her
head. She couldn't believe she was thinking this way. Justify-
ing things that were a whole lot worse than gambling or bribing government officials. So much worse—and whatever she'd
just heard was most definitely in that category. What was Oscar
supposed to have done?

She had to clear her head. She had to figure out the fire neckline for her volcano dress. But Oscar's voice just now . . .

"You okay there?"

"Uh . . . you *were* there just now. Right?"

"Maya—" He stepped in front of her, lifted her chin. "Here's
the thing—you need to pretend like that conversation between
Oscar and his brother never happened. Like we left five minutes before that conversation you *didn't* hear ever happened."

So that *was* Oscar's brother. . . . And it was weird. Sebastian
sounded like his regular old self. But if what he'd just said had
been spoken by anyone else, it could have been taken as a
threat. *Need to. You need to pretend like it never happened.*

A woman in a pink tank top and tight jeans walked by, clutching a cell phone on speaker. She clearly didn't care about who
heard what *she* was or wasn't saying.

Sebastian took Maya's hand again. "Look. I gotta get back
home. I'll text you later." He gave her a quick kiss on the forehead before leaving. Even that gesture was reckless—a kiss
in the middle of the street for all the nosy neighbors to see, to

chew on in their nightly gossiping sessions over coffee and pan dulce. *Oh, did you see Maya with her new novio? Sí, sí, sí. Carmen's hija. With a guy? Who is he? We've never seen him. She'd better be careful. Does her mother know?* Truth was, and she knew the truth—the neighbors were the least of her worries.

17

When Maya walked into her house, it was empty, except for Luna, a note from señora Pérez on the kitchen table. She looked at the clock in horror—two hours had gone by! Oh my God, her mother was going to KILL her! Señora had written on the back of an envelope, in block letters:

MIJA:
VOY PARA MI CASA. ESPERO QUE ESTÉS BIEN. LLAMA A
TU MAMA. ESTA <u>MUY</u> PREOCUPADA.
SEÑORA Pérez

Señora Pérez had gone back home. She was worried. And—she'd gone and called Maya's mother. Shit, shit. Yet something about her handwriting—all in caps—tugged at Maya. She should go apologize. That would be the right thing to do. Her house was just steps away from Maya's. So, before she knew it, Maya was standing in front of the señora's door.

It was just a flimsy piece of rectangular wood, its gold-colored dead-bolt lock only bringing attention to its cheap attempt to keep out robbers. Poor señora Pérez. The image of her loose stockings bunched up around her calves, where varicose veins crawled, pinged Maya in the chest. Maya knew the woman was only trying to do her job. Damn.

Maya knocked. No answer. Layers of lace curtains obscured any attempt to view inside the house.

Maya knocked again. Harder. Still no answer.

Just as she was about to head back home, she heard the faintest muffled sound. Then, the unmistakable scrape of a chair. She looked more carefully at the dead bolt. Someone had messed with the lock. Part of it was hanging off the doorframe like a loose tooth. With wobbly hands, she gently pressed against the door. It opened as easily as if it'd been constructed of feathers.

Again, she heard a chair scraping against the floor. Another muffled moan. What if something had happened to señora Pérez? Oh my God, what if Maya had sent her spiraling and she'd had a stroke or something? Maybe . . . Heart in her throat, Maya tiptoed inside and followed the sound.

Looking back on this moment, later that night, and years later, she'd wonder how different her life would have been if she hadn't stepped inside the house. If she'd chosen to go back home, to her previous life. Because that was what it became, a previous life. Everything after this moment would be known as her life *afterward*.

Careful not to make a sound, Maya took soft steps down the little hallway and toward the muffled noises. They were coming from the courtyard in the center of the house. It'd been a couple of years since Maya had actually been inside señora Pérez's. Like many homes in the colonia, hers had a simple concrete courtyard in the center with a pila, also concrete, used to wash clothes and dishes. She used to throw elaborate birthday parties for Daniel in that small space, until he outgrew the piñatas and the streamers and the games of musical chairs. He turned into a complicated, spike-haired boy-man who swore a lot, who disappeared for days doing who knew what. Señora Pérez—Maya never knew of a *señor* Pérez—covered for him all the time, once even going so far as to tell Maya's mother that he'd gone on a church service trip to build houses in the mountains. But he'd come back with a fresh tattoo on his neck, something in cursive that Maya could never get close enough to read, but was pretty certain that it wasn't a Bible verse. Maya suddenly remembered how, when they were younger, he loved setting off firecrackers. He counted down at the top of his lungs as he ran after lighting one, his forehead glistening with sweat.

And so it was a monumental shock to see that same face now, eyes bulging, forehead again glazed with sweat, a stretch of fabric around his mouth. Daniel—*Daniel!*—was writhing on the concrete floor in the center of the courtyard, tied to a chair that had been knocked on its side.

What. The. Hell? This couldn't be real. It couldn't. Oh, but it was. Maya wanted to bolt toward him, rip the cloth from his mouth, *save him*. The veins in his neck throbbed—looked on the verge of exploding. Ferns in hanging baskets around the perimeter of the courtyard created creepy shadows. Maya forced herself to shrink back, pressed behind the doorframe. It looked like he was alone. But even she knew better than that. Just as she revised the thought—

A toilet flushed. Then she heard, "Just do it, pendejo!"

Maya held her breath. She knew that voice—had *just* heard that voice. Oscar! Pero, what was . . .

She glanced back at the front door. Leave. All she had to do was leave. Put one foot in front of the other and get the hell out of there. But her legs wouldn't move. Her legs were cement blocks.

"You're such a piece of shit, you know that?" he muttered. "I knew this would happen. You can't do anything right!" Oscar appeared in the courtyard doorway. Maya turned her head a centimeter to the right, squinted. He couldn't see her, but oh she saw him.

With. A. Gun. In. His. Hand.

"I'll show you who's a piece of shit!" Oscar's fury grew with each word. And Maya realized he was talking to himself; everything his brother had aimed at him, he was aiming at Daniel.

"Dumbest in the whole gang!" he said now, kicking Daniel in the ribs.

Daniel arched his back, cried out through the fabric. "¡Por favor!" His eyes wild.

Hold on. Was señora Pérez's son in the gang too? The same gang—?

"¿Por favor?" Oscar spat on the ground. "You wanted to go home. Begged! So, welcome home. Pain in the ass to bring you back here, but you know, your mami will be *so* happy to see you."

Daniel bucked and kicked, the chair scraping against the concrete.

"This is what happens to little traitor bitches," Oscar sneered, and stomped on Daniel's head!

Maya stuffed her knuckles in her mouth to keep from crying out.

She had to get out of there.

But she couldn't let Oscar kill Daniel!

Because that was what he was going to do.

And oh my God, where *was* señora Pérez?

Maybe she'd be home any minute.

Maybe she was already dead!

And if Oscar saw Maya, he'd kill her, too.

How were these real thoughts?

In that moment Oscar placed a long, thin tube at the end of his gun—was that a silencer? And just as she processed that, Oscar aimed it at Daniel's forehead, and shot once, twice, and a third time. Imaginary firecrackers went off in Maya's head.

Daniel lay motionless, blood already pooling onto the concrete. Maya let out a whimper, immediately furious that she'd made a sound. Her knees gave out, but at the last second, she caught herself. *Oh my God. Oh my God.* She had to get out of there. Daniel was dead! Where was señora Pérez? She had to get out of there! Thoughts raced, but one was most prominent. She prayed in fast-forward that Oscar wouldn't notice her.

That prayer went unanswered.

18

"What the fuck?" Oscar swung around, gun raised, ready to fire. He must've heard her. Shit! *Shit.* Maya stood like a statue. *Please, please don't let him see me.* Gun still raised, Oscar moved to the left, enough to see into the doorway. Now he was aiming directly at *her.*

She was too stunned to react. *OhmyGod, OhmyGod, OhmyGod,* the words a chant in her head. Oscar lowered his gun warily. He eyed Maya, the body, the giant green leaves glistening around them, Maya again, and whispered, "Fuck."

Maya couldn't stop shaking. She covered her mouth, holding in the scream lodged there, aching to be released.

"What the fuck are you doing here?" Oscar, glaring at her with fire in his eyes, began to pace. Blood spooled from, oh my God oh my God, Daniel, señora Pérez's *son,* just inches away from Oscar's feet.

"I—I—"

"FUCK!" he bellowed.

"I'm sorry—I . . . I just came over to . . ." She was in shock.

"Leave! Do you hear me? Get the fuck out of here. You never saw anything. You never—" He raised the gun.

Maya gagged. "Please! Please . . ."

"GO!"

She swung around, tripped over her own feet, fell hard onto the floor. Her knee throbbed with pain. Ignoring it, she scrambled up and somehow made her way to the front door, convinced that she'd have a bullet in her head before she could get out of the house. But there was no bullet.

At home, night on her heels, she could barely turn the key to get inside. Her hands seemed to have forgotten how to work.

She half expected Oscar to be right behind her, having changed his mind.

Oh my God, oh my God, oh my God.

What just happened? Once inside, she made sure the door was locked. Checked it like seven hundred times. Then grabbed a chair and wedged it underneath the door handle. Her heart wouldn't stop racing. *Think.* Close the curtains. She closed the curtains. Thought about moving the couch over to the door. But . . . but . . . if Oscar had a gun, he'd shoot through the window. And he'd eventually find a way to get inside. The roof! She could see if he was coming. Warn Mama. Holy shit—Mama! She'd be home soon. No! If Maya had thought her mother was a hurricane about to land, now her world was about to become a tsunami. She had to tell her mother what she'd seen. How could she not? She couldn't keep this to herself. Should she call the police? She'd just witnessed a *murder.* Would—would—Oscar kill *her?* He would if she said anything.

Oscar was a *murderer*. Lisbeth! Lisbeth—it was just like with Juliana! She should have listened to her gut, she should have, she should have. And Sebastian. She pressed her fist to her mouth as the awful truth dawned on her—he had to have known this was going to happen—it was why he'd said what he'd said about señora Pérez, why they left so quickly. Ay, no! And señora Pérez—this would destroy her.

Maya reached for her phone. She had to warn Mama! She called her, but it went straight to voice mail. Again, she tried. And again. Lisbeth! Maya called her next. It rang and rang. No answer. Where the hell *was* everybody? She tried texting, but her fingers, she couldn't get them to hit the right letters. She lurched forward and dry-heaved.

And stayed that way, on the floor, praying—*Please, God, please*—until she heard the lock click open. Only Mama had a key. Maya hurried to remove the chair. Enter: hurricane. Mama only knew that Maya hadn't been here with señora Pérez. Maya couldn't begin to imagine how her mother would react if she told her the rest. Luna eyed Maya with an expression that said, *Good luck*. If only Luna knew the half of it. Tell Mama. Don't tell her. Tell Mama. Maya backed against the wall for support.

Mama. She looked . . . she looked like she'd been trampled. Not physically, but her heart. She looked like every step required a summoning up of energy she did not have. The fact that it was all due to her sent a quake through Maya's entire self. And now, how could she tell her? *Oh, I just saw my best friend's boyfriend kill your friend's son.*

"Mija," her mother finally said. "A line has been crossed for the final time."

Did she know? She couldn't possibly . . .

"Mama—before you say anything." Stick with the original plan, Maya: apologize for coming home late. Really, she wanted to say, *Listen, Mama! I just saw a man get killed.* She wanted to scream and cry and run into her mother's arms. But she didn't.

"I'm beyond furious with you, Maya, but first—"

Maya held up a hand. "Before you say anything—I'm really sorry about not coming straight home. I am. But I couldn't help it. Something with the fashion show—I really am sorry. Mama—don't look at me like that. I can't take it when you're so disappointed. Be mad or something. Take away my . . ." She was careful with her words. "I hate seeing you so sad, Mama."

Then she noticed her mother was staring off into the distance, hardly seeing Maya. "Mija, sit down," she said.

"But—"

"*Sit.*"

Luna's ears perked up, probably thinking, *But I'm already sitting.*

Maya sat.

"Señora Pérez . . ."

"I know. That's what—" How could she lie straight to her mother's face? Not tell her what she'd just seen?

"We'll talk later about how you disobeyed me for the last time. But right now I need to tell you . . . They killed her son."

A guttural sound escaped Maya's mouth. "No . . ." Yes, Mama. She knew it. She'd been there when it happened. And she'd been too terrified to stop it. Tell her! Tell her! No. Don't! Don't!

Her mother, stone-faced, ashen, nodded.

"No! That can't be true." Maya hoped she wasn't being too theatrical. She would not meet her mother's eyes. Not for a second.

"Maya. It just happened. Doña Blanca called on my way home from work. She said she could hear señora Pérez screaming from her courtyard. So . . . so Doña Blanca knocked on her door. Then she realized the bolt was broken. She was too afraid to go inside alone, so she got a couple of other neighbors and they went together—" Her mother shook her head.

"Mama . . ."

"That's when they found her . . . beside her poor son . . ." Her mother wiped at her eyes with her palm.

"Daniel?" was all Maya felt safe saying.

"I know. It's horrible. Beyond horrible. They . . . those *animals*, they put his body on display there in the courtyard so that when his mother returned home, she would see him like that. Ay, Dios santo. I can't—" Her mother couldn't bring herself to finish the sentence. "Ay, mija. You don't look so well. This is just . . . demasiado. Come here."

Maya dug her head into her mother's neck, and she pulled Mama close. "Mija, Daniel was caught between the police and the maras. Señora Pérez was paying the mareros, trying to buy time. But it wasn't enough. It rarely is. This is *exactly* why I keep telling you that it's too dangerous here. It's *been* too dangerous."

And, Maya thought frantically, who knew what danger was next? What *Oscar* would do next. She'd brought that danger *home*, to her mother, herself. This she thought as her mother clutched her close. Her mother lifted the curtain, barely an inch, with her finger. "They're lighting candles, incense. Ay, pobre. We should too. I think I have some in the drawer."

Maya dug around and found two thin candles. What had Sebastian said exactly? *How do you know señora Pérez?*

"Maya?" her mother called, keys jingling.

"Coming." She had the worst feeling in the pit of her stomach. Not only was Oscar involved, but Sebastian was too, somehow. Was Sebastian also a—no! She couldn't go there, she couldn't. Not right now.

As they walked toward the neighbors circling around señora Pérez, who was seated on a white plastic chair someone had brought out for her, candles and rosaries and incense and prayers all around, Maya gently pulled her mother's elbow. "Mama?"

"Don't be scared, mija."

She shook her head. "That's not it. I'm just . . ." How could she explain any of it?

"Buenas tardes, señora Silva," a neighbor called to her mother, then reached over to hug Maya tight, holding on longer than usual.

Her mother leaned in, whispered, "We'll finish this conversation later. Right now, we need to be here for señora Pérez, entiendes?"

Maya nodded as another neighbor, señor Padilla, walked up and put his palm on her mother's shoulder. They exchanged solemn nods. He lit their candles using the flames from his own. A little girl clung to her mother's skirt. Another couple passed a baby between them while taking turns consoling señora Pérez, who stared blankly into space, only mumbles escaping her lips, her fingers rubbing the pink rosary in her hands. Someone passed around chuchitos. Someone else passed around little bottles of water. These people weren't just her neighbors, Maya realized. They had lived on this street and in this colonia for years, some of them even for generations. They were practically extended family. And it was clear that something was shifting. Home was no longer this safe cocoon. And from the looks on their faces and their tense bodies, it seemed like everyone was thinking the same thing.

Who was next?

19

By the time they got home, it was after nine and they were both emotionally drained. Maya kept looking at her phone. No Lisbeth. What if . . . She could *not* go there. Lisbeth was just . . . busy. Maya would wait for her to text back. She turned on the small lamp beside La Betty and dug out the fire neck from her backpack.

Her mother placed a hand on Maya's shoulder. "It's been a long day, mija. It's okay to leave the work for one night. You must be tired." True—she *was* exhausted, but there was no way she could sleep. Still, she secured the fitted sheet onto the corner of the mattress. She would try. As her mother fluffed a pillow, she said, "Maya. *Swear* to me. Tomorrow you will come home straight after school. En serio."

"I promise." Maya slowly covered the mattress with the comforter. She was still in some kind of shock. . . . She needed to text Sebastian. And try calling Lisbeth again. And again. And again. "I really do. I'm sorry—"

Mama put up a hand. "I'm too tired right now. Shut off the light."

"Okay, Mama." Maya was all about saying *sí, Mama* and *okay, Mama*. Whatever was necessary to keep her mother at peace, or at least in some vicinity of peace. But as soon as her mother started her soft snoring, Maya reached for her phone. She dimmed the light and turned toward the wall.

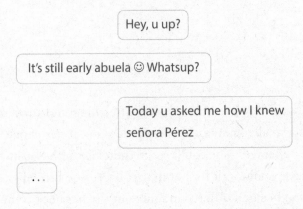

Hey, u up?

It's still early abuela ☺ Whatsup?

Today u asked me how I knew señora Pérez

. . .

Maya waited. She was *aching* to tell him what she'd just . . . what had . . . It still didn't feel real. Didn't seem possible. And it was nowhere near over; she wasn't *that* dumb. Sebastian took so long to reply that the light on her phone dimmed. Finally.

And?

So, do u know her?

You sound like a reporter

> Lol I'm not. So how do u know her? Did u hear what happened to her son?

Yeah. Heard about it.

> Did u know it was gonna happen?

No.

This would have been a perfect time for Maya to type: *I SAW OSCAR KILL THE GUY. OSCAR, YOUR COUSIN, IS A MURDERER*. But she didn't. Her stomach was a knot. If Oscar hadn't even told Sebastian . . . then he really *was* going to keep it a secret. So—maybe he meant it when he told her to pretend she'd never seen him. And maybe, so long as *she* said nothing, and no one else knew, he'd leave her alone. So—Maya would keep it a secret too. Even from Sebastian. But . . . was Sebastian telling the truth? How could she really know? She typed again.

> Ok. It's so sad tho

> Yeah. Gotta go. Good night. See u tom.?

Maya turned to look at her mother, who was sleeping hard.

> I can't. have to come straight home.

Bummer.

I know. But I need to get ready for FS anyway. Designs need work.

Got it. If u change ur mind, text me

Ok ♥

He didn't respond. The phone dimmed once again. Maya sent a quick text to Lisbeth. No response there, either. She placed her phone beside the mattress and closed her eyes, but she couldn't *unsee*—señora Pérez's son . . . begging for his life. And Maya simply standing in the shadows, too paralyzed to make a move. Until it was too late. She'd done nothing to stop it! But what could she possibly have done? Gotten shot herself too, which would have *killed* Mama! She could no longer deny the risks. The danger was surrounding them, closing in. She couldn't stay paralyzed *this* time. The boxes were practically packed. *Move.* It was the only thing to do. It was the only thing that made sense.

Then her phone lit up. She grabbed it. Sebastian. Replying to her last text.

Nothing made sense.

It was going to suck beyond anything ever, but she knew they didn't have a choice. They had to move to San Marcos. Now.

20

5 Days to Go

All night Maya had tossed and turned, the image of Oscar silencing the gun, then aiming it at Daniel, at her, at Daniel, at her, woke her up at least a dozen times. She caught an even earlier bus to school, tried to focus on the chuchito corset—the husks were hard to manipulate and starting to smell. Not good! She glanced at her phone every few minutes, but no Lisbeth. Ana Mendez was in the studio too. She usually stayed after school. But the fashion show was now only five days away. First bell, still no Lisbeth. During Design II, Maya kept texting her when the instructor wasn't looking. Nada.

By lunch Maya felt nearly hysterical with worry. Again, voice mail. Then she texted Sebastian.

> Do u know if Lisbeth is with Oscar?

Nope. Just woke up.

Nice! ☺

Let me check it out. Text u later.

Maya didn't feel like sitting with any of the other girls at lunch. Mostly everyone brought food from home and sat on the front steps or in the wide entranceway. There were a few vending machines and couches there. Others, who could afford it, would leave campus and buy lunch at San Martín or a food truck. Others like Ana. But Maya was too freaked out at this point to eat—so she decided to go back to the studio, focus on anything except Lisbeth and what she'd seen yesterday.

Until her phone buzzed. Lisbeth? Please let it be Lisbeth! But it wasn't her. It was . . . Mama? Had something happened?

Maya answered immediately. "Mama!"

"Hola, mija. Don't worry. I'm okay. I'm at work. I only have a minute."

In the hallway a few girls laughed, their heads together, looking at a magazine. Maya gazed at them longingly. If only she could join them, giggle about something stupid, be consumed by something other than the messy web she was caught in. Damn! How long would Oscar stay quiet about what had happened? Could she?

"Maya? Are you there?"

"Sí, Mama. I'm here."

"I don't want us to fight, mija. Life is too short. Señora

Pérez—" Her voice caught. "Who knows what her last words were to her son? May he rest in peace."

Now Maya was tearing up. Her mother was scared. Maya was too.

"Mija," her mother said carefully, "we *can't* stay. We'll come back for the show, but we are leaving for San Marcos mañana. Punto."

Maya nodded ever so slightly. She couldn't believe she was admitting it, but the words stumbled out painfully. "I know, Mama."

"I'm so sorry, mija. This isn't the Guatemala your father would've wanted for you, for us."

"No . . ." A broken whisper.

"But—" Her mother changed her tone. "We only have one more night here, so I was thinking, why don't you invite your friends over for dinner tonight? Lisbeth and her novio, and the other muchacho. Sebastian."

Maya felt like she was having an out-of-body experience. Her mother wanted her to do *what*?

"Maya?"

Maya collected herself. "Sure!" Forcing pure cheer into the word. "I'll ask them, Mama. But I have to go. Class—"

"Anda, pues."

"Love you."

"Love you, too."

Maya hung up and laid her hands on the table to steady herself. Oscar. At her house. No way. Nooo way.

Her phone pinged again. Lisbeth!

I'm fine. In class. U worry 2 much. XO

First: relief! Second: seriously? Maya *had* to talk to Lisbeth.

In studio, Maya stormed into the room, flung her bag on the table. Whispers from girls around her grew louder. Maya looked up. Ana came over to her. She had this look that was . . . apologetic? "Maya . . . ," she began. "I'm so sorry, but it looks like someone . . ." She motioned toward Maya's pink quinceañera dress draped over the dummy by the window.

Every single balloon had been popped.

"No!" Maya dashed over. Sure enough, pink rubber everywhere—bits on the floor, dangling from the dress, fluttering in the breeze coming through the window.

No.

No.

No.

Maya fell to her knees, scooping the remnants of the balloons in her palms. Obviously, they were unsalvageable. Yes, she could buy new balloons. But it would take forever to blow them up, and there was so little time! And *who* would've done this?

Ana. It was her! It *had* to have been her. But then, why was she walking toward Maya, holding out her hand? "Vamos. Let's get some air. We can buy more balloons at the tienda on the corner."

Could Maya trust her? Maybe she'd popped all the balloons and she was just trying to seem nice now, in front of everyone. Maya didn't know what to believe anymore. "It's okay. I'll just go."

"What's going on?" Manu, hand on hip, approached them. "Ohhhhh," she said upon seeing the mess.

Then, a bang from the hallway. "Patojos! Get back here!" A man in a navy-blue uniform chased after twin boys wearing superhero capes. The boys ran circles around the dummies, nearly knocking over Maya's quince dress—what remained of it, anyway.

"Hey! Watch it!" Maya yelled.

The man, out of breath, the buttons on his shirt threatening to pop any second, raised a hand as he knelt over. "I'm so sorry, señorita. My sons . . . they didn't have school today and so I brought them to work with me."

Maya noticed the lettering on his shirt—Pura Energía. Ah, he was an electrician. Wait. She put two and two together. These kids—had they popped the balloons on her dress?

"I really am sorry, señorita. Please let me at least pay for new balloons."

Ana crossed her arms. "You should pay for that and more. Your kids literally destroyed her design!"

"Yeah!" Manu added.

Maya could barely believe it. Manu, yes. But Ana Mendez? Sticking up for her? The boys whizzed past. All that time . . . all that effort to create this look, and poof! She felt as deflated as the balloons. "I'll figure it out," Maya managed to say to the man through clenched teeth, and left for the store.

A few minutes later Maya was back. She considered scrapping this particular piece for the show, because she had so much else to do, and by the time she blew up the new balloons and stitched them to the dress . . . Ugh. There was no way she could do it all before leaving for San Marcos. To Maya's surprise, there stood Ana once more.

"Don't even think about it, Maya. Here. Give me those balloons."

"But why—"

"Last week the chiffon I've been working with was discontinued at La Fábrica. Entonces, I had to improvise. We're artists. Yes, it's a competition, but we're not in a war. Plus, I was so mad when I saw what happened! It was like *my* dress was attacked. This isn't how we roll here. So give me a balloon."

Maya could barely believe her ears . . . or her eyes. Ana ripped open the package Maya now held out to her and removed a pale pink balloon. She brought it to her lips and started blowing. Maya blinked, stunned. Aware that the world had become a very strange place. And this? Another example. Maybe it wasn't being rich that Maya envied, but the way Ana lived in the world, with this *it'll be fine* attitude, which came from a kind of security that Maya didn't have. Not yet. But Maya was good at fixing things, making something new from the wreckage. This was no different, she figured. So she grabbed a balloon herself, and together, they fixed the damn dress.

After studio, Maya charged straight toward Lisbeth's locker. She was carefully pulling out her iPad. Maya remembered the day they'd each given their lockers "makeovers," buying little stickers and shelves to decorate them exactly the same. It seemed such a long, long time ago. She tapped Lisbeth on the shoulder. *Your boyfriend killed someone. I saw.*

"Hey, stranger," was all Maya managed. *Stay calm.*

"Hey." Lisbeth looked . . . different. Moving in slow motion. Maya watched for a moment. Was she high? Did she *know*?

"Are you okay?" she finally asked. *Your boyfriend is a murderer.*

"Yeah! Why wouldn't I be?" She placed the iPad in a mint-green case and then slipped it into her bag.

"Uh . . . I sent you like a thousand texts."

"Oh, sorry. I was busy." Busy hanging out with a killer? She *needed* to tell her.

"You heard about Daniel?" Maya asked, avoiding eye contact.

"Ay, sí. Pobre. And his mother. She's your neighbor, right?"

Maya nodded. Lisbeth zipped her bag. Neither of them said anything for a few tense seconds.

"Lisbeth, c'mon. It's *me*. Something's up. I can tell. You don't look . . . yourself." Maya's teeth chattered.

"Nothing. I'm just wiped. I told you, I was busy. I was up . . . late. With Oscar." Well, *yeah*. Of course. Although, her huge smile looked genuine enough. Ugh. Maya *had* to tell her!

"Sounds like you two are each other's media naranja lately. I mean—" Maya fumbled with her phone.

"We are." Lisbeth shut her locker. "And why wouldn't we be?" She looked around, then lowered her voice. "Okay, okay— fine, you're right, I have to tell you. You're right. Sooooo, he's been taking me on some jobs with him, and he even let me run some errands for him. But check this out. He pays me to do it. It's basically like a job! Right? It's super easy, too. And I was thinking—you could do it with me. All I do is—"

Maya felt herself spinning—Lisbeth was working for Oscar? For . . . a gang? And she didn't even know—

"Lisbeth—"

"What?" Lisbeth cut her off, her voice laced with annoyance.

"You're running *errands* for Oscar? You sure you want to be doing that?"

Lisbeth looked at her like she was insane. "Doing what? I'm just dropping off sandwiches and picking up six-packs of beer. Maya—you seriously have to take it down like fifty notches."

"Oh . . ." Maya couldn't do this. How could she tell her best friend that her boyfriend . . . that her boyfriend had . . . And now Lisbeth was working for him. Okay, she wasn't dropping off diapers full of cocaine, but still. "But why is Oscar *paying* you to drop off food? Hello—there are things called delivery services—"

Lisbeth propped her hands on her hips. "Maya, think about it. You know they have like, secret places they hang out and stuff, so it's not like he can just have pizza delivered by some flaco on his motorbike who'll tell everyone everything."

Maya considered. "True . . ."

"Anyway, the money is good. And I'm helping Oscar. And then we spend more time together. Speaking of, what's up with you and Sebastian?"

Now it was Maya who smiled brightly, despite the knot in her throat. But no, she had to stay focused. She had to tell Lisbeth the truth. She *would*.

"Mm-hmm . . ." Lisbeth leaned against her locker, crossed her arms. "Well?"

And just as Maya opened her mouth to say, "There's something you need to know . . ." the bell rang.

"Shoot! I can't be late for this class again; catch ya later,"

Lisbeth exclaimed, and off she went, fast-walking down the hall, turning to blow a quick kiss Maya's way. The knot in Maya's stomach tightened. After school, then. She'd tell her after school.

Later, between classes, Maya sent her mom a quick text.

> They can't make it for dinner. 👎

At least that part, the thumbs-down emoji, wasn't a lie.

21

Maya had to tell Lisbeth. She looked for her after school, but Lisbeth had already bolted. At home, madly humming a Bad Bunny tune over and over as if it were a musical pacifier, Maya tried to distract herself by working. She was gathering fabric pieces beside La Betty and stuffing them into a plastic bag to fit into a cardboard box—where the heck had her mother even gotten so many boxes?—when she got a text from Lisbeth.

> Hey, bumped into ur mom while I was picking up burgers for Oscar. For some reason she thought I couldn't make it to dinner. She says to bring Oscar & Sebastian tonight! I'll bring dessert, too! See you soon!

Oh no. Oh no, no, no. Maya's fingers hovered over her phone. What could she reply? *No, don't bring your boyfriend because he's actually a killer?* Instead she managed to type:

> We're leaving tmrw so I'd love just
> YOU to come over, it's our last night!

> ☺ What! See you at 6!

No. *No.* Maya tossed the phone on the couch. She looked around frantically, picked up her phone again, and called Lisbeth. She didn't answer. Argh. Next, Mama. No response. Pick up . . . *porfa* . . . She tried again. Still, nada.

Then Maya called Sebastian. She would explain. She would make up something. Anything. But it went straight to voice mail. Ugh. Luna whimpered, marching in circles. Funny how dogs always knew when something was up.

Think, Maya. Think. She paced the room. How in the world could Oscar be coming over for dinner? Then, thank God, she heard her mother call from outside.

"Maya! Help! I have bags."

Maya swung open the door, reached down for a bag. "You got so much food, Mama! But we can eat it on the bus tomorrow. Tonight, our last night, I think we should go out."

"What?" her mother said, stepping inside. "But your friends are already here."

Maya looked up. Lisbeth, Oscar, and Sebastian all stood behind her, Sebastian with a bouquet of yellow marigolds in his hands. Oscar had an arm around Lisbeth's waist. In his other arm, a bottle of Big Cola.

She was dead. That had to be the only way this was happening.

"Maya Luz!" her mother scolded.

"Oh . . . sorry . . . Please, please come in." Hesitantly, she moved from the doorway, unable to so much as look Oscar's way. Her stomach lurched. She had no idea what to do. Run? And what about her mother and Lisbeth? And did Sebastian still not know? Her mother was already setting the table with glasses and folding paper napkins into triangles at each setting. How. Was. This. Happening?

"The chairs, Maya. On the roof." She spoke to Maya but looked at Oscar and Sebastian. Only Sebastian offered to get them.

"I'll be right back."

Lisbeth laid out plates at the table.

"I'm afraid dinner will be simple tonight," her mother said apologetically. "With us leaving tomorrow and all."

"It's all good," Oscar said. Oscar—*a person who had killed another person like it was nothing*—who was staring directly at Maya now. "It's aaaall good," he repeated, before asking, "So, where are you moving to?" waving toward the stack of boxes.

Maya wiped her clammy palms against the sides of her leggings, willing her mother not to answer even as her mother was saying, "San Marcos." *Please, please leave it at that.*

"Oh, I love that city," Oscar said smoothly. "Where in San Marcos?"

"Hey!" Maya interrupted. "I think Sebastian maybe needs help."

Oscar smirked, then dragged himself up the stairs.

Once Sebastian and Oscar returned with the chairs, followed

by a chorus of *gracias, gracias, buenas noches, encantanda, gracias, que bonitas las flores* . . . her mother put a frozen pizza into the oven and quickly poured a bag of TorTrix chips into a bowl, passed around the soda.

"Please, sit," Mama encouraged. "Carmen, por favor. Call me Carmen."

Lisbeth shook her head, taking a seat. "There's no way I can ever call you by your first name, señora Silva."

"Bueno," her mother said, and put her hands together. "Now, Maya, why did you say these muchachos couldn't make it to dinner? When I bumped into them on the street, they had no idea what I was talking about."

"I . . . just figured it was all too last-minute—I didn't want you to go to all this work when we're still packing," Maya offered pathetically, reaching for Luna. She cuddled her close, silently praying that Oscar would really let things . . . go . . . and that he'd never bring it up—never tell Sebastian or Lisbeth. Praying that he'd never hurt Lisbeth. At the same time, how could he *be* here, in her house, his hand linked with her best friend's—the very hand that had shot a gun— Stop! She could *not* go there right now.

"I'll make a salad," Maya cried out, and excused herself to the kitchen. Her chair scraped against the ceramic tile, the sound whiplashing her back to the courtyard in señora Pérez's house. A wave of nausea hit.

"Maya? ¿Estás bien?" her mother asked.

"I can help," Oscar offered loudly.

All eyes locked on him. "Aw . . . ," Lisbeth said. "That's so sweet. No, I can help."

"No. Really. Let me." He stood before anyone else could protest. Although it was only a few feet away, he and Maya were suddenly alone, hovering over the counter, where she had placed a cutting board and a . . . knife. She would not look at him. Would not. Look. At. Him. Her hands went fumbly and she almost dropped the knife. Oscar grabbed it and placed it on the counter. "I got it," he said. Maya searched for any hidden meaning in his words.

"Thanks," she managed to say. "The tomatoes . . ." She cleared her throat. "And cucumbers are in the fridge." He gathered them while she plucked a lonely lime from a bowl on the countertop. She reached again for the knife. *Steady, steady,* she willed herself. *You can do this.* She lifted the knife and brought it to the lime. She would cut it into wedges, just like she had done a thousand times. Like her mother had taught her, she'd keep the pieces even. She was concentrating, holding the knife, didn't realize she was sweating until a drop fell onto her wrist.

Oscar leaned in close.

She gripped the knife.

He balanced the cucumbers and tomatoes in one hand while he tucked a piece of hair behind her ear. Maya stopped cutting. It took all her strength to hold the knife still.

"Are you two okay over there?" Maya's mother called from the table.

"I don't think Oscar's ever been in the kitchen before," Sebastian said, and everyone laughed.

"Ay, let me help!" Lisbeth bounced over, grabbed the tomatoes and cucumbers from Oscar, and shooed him back to the table, the yellow marigolds alert in a clear vase at the center.

∧∨∧

At least—AT LEAST—they ate quickly. First, chips and Big Cola, then the salad, and finally, the pizza. Maya barely touched hers. Her mother gave her a knowing smile, probably thinking she was too self-conscious to eat because of Sebastian. But Mama had no idea. No. Idea.

"Wow," Sebastian said, bringing his hands to his stomach after having seconds. "I'm seriously full, gracias, señora Silva."

"Ay, de nada, Sebastian. Entonces, tell me. How long have you been here?"

"Almost two whole months." There was something about the way he said it, *two whole months*, like he deserved an award for making it that long. If he could move back to the States tomorrow, would he? What if he could go back to the day he'd been playing basketball and ICE officers charged the court? If he'd managed to escape, he never would've come to Guatemala. She never would've met him. Maya thought of the baskets he shot that day at the park. So much of life came down to luck, she thought. And timing.

"And your mother? Is she still, where is it, in California?"

He shook his head. "She, um, died when I was real young."

"Ay, lo siento mucho. I'm so sorry. I didn't mean to bring it up. I didn't know. Que Dios la bendiga." She gave Sebastian a sympathetic look.

"She died while crossing," Oscar tossed in, all matter-of-fact.

Lisbeth arched her perfect eyebrows. She laid her hand over Oscar's. Maya's mother made a sign of the cross.

"I'm so sorry," Maya gasped.

"Oh, I thought you knew," Lisbeth said, her voice apologetic.

"No. I mean, I knew she— I didn't know *how*—"

"Yeah," Sebastian went on. "I was only eleven months old. We crossed the border with my father, and well, she didn't make it."

"I'm so sorry," Maya said again, pushing her plate away. Now she *really* didn't have an appetite.

"It is what it is," Sebastian said with a wry smile. "My father raised me. And I have lots of family in San Jose."

Oscar punched him lightly in the arm. "And here, vos!"

"Yeah. And here," he said, blinking like crazy.

"Maya, how far along are you with those dresses? You got like negative days left?" Lisbeth said, redirecting the conversation, scooching her chair closer to Oscar.

Now Maya locked eyes with Oscar. She couldn't help it. It was a reflex. Another wave of nausea came over her.

"Maya? What's wrong?" her mother asked. "You look like you've seen a ghost. Mija, it's just a fashion show. Remember that. It's not life or death. If you win, you deserved to win. And if you lose . . ."

"Then you still deserved to win, and it's just that the judges were paid off or something. Am I right?" Sebastian said, overly enthusiastically. He *knew* something was up, Maya could tell! "Right?" he prompted.

"Right!" Lisbeth offered.

"Right," Oscar echoed.

Her mother laughed. "Right," she said, a version of a smile on her face, for the first time in far too long.

Afterward, Maya's mother and Lisbeth cleared the dishes. Sebastian insisted on helping, so he and Maya picked up the dirty napkins and wiped the crumbs off the table. Oscar had gone outside for a smoke. Over the clinking of glasses and the running faucet, Maya heard her mother ask Sebastian, "So, your cousin Oscar."

"¿Sí, señora?"

"He's related to you by blood?"

"Jeez, Mama! That's so—nosy!" Maya interrupted.

Sebastian waved her off. "No, it's okay."

Her mother added, "He's just . . . quiet. I thought maybe Sebastian could share more about him."

Maya placed the smudged glass on the counter. "Lisbeth probably knows more about him at this point," she murmured. Lisbeth poked her in the ribs.

"Well," Sebastian said. "He's super into stand-up comedy. I know—you wouldn't exactly expect that from looking at him, but he can really get into it. He watches comedians on YouTube all the time."

"Oh?"

"Yeah. He has this big dream of opening a performance space where there's like competitions for funny skits and stand-up. He wants to charge an entrance fee, and then get sponsors and everything, you know, for the prizes."

"Hmm. That's thinking like a real entrepreneur. You know, Maya's father studied business."

The mere mention of her father changed the weather in the room. Why did she have to bring him up?

Sebastian passed her mother a dirty dish, and when her mother turned away, he brought the same hand to Maya's arm and squeezed once.

"Anyway," her mother continued. "That's wonderful that Oscar is thinking like a businessman. It's also something that would bring joy to the community, verdad? People still need to laugh even when—" This time she caught herself. "Well, everyone needs a good laugh now and then, sí?"

"Sí, señora."

"Ay! Muchacho, call me Carmen."

Sebastian dipped his chin. But he didn't say her name.

On their way out, Maya brushed her hand against Sebastian's arm. It killed her not to hug him tight, not to kiss him. Meanwhile, Lisbeth and Oscar were glued to each other's sides. Clearly, Lisbeth knew nothing. And clearly, Oscar wanted to keep it that way.

"He seems nice," her mother said the moment Maya returned. She stacked the three folding chairs, the dinner party already a thing of the past. The chairs would remain in the apartment with the rest of the minimal furniture—a table, a sofa, a television. Their landlord had agreed to pay them for these items, hoping to rent the apartment as furnished. Mama said they'd start fresh in San Marcos, build their way into a new life bit by bit.

Maya nodded. "He is. Sebastian. He's really nice." She was grateful that her mother had given him a chance. This was huge. And yet, Maya waited for it. She knew it was coming . . .

"But Oscar . . ." Boom. There it was.

"What about him?" Maya turned around, began pulling out the mattress, anything to avoid her mother's stare.

Her mother helped her ready the bed. "No sé. Something is . . . off. Como si tuviera mala sangre, you know?"

Maya stiffened. Her mother was right, after all. Oscar was *not* a person with integrity. And ohhhh God, she still hadn't told Lisbeth about Oscar yet. She stifled a moan, then swallowed before saying, "I'm tired. Okay if I go to sleep? Unless you need me for more packing?"

"No, mija. The kitchen is clean. That was nice of Sebastian to offer to help. Not like el otro."

22

4 Days to Go

Early Saturday morning, Maya woke to the sounds of Mama rushing to work. Her keys. The coffeepot. Zipping of bags. She was usually so quiet.

"Mama?" Maya yawned. "What's wrong?"

"Sorry, mija. My boss called. Says there's some kind of an emergency. My last day. Of course! We'll catch a bus to San Marcos after my shift. Eat dinner on the road. I love you. Now go back to sleep."

Didn't have to tell her twice! Maya pulled the covers over her head and burrowed into her pillow, Luna by her side.

At school, the studio was open specifically for finalists to prep for the fashion show—it was only four days away! Maya knew she was behind, and heading to San Marcos would only seal that fate, but she hoped that seeing the accessories would give her the kick in the butt she needed, and just maybe, she could still win this thing. She'd also decided—finally—on the three looks. She couldn't take the balloon dress with her to San Marcos, but she could take the volcano dress neckline and the zipper dress and work on them for the next few days until she returned to the capital. Maya asked Lisbeth to come and help. But more importantly, then she could talk to her about Oscar, for real. In the large studio room, they spread out the pieces that Maya had mostly finished and began searching through the plastic bins full of accessories that finalists could use to boost their looks.

"So, what'd you think of dinner with the guys?" Lisbeth asked as she held up a hot-pink bandana.

Maya squinted at the bandana—could it work with the zipper dress? Hmm . . . "Oh," she answered. "It was nice."

"Nice?" Lisbeth echoed, hand on hip.

"I mean, yeah. It was good for my mom to finally meet Sebastian, I guess. Even though . . ." She swallowed, her mouth like cotton. How long could she—she *had* to warn Lisbeth!

"Totally," Lisbeth was saying. "This feels like old times, no?" She held up a yellow-and-silver brooch.

Maya debated whether to add this instead to the jean zipper dress, let the change of subject distract her.

Lisbeth stood beside Maya, eyed the brooch too. Shook her head. "No. I don't think it works."

"But the dress needs something else."

"What about if you do the model's makeup super interesting, like unexpected? Or her hair or something? Or . . ." Lisbeth pursed her lips. They were purple today, probably another present from Oscar. Or maybe she'd bought the lipstick with her own money. She *had* her own money now, from her "job."

"That could work," Maya said. A few feet away another student was using a glue gun to put together a jacket. With the smell came a memory—something she hadn't thought about in years—the time when she was ten and she and her mother used a glue gun to decorate the bottom of Maya's jean jacket with tiny green rhinestones. She had lived for that jacket, until one day she'd accidentally left it in a booth at a pizza place. When they went back the next day to see if it was still there, of course it wasn't.

Lisbeth touched Maya's shoulder. "Don't worry—we'll know what works when we see it, right?"

Lisbeth was right. Maya linked her arm with Lisbeth's. "I'm going to miss you."

"Well, right now I'm right here!" She bumped hips, then reached for her iPad. "I'll find you some inspiration."

"Thanks, amiga." Maya watched as Lisbeth scrolled and scrolled. Her best friend. Her only real friend in the world. Maya would do anything for her. And she knew Lisbeth would do the same. So how could Maya keep this monumental secret from Lisbeth? She had to tell her. It would shatter Lisbeth, Maya knew that too, but Lisbeth HAD to know. Right now. Right here.

"Lisbeth . . . I have to tell you something. About Oscar."

Lisbeth's eyes narrowed instantly. "What?"

Maya glanced around, took Lisbeth by the elbow into a nearby closet. She leaned in close. "Lisbeth—you've known me for forever. You know I'd never do you wrong. So trust me when I say this. You really have to be careful with him. I don't think you should make any more deliveries, and I think you should just, try to . . . like . . . not see him.”

“Maya! What are you *talking* about? And what about *you*? And Sebastian? Oh, so Oscar isn’t good enough for me, but Sebastian is for you? You sound like a hypocrite, you know that?”

And out it came. “He killed someone, Lisbeth.”

Lisbeth froze, but then she started laughing. Like, cracking up. “Oh, Maya,” she said at last, with a *you’re so naive* sort of sigh.

And it was Maya who was stunned. Lisbeth already knew?

Lisbeth continued. “Maya, just because he’s in a gang doesn’t mean he kills people. Why are you so, like, simpleminded? There are gangs, and then there are *gang* gangs. We’ve talked about this already. C’mon.”

“Lisbeth . . .”

“No, seriously. I know maybe people in the gang do crazy stuff, but not Oscar. He’s not even at that rank yet. Besides, he isn’t that type of guy to just hurt someone for no reason. I mean, if it’s self-defense—”

Maya hesitated. Once she said it, she couldn’t ever take it back. She thought of Juliana. Nobody tried to help Juliana. She was *not* going to let it be the same for Lisbeth. No. She wouldn’t let Oscar do anything to Lisbeth, not if she could help it. She couldn’t help Daniel, but Lisbeth—

“I saw him!” Maya blurted, her voice a harsh whisper. “I was there, at señora Pérez’s house, when . . . He didn’t know I was there . . . And in the courtyard, I saw him . . .”

“You what?” Lisbeth pulled back, her face draining of color.

“Lisbeth . . . I *saw* him . . . kill señora Pérez’s son.”

Lisbeth went paler still.

“I know.” Maya reached for her.

"Oh my God," Lisbeth gasped, hugging Maya back.

"You have to be so, so careful, Lisbeth. I mean . . ." She looked down at her Converse. "I guess we both do," she said, pulling away.

Lisbeth nodded, but she seemed to be staring off into some other world. "I just . . . I'm just . . . I don't know. You're sure? A hundred percent sure?"

Maya nodded.

"I'm sorry—I'm so sorry—"

"This is all so crazy, Maya." She lowered her head.

"I know. I know it is." Maya hugged her again.

Late that afternoon, before Mama came home and they ate a quick dinner before taking a night bus to San Marcos, a bang at the door made Maya jump a million miles. She peeked through the curtain. Well, that didn't take long. It was Oscar. Maya hesitated, then opened the door an inch, the chain still on. He shoved his finger into the space. "You'd better be careful, bitch."

"Stop!"

"*Stop!*" he mocked her.

He removed his finger from the door, and—slowly dragged it across his neck. "I mean it."

"Why are you doing this!" Maya cried.

"You couldn't keep your stupid mouth shut, could you? Lisbeth broke up with me. I knew I should've—" And he turned and left.

Maya sat, trembling, on the couch under a comforter. Luna jumped onto her lap. They stayed that way until it was dark enough to need a light. Even then, she didn't move. *Be careful. I mean it . . .* Sebastian. Lisbeth. Maya reached for her phone, but then hesitated. What would Oscar do if she told someone what she'd seen? She put the phone back down.

When Mama came home, her hands were full. She was holding . . . a wedding dress? "Maya?" she asked warily.

"Hola, Mama."

"Ay, Dios! You scared me! Why are you sitting in the dark? And under a colcha? Are you sick?"

And it was in the dark that Maya told her mother everything.

That was one version she had planned in her mind while sitting in the dark for the past hour. But it wasn't the version she went with.

Instead, she told her mother, "I have a migraine."

"Ay, mija, let me bring you some papa. I think we have one left. Unless I packed it!"

"Uh . . . Mama? Better question—why do you have a wedding dress?"

Her mother gently draped the dress over the edge of the couch, then dipped into the kitchen. She soon returned with two wheels of raw potato, telling Maya to lay them on her temples. She then wrapped a thin bandana around Maya's head and secured it in a knot. It was a remedy her abuela used for headaches, and Maya felt comforted . . . sort of.

"Thank you, Mama," Maya whispered, sick with guilt.

"I'm sorry you're stressed about all this change, mija. And the show. But I have news."

More news? Maya pulled the comforter around her. She wasn't sure she could take any more news. "What is it,

Mama? I thought we had to catch the bus. Like, now."

"The emergency from this morning? Well, my boss needs me to expand this wedding dress for a bride who is pregnant! She wants the same dress and is willing to pay—a *lot*—for the alteration." Mama turned on the lights.

"Hold on a second—so what does this mean?"

"So, as much as I can't believe I'm saying this—what's a few more days? Si Dios lo quiere . . . we'll move the day after the show. No bus tonight."

No. Maya couldn't believe *she* was saying *this*, but she did. "Mama, no! You said we have to . . . I can come back for the show . . . Really. I think you're right. We should really move. And besides, didn't you already pay for our bus tickets?"

Mama gently kissed her on the head. "You're being sweet, but your head must be worse than I thought! Why aren't you thrilled? Mija—the pay—it's a month's wages! The customer, she's from Zona diez." Her mother got out her sewing kit, picked up the dress. "We will be careful. Mind our own business. Then, after the show, nos vamos!"

Maya spent the next twenty-four hours on absolute edge. At least she didn't have to make excuses to Sebastian—he and Oscar and Oscar's brother were going to the coast, some job in Puerto Barrios, for a few days. Thank *God*. Sebastian promised he'd be back for the fashion show. Maya was secretly glad he was away—it meant Oscar was! But she couldn't stop checking her phone for even a cute emoji. She tried to home in on the remaining details for all three dresses. All her waking hours she ate, slept, and breathed trashion. Mama in tandem worked on expanding the wedding dress. The two of them were like mirror images of each other at night, on opposite ends of the couch, sewing, sewing, sewing. The remaining days dissolved into endless decisions about her designs.

Zipper dress—shortened the dress.

Pink quinceañera dress—substituted the plastic tablecloth material for a cotton tablecloth.

Volcano dress—spray-painted the fire neckline with slashes of orange and yellow for dramatic effect.

Zipper dress—lengthened the dress.

Volcano dress—fabric on neckline drooped. Tried cardboard.

Zipper dress—shortened it again.

Volcano dress—cardboard was too stiff. Tried coffee filters instead.

Volcano dress—to cinch the waist or not to cinch the waist? That was the question.

Pink quinceañera dress—sprayed fabric glitter over the plastic tablecloth. Loved how the light hit the glitter. Swapped the cotton tablecloth out for the plastic again.

Maya perfected the hemlines, the stitching, and the "fire" on the neckline for the volcano dress by using a ruffle that she carefully rolled from one end of the fabric to the other, trying a slip-stitch method her abuela had taught her. In the studio, before and after school, Lisbeth was at her side for every last stitch. And thank goodness, or she might have made the zipper dress so short it would've been mistaken for a swimsuit. Lisbeth was a fierce wing-woman, but there were times, like early Monday morning, the two of them at Maya's workstation, when Lisbeth suddenly burst into tears.

"I know it's crazy, vos. Like, with everything . . . But I still miss him sometimes. You know?"

Maya put down the steam iron she'd been pressing against the denim on the zipper dress. What could she say? "You're not crazy."

Lisbeth wiped her eyes with the back of her hand.

"Here," Maya said, handing her a tissue from her backpack. "Besides, you don't need him. I can always take you out for caramel coffee."

A half smile. "Well, you're leaving me too." Her eyes filled once more.

"But you'll visit!" She put her arm around Lisbeth. "Right?"

She nodded, lay her head against Maya's. After a few seconds, she said, "Bueno, vos. Let's get back to work."

Maya's fingers ached, but she couldn't keep from fussing and finessing. Yes, she desperately wanted to win—*needed* to win—but she also welcomed the distraction from the Oscar drama. Still, sometimes at night as she fell asleep, or when she was alone in the apartment before Mama came home from work, holding a pin in her mouth, visions of poor Daniel writhing in the courtyard as he pleaded for his life hit her like a slap, and she'd sit up or drop the pin and quiver all over.

Then, the night before the fashion show, there was a loud knock at the door. Maya sprang up and shoved her back against it. "Don't open it," she yell-whispered to Mama.

"¿Mija?" Mama paused, a swath of beaded lace for the wedding dress in her hands, Luna yipping in circles at her feet.

"Buenas noches," a voice called from the other side of the door. "Capital police."

The lace dropped to the floor, landing on top of Luna, who began to bark like a crazy animal. Mama scooped her up, but her face in that moment . . . full of so many questions. *What is going on? Why is there a police officer at our door so late at night? Does this have to do with those muchachos you've been hanging around with? Ay Dios, I hope nothing happened to a neighbor. Señora Pérez! God bless her. Or maybe one of Maya's friends? Lisbeth . . . Maya. Mija . . .*

"Move, Maya. Let me answer it."

Maya started to—but then stopped.

"Move," her mother said sternly.

Another knock, louder this time. "Señora Silva. Open the door."

"Mama . . ." Maya mouthed the word but no sound came out. Her mother brushed past her, swinging open the door. "Buenas noches. What can I help you with, señor?"

The man instantly looked inside the house. The boxes were now stacked vertically in the corner and as end tables beside the couch. He scanned Maya up and down, his hand on his belt by a gun in its holster. "I know it's late, señora. But if I can have a few words." It wasn't a question. He stepped over the threshold, uninvited. Maya fought nausea, every nerve on fire.

"Sí, sí," her mother said, worry etched in her voice. "Apologies, we only have the one couch. Maya—go get a chair!"

Maya did as she was told, glad for something to do. She returned, placing it near the couch, but not too close. "Por favor, sit," her mother said. She and Maya shared the couch.

"Is there a problem, señor?" her mother asked politely. Maya followed Mama's gaze as it darted from the clock on the wall to Luna sniffing the officer's black boots to the gold-painted cross hanging above the television.

"Señora," he said. He took off his hat. He looked much younger without it. "Señorita," he said to Maya, who linked her arm with her mother's. "There's been a lot of gang activity in the area recently. As you know, your neighbor señora Pérez's son was murdered recently. I assume you are aware of this tragedy."

"Sí, señor," her mother said. Maya felt like she was cracking into a gazillion pieces. But she nodded dutifully.

"We think he was murdered by a local gang member." The officer reached down and scratched Luna under the chin, her favorite place.

Oscar. Oscar. Oscar. Maya crossed her legs, uncrossed them, crossed them.

"In addition to being careful, more careful than usual, I ask that you come forward with any information you may have about the murder."

"Information?" Her mother sounded defensive, Maya could hear it in her voice. *What would we have to do with a murder? Why would you assume I would—that my daughter would—we're not those kind of people. We're not involved with those kind of people. . . .*

"If you see or hear anything, that is." The officer put his hat back on. "You, as well," he said, looking pointedly at Maya.

Her heart pounded. "Sí, señor."

But her mother couldn't let it go. "We don't have anything to do with this . . . tragedy," she said. "Officer, we keep to ourselves. And God willing, you will find the murderer. But please understand that we have nothing to do with—"

"I'm not suggesting that you do. I am merely urging you to share anything you might know." He glanced at Maya. "That is, if and when you hear of something, anything. We all know how news travels in colonias, especially ones with neighbors as close as you were to señora Pérez."

"Are," Maya's mother corrected him. "As close as we *are*."

"Precisely." He stood up, now looking directly at Maya. "Remember, señorita. It is your duty to come forward. Otherwise, you are considered an accomplice."

Her mother placed her hand on Maya's arm. "Now you're scaring her. Señor, again, we have nothing to do with this. *My daughter* doesn't. She's just a child."

He smirked, which Maya thought was odd, before making his way to the door. Another officer had been waiting outside, smoking a cigarette. He seemed bored, but when he caught sight of them all in the doorway, he perked up. One look at his partner's face and something passed between them. Maya knew it. She could *feel* it.

"Buenas noches," the officer said. "My card. In case you . . ." He paused. Static spit out of his walkie-talkie. If Maya's heart was beating fast before, now it was sprinting.

"Hold on a minute," the other police officer said. "You're the girl from the roof."

"I . . . I . . ." Maya shook her head. "I think you have me confused with someone else." She tried her best to sound calm.

The officer continued. "Sí, sí. I'd thought señora Pérez lived here. Yes, it's you. I knocked and you called out from the roof, explained that she was two houses down, that I had the wrong house."

"I wasn't . . . I don't remember." She struggled not to so much as blink, not to give herself away.

Her mother, somehow, avoided glaring at her, though Maya knew it was taking superhuman restraint.

"That's enough for now," the first officer said, giving a little salute. Maya never got his card.

"Buenas noches, señores," her mother said, the queen of calm, and shut the door behind them. Secured the lock. Closed the curtains. And when their footsteps were far enough away, she let out the longest sigh in the world.

Maya and her mother hugged. Held on. So tight. Until they didn't.

"I'm so glad we're moving," Mama whispered, and returned to adding final touches to the wedding dress. She was basically done, going to drop off the dress in Zona 10 tomorrow before coming to the fashion show, but her mother was a perfectionist— just like Maya! Mama had been so creative—taking fabric from the bottom of the dress and using it to expand the middle, for the baby bump. At the bottom she attached lace over the white fabric, and you really couldn't tell the difference.

Later that evening, late-late, when her mother was sleeping hard beside her, Maya reached for her phone. Sent Sebastian a text. He replied right away.

Hey you! Whatsup?

We gotta talk

k . . . am I in trouble? ☺

No. but can u talk now?

K.

With her mother asleep, Maya quietly tiptoed into the bath-room and crouched in the shower. She dialed Sebastian. She hadn't asked him what exactly he was doing in Puerto Barrios, but she felt the chill of it. If he was with Oscar and Oscar's brother, it probably wasn't sightseeing that filled their days. But she knew better than to ask. Maya wanted to tell him about the police just now, but when she heard his voice for the first time in days—they'd been texting, not talking—all she managed to say was, "I miss you."

"I miss you, too. I'm heading back in the morning."

"You're going to make it in time for the show, right?"

"Oh, wait. Is that tomorrow?" he asked, the connection full of static.

Maya's whole body sank. "Seriously?"

"Maya! I'm just kidding! No way would I miss it. I know it's tomorrow. I'll be there."

Relief washed over her. "I know we've both been crazy busy . . . but maybe . . . after . . ."

"I can't wait to see you," he said, making her smile.

"Me too."

"Tomorrow."

"Tomorrow."

She hung up, returned to the living room. Tired as she was, it took her a long time to fall asleep.

Then the day was finally here.

23

Show Day

Early that morning Maya's mother hugged her tight and handed her a gift—a flower brooch that had belonged to her grandmother. "It's a little rusted here"—she pointed—"but it's full of good luck. Although you don't need it, mija."

"Mama!" Maya ran her finger along the delicate jade stone at the center of the flower. This was totally something her abuela would have owned. It gave her all the good vibes. "I love it! Thank you."

"Listen, I'll be there. I'll come straight from work. Actually, I'm going to try to leave early. Either way, I'll be there. You reserved my seat?"

"Sí, Mama. Front row!"

Her mother kissed Maya on the cheek and then left, holding the wedding dress in a garment bag. Today was the day. *The* day. Maybe, just *maybe*, if Maya won, she would be one step closer to reaching her dreams—starting her own label, opening a store with Mama. Maybe even in San Marcos, why not? But first things first. Maya gave Luna a treat, made a quick sign of the cross over her chest, grabbed her purse, and off she went to win this thing.

Maya could barely walk up the concrete steps, she was so wobbly with excitement, but she did it, she made it. She searched the crowded hallway for Lisbeth. Sure enough, there she was, holding a clipboard and barking orders to girls left and right. She'd come in early to help with production. "You're on the lights! You—go help her. And you, get bottled water, lots, for the models. Make sure they drink throughout the day. We don't want anyone, like, fainting on the stage tonight."

"Like a boss!" Maya called out.

"There you are! Finally!" Lisbeth was wearing her black baby-doll dress with a red rope as a belt, cinched supertight on her super-tiny waist. Maya felt a surge of pride—Lisbeth was *so* into it, even though she wasn't a finalist. Even though—*no*—she was not going down the Oscar rabbit hole *today*.

"I've been here for an hour already. Listen—you need to eat something. Or maybe, don't. Rosa Sánchez just threw up in the bathroom. The one in the annex. Don't go in there. Trust me."

"Ew."

Lisbeth eyed Maya up and down. "Well, you *do* look like a fashion designer." Maya was glad to hear it. She'd dressed the part in her black jeans with pink blotches she'd made herself using bleach and an old toothbrush, and a button-down denim shirt, sleeves rolled up. She even wore a fanny pack so she could easily access pins, scissors, and thread if she needed them. The night before, her mother had braided her hair so in the morning all Maya had to do was pin it in a tight bun that sat just behind her neck. The last thing Maya needed was bangs in her face as she made final adjustments to her designs.

Lisbeth clapped again. "Vaya, pues. Let's go."

Maya reached for Lisbeth, hugged her so tight that she actually cracked Lisbeth's back. They both laughed.

"Hey—if tonight doesn't work out, you can always become a chiropractor!"

Maya shook her head. "Nope. Fashion designer Maya."

"¡Eso!" Lisbeth grabbed her hand. "Come on. We have tons to do."

She was right. Just the sight of the other students busy, busy—even though it was barely eight in the morning—fed Maya energy, like she'd just guzzled an entire can of Coke. Everyone was buzzing like bees in a hive. The honey: the fashion itself.

The next few hours seemed to evaporate. The workroom was getting ridiculously hot with so many girls in there making last-minute design adjustments. No fans allowed; they would interfere with glue guns, and send fabric fluttering, and no one could handle that added stress. Maya was sweltering. Why hadn't she worn a tank top? Her forehead had a glazed-donut look. Not cute. Finally someone opened a window.

Suddenly la directora strode in. She wore sneakers, which everyone seemed to judge simultaneously, and which she noticed, because she began her remarks by saying, "I'm going to change into heels later. Listen, everyone."

Every girl looked up, except for the finalists. Maya held two safety pins in her mouth as she used a tiny pair of scissors to fray the bottom of the zipper jean dress. Every minute was valuable.

"¡Señoritas! ¡Atención!"

Okay. Now Maya looked up. Was this the good kind of announcement or the bad kind? Was she about to share that a generous donor was having tacos delivered for everyone? Or was she about to tell them that the show was canceled due to some technical difficulty with the stage lights?

"I have something important to say," la directora said.

"So then say it already," Lisbeth mumbled. The girls close by heard her and started giggling.

"Listen up, ladies. I just want to say that I'm proud of all of you."

"That's it?" Lisbeth said, this time loud enough for everyone to hear. And everyone laughed. Even la directora. But not Ana, who looked like she was going to throw up.

"That's it, Lisbeth," la directora said, raising an eyebrow, but smiling.

Maya exhaled, the safety pins falling to the floor. She hadn't realized how badly she needed to laugh. To feel proud of herself, even for a moment.

24

By three p.m., things got capital *B* Busy. Everyone moved to the auditorium, where backstage, people began dressing their models and applying makeup and reapplying makeup and blow-drying hair. Doors opened a quarter to start time, which was six p.m. sharp. Maya was too busy to watch the clock tick. She *knew* she was obsessing as she continued to fray the edges of the inside-out exposed zipper running down the length of a model's torso. She wanted it to look messy, messier. Obsession—attention to detail—mattered in this line of work.

"¡Qué cool!" Lisbeth practically squeaked. "But I think you're good, no? Pretty soon there won't be any more fabric to fray."

Maya leaned back, squinted, rolled her neck to get out the kinks, then went in and frayed some more. It had to be perfect if she was going to win. She had decided against using the chuchitos design only because they'd started to smell, but if and when she sold that design in stores, she'd have to problem-solve. For now, adios chuchitos.

The first look—Lisbeth in the pink, frilly quince dress made from plastic tablecloths. Sebastian's balloon idea was truly *perfect*. Right now, though, Maya couldn't go down memory lane. She had to *concentrate*.

The second—on another student whose designs hadn't been selected for the show but who jumped at the chance to wear one of Maya's—the exposed zipper jean dress. Sleek and sophisticated and unexpected. Maya could *totally* see this in a store at the fancy mall in Zona 10. Fingers crossed!

And the third—was on last year's winner, who had agreed to model Maya's volcano dress with the fire neckline, made, at last, from coffee filters.

Maya was so focused, she didn't so much as blink until Lisbeth waved her arm in the air at her like a matador. "Come on, Maya. Take a moment to at least, you know, take this all in."

Maya looked up, looked around. "You're right. It's . . . it's the best day of my life."

"Now who's the dramatic one?" Lisbeth said, grinning. "Here. Drink."

Maya took the water, chugged the entire bottle in one long gulp. "Thanks."

"No problem."

They exchanged a look. "Any word from Sebastian? He's coming, right?" Lisbeth asked.

"He'll be here. Even if he has to take a camioneta, he'll be here." Maya pictured Sebastian riding a crowded bus, chickens and roosters riding alongside passengers, just to make the show.

Lisbeth looked away. The elephant in the room: Oscar. Of course he wouldn't be joining Sebastian. She pivoted like a pro amiga. "Not for nothing, that is something I'd like to see—Sebastian riding a chicken bus all the way to the fashion show."

Maya cracked up, then her stomach gurgled, loud.

Lisbeth eyed her. "Did you even eat lunch, Maya?"

"No . . ."

"I'm going to get you a sandwich or something. You have to eat. I'll be right back."

"You're the best. Thanks, Lisbeth."

"Yeah, yeah. You better remember me when you're famous."

"Ha! I will."

Maya couldn't stop—she added a tiny bit of glitter to the fire neckline, took a mini hot iron to the smallest of wrinkles on the zipper dress, lengthened the black eyeliner on her models. Everyone both onstage and backstage was hurtling about with last-minute preparations. A team of girls placed pieces of printer paper that said RESERVED on each seat in the first two rows in the auditorium for board members and family. Another team folded lavender-colored programs. And another pair roamed around, holding up small battery-operated fans to girls' faces. It was ridiculously hot in the auditorium, too, and it was nearly empty. Once the audience filled all these seats . . . But Maya couldn't think about all that now. When Lisbeth returned with a ham and cheese sandwich on French bread, Maya bowed—with a wink—then ate the sandwich in four bites, standing up.

Impossibly soon, an announcement came over the loudspeaker: "We're on in thirty minutes!"

What? Thirty minutes?!

Then, in what seemed like a blink, she heard, "Five minutes until showtime!"

Maya glared at the loudspeaker. Was her mother here? She reached for her phone. Called her. No answer. Sent text after text. Nerves. Anxiety. She peeked behind the curtain. No Sebastian, either. But Mama . . . Each of Maya's texts was less patient than the one before.

> Mama—call back.

> Mama??

> Mama, show is about to start. Where r u?

> Mama—it's time.

> Mama, are you . . . going to miss it??

> Mama, I will never forgive you if you seriously miss this.

Then she went weak. What if . . . what if . . . something had happened to her? An accident? Oscar? Oh God. No—Maya shoved that thought away. He was still in Puerto Barrios doing a job!

Lisbeth suddenly towered over Maya—even more so in her five-inch heels. "Maya, you know we're starting in like a negative minute, right?"

"I know . . . ," Maya managed a whisper. So maybe Sebastian got stuck in traffic, or he couldn't catch a bus, or . . . but her mother? A knot formed in her throat. Her mother couldn't miss tonight. Her mother would *never* miss tonight! This was the fashion show!

The fashion show, where right now the models were getting ready to walk onstage, and multicolored lights—fuchsia and lemon and turquoise—blinked from the ceiling and spilled their colors all around, where the sound system was getting a last-minute mic check, one two, one two. Maya pressed her palms against her temples, but it only made her think of her mother again, the potato slices she'd used to help Maya get rid of that headache a few days ago. Two girls fanned a third, who was wearing a black velvet bodysuit. Oy. Not the best fabric for the runway. It showed every flaw—on the fabric and the model. Plus, it was insanely hot. Poor Lisbeth. She was probably melting in the plastic quince dress. But as she strutted over to Maya for one final check, swinging her hips as if on a catwalk, the skirt with just the right bounce, Maya couldn't lie—she looked phenomenal.

"Showtime, Maya! Come on." But—Mama!

"Can you go tell them that I have . . . a headache?" she said quickly, desperately. "Maybe my girls go last?" Maya checked her phone again. Nothing.

Lisbeth brought her hands to her lips as if in prayer. "Maya."

"Yeah?"

Lisbeth adjusted her librarian eyeglasses, which were adorned with little pink diamond stickers—a perfectly chosen accessory. Sighed. "Maya. The. Show. Is. Starting. You realize that."

"But—my mother—she's not here yet! Please, Lisbeth! At least try." Maya looked toward the double doors. A school officer was ushering in stragglers. "Please."

Lisbeth returned a minute later, crestfallen. "I'm really sorry—they can't change the order now; it's how it's printed in the programs. They've already handed them out to the audience."

And as if on cue, la directora announced over the intercom, "Bienvenidos! Please take your seats. We are about to begin." La directora had changed into black leather leggings, a black tank top, and a long leopard-print suit jacket. And red heels. No more sneakers. She looked as stylish as Maya had ever seen her, and she half wanted to snap a picture of her, but then the bass of the intro music hit Maya in the chest. Instead of pumping her up, she felt almost, unexpectedly, hollow. Where. The. Hell. Was. She? Mama had been as excited about this as Maya had been! La directora was onstage, making some welcome speech thingy, then explaining how the winners would be announced at the end of the program and blah, blah, blah, but Maya could only half listen. From behind the curtain on the stage, she could not peel her gaze from the double doors.

Then the lights flashed extra bright and blinked. It really was showtime.

Don't cry. Don't do it. Maya wiped her eyes with the back of her hand. If anyone noticed, she'd just say she was emotional because it was her first show.

Then Maya reached for her phone and finished typing her last text.

It's starting . . .

Maybe Mama was stuck at work after all, something to do with the wedding dress for the pregnant bride. Yes, surely that was it.

The stage lights went black, the music off. People whispered in the audience and then it went quiet, so quiet that Maya wondered briefly if the power had gone out. But no. A second later, dramatic pink lights fired onto the stage. Showtime.

The first designer's models walked the runway, one at a time. Three suit looks: one ankle length and tan, one cropped and zebra print—very cool, that one—and the third, a see-through number. Maya had seen Gabriella working on these designs for weeks, but with the music and lights and the models wearing makeup (heavy blue eye shadow edged with silver glitter for all three), it looked really . . . impressive. Okay, maybe Maya could just enjoy this show. Maybe her mother was walking in right now.

The energy from the crowd was contagious. From stage left, Maya cheered on her classmates. They *were* all in this together. Yes, it would certainly matter who won, hello, but in this moment, the show was for the art itself. At the same time— she couldn't help herself—Maya kept scanning the auditorium for a woman frantically searching for a seat. As much as Maya willed her to appear, she didn't.

Next up was Manu. Everyone loved Manu—even during the days leading up to the show she somehow always found time to write her little inspirational notes on pastel Post-its and leave them on each finalist's work space. *You are enough* and *You are a boss bitch*. Manu's final designs were *incredible*—a hot-pink furry crop top paired with electric yellow tights and white platform boots; a black sweetheart neckline ball gown paired with purple boxing gloves, and jean overalls over a white tee. The last look was surprisingly simple, thought Maya, until the model arrived downstage and unfastened the overall bib's buttons, revealing a giant *5272* in bloodred paint. The crowd went wild. 5272 was the bill that once banned same-sex marriage and defined a family as a man and a woman who were raising children together. Many people in the audience stood and clapped, but Maya spotted a few parents who shifted uncomfortably in their seats. Seriously? Mama wouldn't be one of those parents—Mama, who believed you should never apologize for who you are. Mama . . . Where *was* she? Maya scanned the rows with desperation, her eyes darting to the entrance and reserved seating and back again. No Mama. No Sebastian.

Next up was Ana Mendez. Okay, a good distraction. Interesting. All three of Ana's designs were in the same fabric—pale blue chiffon. An A-line dress (cute for a wedding), a fitted halter dress (sexy!), and a pantsuit (swoon). As the models strutted across the stage, Maya realized this was actually genius. A store would totally pick up this line. Maybe a bridal shop. Yes! These looks were dead-on for a bridal party. Go, Ana!

Lisbeth appeared beside Maya and whispered in her ear, "Don't worry. You still got this. Anyway, blue is so . . . basic."

Maya threw her arm around Lisbeth. She knew Lisbeth was just trying to calm her, but honestly, Maya felt happy for Ana. And for herself. And for all the finalists. *Tonight* was a total dream. *Their* dream. It was why they'd enrolled in Salomé Fashion Institute, and why they worked so hard. Then Maya spotted Ana's parents and sister in the front row, aiming their phones and smiling from ear to ear. Maya squeezed Lisbeth tighter.

The show went on—with oohs and aahs from the crowd, including a little girl with pink hair who watched the models wide-eyed. There were flops, too. The one model whose tangerine tube top threatened to slip down as she pranced across the stage. Oops—that designer hadn't accounted for movement in designing the piece. Big no-no. Then there was the model who totally overdid her walk, like major. She took enormous strides, as if she were stepping over invisible hurdles. And the model who rushed across the stage, doing a little dance as if she had to pee. Another mishap: a model losing the oversized nineties clip in her hair, making her fumble to catch it, causing her to trip, and then . . . fall face-first. The drama brought different oohs from the crowd. Luckily, she was fine!

And then it was Maya's turn.

She had selected classical electronic music to accompany her designs. The rhythm matched the attitude of her pieces—the glint from the zipper, the S shape in the ruffles, the edges of the fire neckline. Maya knew the competition was fierce, and still she'd been confident, but now . . . she wasn't sure. Manu and Ana . . . But as Maya's first look appeared onstage, she shoved those thoughts away. This was her time.

First up: the oversized zipper dress. The way the stage lights reflected off the actual zipper was . . . superb. It made it seem like the zipper was fuchsia, then lemon, then turquoise. Like magic! The audience clapped as the model walked, something they'd only done for Manu's 5272 look. Maya had teased the model's hair into a giant beehive, complementing her lace-up wedge sandals. The fabric—denim—looked sturdy, yet feminine with the fraying. Maya was glad she'd taken her lucky scissors to the edges. No detail was too much. . . . Ooh! Maya did a little jump.

Next: the quinceañera dress! And there she was to model it perfectly—Lisbeth. When Lisbeth appeared onstage, some people in the audience actually gasped, their mouths in little Os. The balloons! The balloons . . . they took this look to the next level. Maya whispered, "Thank you, Sebastian." Even if he wasn't here to see it. Because what mattered was that the judges saw it! And they scribbled furiously on their notepads at the table in front of the front row. *Breathe, Maya. Breathe.* Lisbeth wasn't at her side to calm her down—she was onstage! And oh, was she ever. Her back ballerina-straight, core tight, and shoulders back and down—just as they'd practiced. She moved with such energy and poise—her catwalk was life! At downstage, she posed for just a couple of seconds, even smiling for pictures. Everyone in the audience, it seemed, held up phones. Oh, Lisbeth!

Finally, the volcano dress. This was it. The music bum-bum-bummed in Maya's chest. The stage went black, then red and orange and yellow (like fire!). The lights flickered (like fire!). And Maya braced herself. Her final look. She'd chosen an especially tall model for this one, and even then, Maya had asked her to wear four-inch heels. The taller, the better. The volcano needed to have . . . presence. Maya had sewn scraps of newspapers into the charcoal fabric to add texture, and incorporated tiered rings underneath—wide, wider, widest—to give the

dress a volcano shape. It worked! It looked like an actual volcano! Especially with the fire neckline, which glowed! Maya
had taken it up a notch by stitching little battery-operated light
bulbs underneath it so that when the model clicked a remote
control that she had tucked in her palm, the lights turned on,
creating a neckline that truly glittered like fire. The audience
cheered!

At this point, Lisbeth reappeared by Maya's side. She was
for real crying. "Maya . . . it's gorgeous. You're amazing, amiga!"

Maya swallowed tears herself. "Thanks, Lisbeth." They gave
each other fist bumps, and Lisbeth dashed back to join the
other models, who had to prepare for the finale, when they'd
all appear onstage together.

All the days, weeks, months, and even years, and here she
stood, proudly watching models display *her* designs onstage.
The crazy part was that it was all over so fast. The remaining
designers had their turns, but it was all a blur. Then there was a
short intermission where the judges conferred, and the designers huddled together backstage, complimenting one another,
wishing each other well. Maya caught snippets—*You're gonna
win! No, you are! I loooooooved that see-through suit!* But instead of
joining them, she took sips from her water bottle, opening and
closing the cap to give her hands something to do.

The time had come. Again, the stage went black. Then a
single spotlight—a soft yellow—shone above la directora. Her
face was a montage of shadows. Maya stole a look at her phone;
still nothing from Mama. Her insides felt strangled, but she
wouldn't let her mind go to the possibilities. Of course Mama
was okay. She just . . . wasn't there.

The audience was quiet, except for one girl in the front row who had two fingers in her mouth, whistling. Then la directora smiled wide, her bright red lipstick glowing—the color looked kinda good on her, actually, and it matched her red patent-leather heels—and, after thanking everyone for coming, sang out, "The third-place winner is . . . Manu!" Manu screamed, and as she speed-walked to the center of the stage, she raised a fist, bear-hugged la directora, and accepted a plaque from her. She reached for the microphone—was she actually prepared to make an acceptance speech? Should Maya? But la directora kept her grip on it. "¡Felicidades!" she said, and nudged Manu to the right. Manu posed for a few pictures, waved to her mother and abuelos, and walked offstage.

Next, next . . . was second place. Maya needed to steady herself on something, a railing, a wall, anything. But there was nothing nearby, so she widened her stance, took deep breaths. All around her, other girls muffled their squeals.

La directora continued, "And I'm so proud to say that the second-place winner is . . . Ana Mendez!" The audience clapped and whistled. Ana Mendez was second place. It sank in. *Ana didn't win.* Even with her wealthy father, and her incredible chiffon designs, which Maya was sure could—no, *would* be sold in stores. Maya felt for her. To come this close . . . but second was still great!

That meant—Maya couldn't breathe. At all. That meant—there was a chance, there was!

La directora looked across the audience, clearly enjoying this moment. And why not? The show was her own kind of finale—of years of teaching and training and lifting up others. She lowered her glasses—ones with hot-pink rhinestones—and stepped forward once more. "And the winner . . . I'm *thrilled* to say the winner is—"

La directora lifted her chin. Maya pinched her lips so hard, she thought she might bleed.

"Oh!" la directora interrupted herself. "I almost forgot to mention. The prize includes a gift certificate for 2,500 quetzales to La Fábrica." She nodded, as the audience applauded.

"Announce the winner!" someone yelled playfully.

Maya couldn't take it anymore, and then—

"The winner is . . . Maya Silva!"

That was her name. Hers! She'd won! Maya had won first place. Wait—really? Again, Lisbeth showed up beside her, out of breath, and grasped Maya's shoulders.

"Did she say *my* name? Lisbeth, am I hallucinating?"

"Yes. And no! And you're totally making me sweat coming back here in these heels," she said, jumping up and down.

"Is this really . . ."

"Maya Silva!" la directora announced again, the tiniest bit of a question in her voice.

"Maya! Get out there!" Lisbeth not so gently shoved her.

Maya floated onto the stage and hugged la directora, who upon a closer look had red lipstick on her teeth. That was one bizarre detail Maya would remember forever from this blurry exchange. La directora handed Maya an envelope with the gift certificate, and the knowledge that Maya's designs would be displayed *and* sold in the storefront this summer. Maya would work on making more of these exact designs, in various sizes, until then.

"Congratulations!" la directora said, and whispered in Maya's ear, "The cash prize will be granted within the next few weeks." Maya nodded gratefully, hardly believing any of it.

This is it, Maya thought, thunder in her chest. This is it. I won. I won! I won. . . . But she couldn't ignore the pang in her heart, and worse, the worry in her gut. But *no*. Mama was finishing *her* dress.

Afterward, the girls all celebrated backstage with soda and pizza and lots of debriefing between hugs and more pictures and laughter. Maya was there, but not there, moving between congratulations in a daze. Eventually, the crowd dispersed, and when the last pizza slice in the box was eaten, she and Lisbeth headed back to the colonia. Arm in arm, they debriefed each other on every delicious detail.

25

Maya practically ran-walked the rest of the way home after she and Lisbeth separated at their turnoffs. Lisbeth was supposed to come home with her, but then she got an angry text from her stepmom, something about how she'd left the kitchen a complete mess that morning and she'd better come straight home, blah, blah, blah. "I'm so sorry," Lisbeth had said. "We should be celebrating! Together!" Normally Maya wouldn't walk by herself at this hour, but her mother was supposed to have been with her . . . And the truth was, Maya just wanted to be alone, anyway. Her mother had missed the most important night of her life. And the disappointment was hitting Maya hard.

Still, her mom, she got. But Sebastian? WTF? Why didn't he show? Maya stopped for a quick moment and sent him a text.

In case u care . . . I won!

OMG!!!!!!! Congrats maya!

Where r u?

...

She wasn't going to wait in the dark for him to respond, so she broke into her run-walk. As she turned the corner onto her street, she felt instantly uneasy. There was no one around. Not the tortilla lady selling her last docena of the day, or some guy on a motorcycle whispering into his girlfriend's ear, or a tired señor coming home late from work. The avenida was empty, save for a stray dog whose ribs Maya could make out even in the dark.

A surge of relief—she was home! Then, about to unlock the door, she saw it was already open a crack. She took a step backward, instantly wary, remembering señora Pérez's door, then pushed it open carefully. She heard someone laughing. Who was *that*? Mama would never deliberately miss Maya's big night. They'd both been looking forward to the show for two straight weeks. Mama would never—she would never miss it. . . .

"Mama?" Maya called out hesitantly. The kitchen lights were on—and what was that strange smell? Smoke—cigarette smoke.

Again, a laugh. A man. A man laughing. Not a celebratory kind of laugh, not one that had been watered with jokes or chisme or . . . This laugh scraped her from the inside.

Maya dropped her bag soundlessly. Smoke, and bottles clinking, and men—two?

She took a step, then another, quietly, quietly, until she could peek around the corner into the kitchen. There, at the round table with the plastic tablecloth—the one with mother hens feeding little chicks, a pattern repeated—sat her mother.

Tied to the chair.

Two men in black masks and gray hoodies surrounded her. Maya fixated on one—the one gripping the gun. *No, no, no.* He held it to the back of her mother's head. Mama! Her face was wet with tears. A gag covered her mouth. Teal. *Their* fabric.

"Mama." The word escaped in a tangled whisper. As if she heard, Mama glanced up.

Shook her head ever so slightly. *Don't talk. Don't say anything.*

Maya briefly registered Luna whimpering somewhere, but she couldn't, she *couldn't*, look away from her mother's face. It was her face too.

The face that shifted Maya's interpretation of the last six hours—facts to replace all the guessing Maya had done. Mama had missed the show. But it wasn't because she was at work. She'd been here . . . Oh my God . . . she'd been *here*. For how long? Oh God, for how long? Since—oh God, oh God, before five o'clock. What had they been doing to her all that time? *No*, she couldn't go there, not yet. It felt like an anvil was crushing her chest as her mother pleaded to her with her eyes to run, leave. But Maya wanted to run *to* her, to scream. Still, still, she knew that what she chose to do in the next several seconds would determine everything.

The man without the gun noticed Maya. "Always hiding in shadows," he said to her. "How was your little fashion show?"

Maya went cold. Oscar. He lowered his mask.

"Why . . . why are you doing this?" she sputtered incredulously.

"What do you want?" She had to stay calm, had to. Had to. All the while her brain was screaming, shrieking, *Don't shoot my mother*, and *It's all my fault!* Then, "Mama—are you hurt?"

Her mother moved her head a centimeter.

Oscar tsk-tsked. "Oh, Maya. Some questions have long answers. And for you, it's better if you just don't ask at all." He gave her a hard look. "You know, I wondered if you'd make a better investigative reporter than fashion designer. Actually—"

"Shut up! Shut the fuck up!" the man with the gun bellowed. His was the same chilling voice she'd heard at Oscar and Sebastian's house. "That's your fucking *problem*, hermanito. You talk too damn much. You and your big mouth have made a major mess. And now *I'm* cleaning it up."

Maya needed to think. Quick. The man lowered his mask. "It's so fucking hot in here." Placed his gun between his legs while he ripped off his hoodie. Maya hadn't seen him then, but now, she'd never "unsee" him. In his tank top and jeans, his tattoo-covered face and neck and arms were all on display. Even his eyelids had tattoos.

"You checking me out?" he leered, picking up the gun. "You interested in something?" He grabbed himself with his free hand, the other one steady, still aiming at Mama.

Maya shook her head, her eyes begging Oscar to end this nightmare some way, somehow. But Oscar looked past her. How could he do this? In this same kitchen where he'd shared a meal with them. *Please, God. I'll do anything. I'll move to San Marcos. Tomorrow. Tonight! I'll give up my prize from the fashion show. I'll pray every day for the rest of my life. Please. Please.*

But instead of her prayers being answered, things only got worse. Footsteps. Climbing down the bathroom staircase. Someone had been on the roof. She turned, not wanting to see who she knew in her gut it would be.

Sebastian.

26

She knew it'd be him, coming down those stairs, but even still, her soul felt gutted. *How could you? How could you? How could you?* He'd been the lookout, she realized. That was how Oscar knew she was in the house! Sebastian would have seen her walking down the sidewalk. Then a new thought flashed through her brain. He could've *warned* her, sent her a text.

Oh my God. They'd been texting. Just two minutes ago! He told her *congrats* as he watched her walk straight into this hell. Why??? Why? Had he been in on everything all along? Had everything between them been . . . a lie?

His face was stone. He just . . . stood there, only his jaw clenching, unclenching.

How could he— What could she— But there was no time to even finish a thought. Oscar's brother unlocked the gun, a horrid clicking sound, and then he held it out to Sebastian.

"Since my hermanito fucks everything up, how about *you* climbing the ranks, primo?"

Sebastian took the gun and aimed it at Mama.

Mama began full-on weeping. Maya could not breathe.

Oscar instantly got in his brother's face, fist clenched. "Come on, Martín. I can do this."

"I *told* you to shut up!" the brother spat. "Our primo is more of a man than you are, sí?" He lifted his chin at Sebastian. The gun looked so out of place in Sebastian's hand, it could be a plastic toy.

"Sí, primo," Sebastian said, cool, chill, like he did this every day of the week.

A vein on the side of Oscar's forehead was throbbing. His face had gone scarlet with fury.

"No . . . Sebastian—please—don't do this!" Maya begged. "I don't understand— Why are you—"

Fast as a viper, Oscar lunged around the table and back-handed Maya across the face. She dropped to the kitchen floor, her cheek burning. The corner of her mouth was wet with . . . blood. Her mother now wailed, rocking the chair.

Sebastian's eyes. The gun facing Mama. Oscar's sneer. From the floor, this was what Maya could see. Stay calm. Stay calm. Breathe. Breathe. Then, carefully, oh so carefully, she lifted herself up. She glared at the others, dared them to try to stop her. And she walked to Mama, placed her hands on her trembling shoulders, whispered, "I love you," and stood tall. "If you're going to kill her, then you're going to have to kill me, too," she told Sebastian. Luna began to run in circles, howling.

Martín laughed, harsh, mirthless. "This is some goddamn novela, vos!" He and Oscar cracked up. "Look, chica, we only wanted you. But then your mami had to go and do some investigating with the police, something about a murder in the colonia. Entonces . . . you know how it goes."

"Just do it already," Oscar said. "I'm hungry."

"You know what?" Martín said. "Let me just fucking do it. You're both little bitches, you know that?" He snatched the gun back from Sebastian. "Let me show you little girls how it's done."

"No," Sebastian said furiously. "*I* will." He snatched it back.

Then, out of nowhere, Luna charged. She clamped down on Martín's ankle.

"Fuck!" Oscar's brother yelled.

Oscar leaped forward, tried to yank Luna off, but the dog did not let go. "Fuck!" Martín said again, and swung his leg hard.

Luna lost her grip, but then charged again, this time sinking her teeth into Oscar's calf, clamping down. He roared, kicking wildly. Luna hung on. The roar grew louder, more hysterical, and it all began to blur—Martín dropped to his knees, pulling at Luna, who was growling with the ferocity of a Doberman. Maya tore her eyes away, slipped over to her mother. To her shock, the tie was already loose. She heard, "Let the fuck go!" and "Get it off!" Did someone say *run*? Mama? Then Luna gave a great cry, a sound that clawed at Maya's heart. But in a flash—how?—Luna had leaped at Martín's face, biting and biting, his nose, his lips, and now both brothers were swearing and pulling and Maya and her mother inched toward the door, and somehow were almost there when Sebastian yelled out, "Stop!" but they didn't. They didn't. They bolted, literally ran for their lives. Out the door. *Their* door. Down the street. *Their* street. Maya heard a gunshot in the air. She heard Sebastian call, "I'm on them!"

Maya and her mother ran and ran and ran until Maya's muscles and lungs and heart were surely on the verge of collapsing. But still they ran. They were going to die either from a bullet or heart failure. Maya could hear Sebastian pounding after them, calling her name. She grasped her mother's arm. Thank goodness, as just then Mama stumbled. "Noooo, Mama! Noooo! We have to keep going!" She eased her mother back up. "We can't stop, we can't!" Her mother was coughing, out of breath entirely, trying to keep running, but moments later, Sebastian caught up with them anyway.

This is it, Maya thought. This was the last line of her life. It ended here. But then she remembered. *Run.* It was Sebastian who'd said, "Run." She looked at him, his face in the shadows. What did he want? What was he going to do? He had a *gun*!

"We have to keep going," he urged them breathlessly.

"*We?*" she spat out.

Her mother dropped to all fours and vomited onto the pavement.

"Oh, Mama!" Maya dropped down beside her, tried to help. Her mother wiped her mouth with her sleeve.

"Maya, look—" Sebastian glanced around. "I'll explain everything later. But you have to listen to me. We *have* to keep going. They are going to make sure that I've—finished the job. If I don't have bodies to show them, then it's mine they'll go after next. So please, please, we've got to go!"

Maya's head was exploding. "Sebastian, how could you do this to us, to ME?"

He yanked at her arm. "Maya—we HAVE TO GO! Now!"

"He's right, mija." Her mother. She reached for Maya's arm, and Sebastian quickly helped her to her feet. "We don't have a choice."

"Mama! No. We can't trust him. Let's go on our own."

"Mija," her mother gasped. "The knot—behind the chair. *Sebastian* loosened it so I could try and escape. The goal was to somehow alert you before you walked in . . . But then Oscar's pinche brother showed up and that plan went out the window. He made Sebastian go up to the roof as lookout."

"Señora—por favor, we *have* to go." Sebastian pulled at her arm, half dragging her into a run. Her mother ran. And so did Maya.

On the main avenida, Sebastian leaped into the street, nearly getting hit as he hailed a taxi. "Where to?" the driver asked as they scrambled in.

Mama leaned forward from the back seat and gave the driver an address just outside the city. Sebastian told the driver he'd pay him double if he sped.

And that driver sped. Along the periférico, the main highway in the city, buildings flashed by. Maya watched, stunned, as Sebastian lowered a window and chucked his phone out of it. But not the gun. *That* he held on to. Maya's own phone was in her backpack, along with the La Fábrica gift certificate, at home. So was Mama's purse! They had no way of contacting anyone! No one said a word until the traffic thinned and they were on quieter, less lit streets. Her home. Their things. Everything they owned, from her baby pictures to her sewing machine, La Betty. All in the rearview mirror. Lisbeth! Oh my

God! What about Lisbeth! She had to call her—warn her! Shit! There was no way! Then she thought of Luna and choke-sobbed. She couldn't bear to imagine what they might do to her. . . . So she prayed.

"Maya." Mama was stroking her hand.

"I'm okay, Mama."

Sebastian turned around from the front seat. "I have a lot to explain. But first, please listen."

"Not. Ever. How could you? How *could* you! I was— We could've—" Maya pressed into her mother. Her mind was reel-ing. Sebastian was *there*, he could've stopped it all before it got to this point. What would've happened if—

"Up ahead, take a left," her mother told the driver.

"Maya," Sebastian said again, this time in a whisper. "I'll explain everything. I swear. But right now, we have to focus on getting out of here."

Maya's mother held her tight. "Mija, listen to him. We *have* to leave," she said in a firm voice.

"Mama! Are you even okay? Did they hurt—"

Her mother put her fingers to Maya's lips, interrupting her. "Mija. There's no time right now. Ponte las pilas." *Get to work.* Her voice went even lower. "Maya, we have to leave the coun-try. Leave Guatemala."

"But . . . Mama . . . What about San Marcos? I thought you wanted— I mean, couldn't we live under new names or some-thing? They couldn't trace us there! Right? Mama? Mama— this is when you say, 'Right, mija.'"

Her mother gave her head a slight shake, her skin a ghostly yellow from the streetlights' glow. She leaned in, even though the driver was singing softly to the reggaetón radio station and probably couldn't hear her. "I think they'd follow us, mija. They'd find us. They know we were just there a few weeks ago. And the cousin, Lisbeth's novio, he asked the other night! The maras have tentacles everywhere. I just . . . I think this is the only way. . . ."

And though Maya's every molecule was screaming *noooo*—it sank in. Major. And it was all her fault. All. Her. Fault. They were in this position, this *mess*, because of her. And no prize money or gift certificate would be enough to get them out of it. "But—Mama . . . What are we going to do now?"

"Right here is fine," her mother was telling the driver, interrupting Maya. "We'll walk from here. Gracias." He hit the brakes. Sebastian paid as they all got out, and they watched until he drove away, till they couldn't even see his taillights.

Then Maya swung around. "Sebastian is coming *with* us? But, Mama—he . . . he . . ."

"He tried to *save* me. I told you!"

"*Yeah, well, he didn't, did he?* But—he *did*—he said to run! But why didn't he send a warning text? He *saw* me coming down the street!"

"Hello—I'm right here, Maya. And I *couldn't* have done that. What would've happened to your mother then? Oscar and Martín were getting stir-crazy, itching to make things happen!"

At which point her mother said, "Enough. Come on. It's half a kilometer this way." And she turned to the right.

"Half a kilometer!?" Maya exclaimed. "Why didn't you just have the taxi drive us all the way?" Maya deliberately walked on the opposite side of Sebastian.

Her mother wiped her brow. "Ay, mija. I've sheltered you too much. Listen, you never know who is watching, or if someone is following us. You can't be careful enough."

"Wait—is that why you threw your phone out the taxi window?" Maya hated that she was even talking to Sebastian, but she had to know.

"Yeah. And I bet your mom would've done the same thing." Her mother nodded.

"Mama." Maya's voice cracked. "I'm so sorry. I'm so sorry!"

Her mother stopped and hugged her tight as Maya sobbed. "I'm the one who invited Sebastian and Oscar over in the first place . . . and I kept hanging out with them even when you said no. . . . And now . . . and then . . . Mama— I didn't tell you—I didn't tell anyone—he said he'd kill me, but I saw Oscar kill . . . señora Pérez's . . . her son. Ay, Dios." Now she was crying so hard, she was choking. Still, she choked out, "This is all because of me. You could've been killed! Mama—I don't know what I would've done. I'm so sorry!"

Her mother held her and held her. "Mija . . . We're okay. For now. At least that!" Eventually she said, "I love you, Maya. There is nothing you could do that would change that. ¿Entiendes?"

Maya suddenly grasped her mother's hands. "And, Mama! I won! I won the fashion show."

Now her mother was crying. "*Of course* you did, mija. I'm so proud of you."

"I won . . . ," Maya said, still squeezing her mother.

"Mija, I'm so proud, I am. But right now, we have to keep going." She started walking again.

"But to *where*? And—Lisbeth! We have to warn Lisbeth! Oscar could—"

"He's not going to do anything to her," Sebastian said firmly from where he was walking behind them.

"But how do you know? For sure? Mama—we have to warn her!"

"I swear on my life he's not. We talked about it."

Maya felt the bile rise in her throat. "And you *believe* him?"

Her mother grabbed Maya's shoulder. "Mija. Listen to me. Right now, we need to talk to a coyote."

Sebastian looked at her skeptically. "Where are we going to find a decent coyote, one who won't take a bribe from my cousins? They're for sure going to guess that's what we're going to do. And then—"

"Chicos, listen to me. We're nearly there."

27

The coyote lived in a house on a hill where the sky started and the trees stopped. At least they had the moon and its loyal light following above as the threesome took careful steps single file across a rocky path and up over a bend. The moon. Luna. Little Luna. She'd saved them all. What would happen to her? And Maya felt her heart shredding all over again.

"Maya," her mother said as they approached a house. *The* house. "You've actually met this man before."

Maya frowned. "I have? Who is it?"

"It's Fernando," she said, face forward, determined.

Dark eyebrows. Earring. So very much in love with her mother.

"He still crosses people?"

Mama nodded, then amended that by saying, "Well, not since . . . His last job didn't go so well. He tried to cross his brother, Raúl."

"And?" Maya was getting winded, was surprised at how at

the same time her mother seemed to be moving *faster*.

"And . . . la migra caught them. Up until then Fernando had a perfect record as a coyote. Crossed people every single time. But not this time . . . Border Patrol shot Raúl—right in the throat. And after that, Fernando never crossed anyone again. In truth, after that, Fernando was never the same again."

"Was that why you broke up?" Maya had always wondered why he'd stopped visiting. He always brought a treat for Luna. He always made Mama smile.

Her mother turned around abruptly, nearly knocking Maya over. Sebastian paused, giving them their privacy.

"We'd actually . . . things ended before that. But tonight, we need to convince him to help us, to cross us, mija. We have to do anything—everything—we have to . . ."

"I understand, Mama."

Her mother opened her mouth but hesitated to say whatever it was she was thinking.

At the entrance to Fernando's house, Maya took a deep breath. Placed her hand on the gate. Its cold touch felt even colder in the dark night. The moon had dipped behind a cloud.

Then, "Fernando?" her mother called out. There was no way he could hear her. Maya nudged her. "Mama. You have to say it louder."

Her mother cleared her throat. "Fernando! It's me . . . Carmen!"

Inside, a light turned on.

At first he was a shadow in the doorway, but when he stepped forward, it all came back to her—his dark eyes, wide shoulders, and now . . . beard. He looked distinguished, still the tall and sophisticated man her mother had dated all those years ago, but there was white hair along his brows, and he appeared far away, even though he was standing right in front of them.

"Carmen," he said simply. Then, "Maya."

"Don Fernando," Maya replied politely. She wanted to say more—*thank you, please help us, I'm sorry about what happened to your brother*—but Mama took over.

"Fernando," she said, rubbing her thumb against her palm. Mama was nervous. "This young man is Sebastian. It's a long story, mi—" She caught herself. The words *mi amor* hovered in the air. "We need your help." Her voice explained so much.

He looked beyond them, then, "Come inside," he said firmly.

"It's just us," Sebastian assured him quickly.

Fernando searched him just as quickly, effortlessly, and when he felt the gun in Sebastian's back pocket, he simply took it out, emptied the bullets right then and there, and shoved the gun in his own jeans. No one said a word.

Inside, Maya sat miserably on one end of the couch in the living room while Sebastian paced while a muffled conversation was taking place between Mama and Don Fernando in the hall. A part of her wanted to hear each and every syllable, but the other half willed time to tick. She felt wild with worry, imagining Oscar and his brother bursting through the front door any second.

"Maya . . . ," Sebastian began.

"Don't!" She crossed her arms like a makeshift barrier.

He hesitated, looking at her with pain-filled eyes, then resumed pacing.

Mama came out of the hallway, her head low, and as she made the sign of the cross, whispered, "Vámonos, chicos."

Don Fernando, with a quick nod to them all, rummaged in a closet and handed Mama an empty backpack. "Fill it with whatever you can find in the kitchen," he said matter-of-factly. Then, as if noticing Sebastian for the first time, Fernando cleared his throat. "My favor is to you, Carmen. Y tú hija. Pero este chico . . . no se."

He shook his head. He wasn't going to help Sebastian cross. Or at least he wasn't sure.

Maya looked quickly from Fernando to Sebastian. Could Sebastian even make it over the border . . . especially without help? Served him right, Maya thought coldly. He'd betrayed her. Why *should* they help him? Yet . . . seeing him go pale at Fernando's words, she couldn't help but think that he *had* helped them—otherwise they would surely be dead right now.

To her surprise, her mother was the one to ask, her voice pleading, "¿Porqué no?"

Sebastian looked up in surprise. As surprised as Maya was. Her mother was actually vouching for him?

"Fernando," her mother continued gently, her eyes beseeching. "If he goes on his own, he probably won't make it."

Don Fernando took a folded handkerchief from his jeans pocket and wiped his brow. He looked through the window— at what, Maya didn't know. But then he said, "Vaya, pues. Lo hago para tí, Carmen." *I'll do it for you.*

Maya swore she saw her mother turn red.

"Now go fill this bag with food. And water," he added, all gruff. "I'll find another backpack."

Her mother mouthed, "Gracias." Their eyes met for a very long time.

Then Don Fernando began digging in the closet once more while Sebastian went back to pacing, looking like he'd dodged an actual bullet. But what had he expected? To be welcomed with open arms? He was part of why they were in this mess . . . Okay . . . she was too. Okay, okay, she was *more*. And okay, she wasn't *totally* angry that Don Fernando was letting him join them. She definitely wanted to strangle him. But . . . she didn't want anything *bad* to happen to him either.

Within minutes, they were in Fernando's car headed north. Sebastian sat up front and Maya sat with her mother in the back seat. How had her mother convinced him to take them in the first place? What had she said? But now wasn't the time. As if reading her mind, Mama leaned in, stroked Maya's hand. As she did, she whispered, "He's a good man," then paused, before adding, "And . . . he said he'd never forgive himself if something happened to you." Maya must have looked shocked because Mama added, "Yes, to you. You always reminded him of his younger sister, Isabel. It's true. A señorita crossing the border without a coyote? He said he'd never sleep again."

Maya pictured herself walking alone down a long road, shadows surrounding her. She leaned her head against the window, never letting go of her mother's hand.

The trip itself would take about thirty hours. But that's only if they drove straight through on major highways, and all went well. And of course, they'd also need to stop to eat and use the bathroom and maybe sleep for a few hours. No trains for them—certainly not the Bestia. No sleeping on cardboard by the train tracks. They would drive and drive, and at checkpoints and tolls in Guatemala and Mexico, Maya and her mother would cram into the trunk, sometimes for a few minutes and other times for up to an hour, just to be *safe*, while Fernando paid bribes to the guards.

The first one came at the Guatemala-Mexico border. In the darkness of the trunk, as Maya and her mother listened to the damn song "Despacito," which Fernando had on repeat, holding hands, close, closer, Maya had the odd thought that maybe this was what it was like to be in the womb. Regardless, they were together. And for now, that was enough.

"Mama?"

"¿Sí, mija?"

"What happened before . . . before I got home?"

They were long past the checkpoint, the only sound the whoosh from the tires moving over the paved carretera. But they had to stay in the car before and after the checkpoints so the guards wouldn't see them getting in and out of the trunk. It was safer this way, Fernando had insisted. With every minute, they were that many more kilometers away from home, closer to . . . she couldn't fill in the picture, not yet. That whoosh was almost comforting. It meant that they were that much farther from Oscar, from his brother. "Mama?"

Her mother was shaking—no, she was crying. "I was so scared, mija. I thought—I thought they were going to do something to you."

"To *me*? I was at the show. How could—"

"I don't know. They have people. Everywhere. And besides, even if not, you would have come home, as you did, and—"

"It's okay, Mama. You don't have to say anything more. We're here, we're together."

"Gracias a Dios." Her mother sat up with a sniffle, cleared her throat. Her voice suddenly serious, she said, "Maya. Listen. We have to stay alert. We can't trust anyone. You understand?"

Wasn't it a little too late for that? "Not even Don Fernando? *Or Sebastian?*" Her voice rose above the sound of the tires on the road beneath them.

"Besides them," Mama said. "What is coming up . . . Well, Fernando will help us cross, God willing, and then we'll seek asylum. If we don't, we'll be running for the rest of our lives, entiendes?"

"Stop asking me if I understand. I do. But—this is all . . . nuts."

"Mija . . . Asylum is the only way we can be allowed in, and stay together." She hesitated.

"I get that, Mama. But . . . then what?"

"Then we're going to make it work. Survive. Little by little."

Despacito, just like the song.

The trip itself was also despacito; it felt eternal. Still, two, even three days would be nothing compared to the stories of migrants they'd heard about on the nightly news from the safety of their living room, a million years ago. Maya knew that much. Her mother knew it too.

At one point the following day, they stopped in a dusty town at a gas station, somewhere far off the carretera. Don Fernando didn't want to take chances by only taking the main freeway, so occasionally, like now, they had veered off onto back roads.

So far, the Mexican landscape looked so similar they might as well have still been in Guatemala. Maya used the restroom. When she came out, Sebastian was standing there, offering her a cold can of lemonade. She hadn't spoken to him directly since they'd reached Fernando's house. He had a huge tear in his jeans. A part of the fabric was hanging out like a tongue.

"I know what you're thinking," he began.

"Do you?" It was so hot that her shirt stuck to her back. She took the lemonade. Deliberately didn't thank him.

"How could I do this, right? How could—"

She pulled back the tab, took a long sip. It sent little needles of ice-cold down her throat, but she didn't care. She was thirsty. And way more pissed.

He pressed on. "Maya, you have to believe me. If I could've warned you, or if I . . . I didn't know how to . . . Basically, Oscar was going to—"

"You're doing a pretty shitty job of apologizing," Maya interrupted. "I mean, just saying."

He looked so sheepish, it was impossible not to let him continue.

"Look," he said, squinting into the sun, then back at her. "At first Oscar just wanted to scare you. Like, he didn't trust that you'd keep your mouth . . ." He sighed. "About what you'd seen. So that's why he sent those cops over—"

"Are you kidding me? The cops were . . . ?"

"Yeah. They work for the gang. Oscar was testing you to see if you'd fold, if you'd snitch."

Maya tipped her head back, barely able to process what he was telling her. The sun was so strong that her scalp was burning. "But—but . . . one of them . . . the one outside said that he'd seen me before, on the roof. He sounded so . . . genuine."

"Well, I guess enough quetzales will make anyone sound genuine. But, yeah . . . you passed. But then . . . your mom . . ." He trailed off as Maya scowled.

"My mom what?!"

"C'mon, you can connect the dots," he said at last. "She went to the police, Maya. First thing the next morning. Asking questions about the murder. She was going to be . . . a problem. So they had no choice."

"No choice? Seriously?"

"Please. Here, let's get out of the sun." He reached for her. Maya swung her arm away.

Just then her mother and Fernando came out of the gas station, loaded with plastic bags full of snacks and big bottles of water. Fernando was paying for everything—wouldn't touch Sebastian's money. Maya knew that her mother was keeping track of every quetzal, was going to pay him back every last one, someday. Mama eyed them, a look of pity crossing her face, but she said sternly, "Maya Luz, let's go." Fernando gave Sebastian a sympathetic look, handed him a bag.

Even with the AC on full blast, Maya felt sticky with heat. Yes, she wanted Sebastian to finish what he'd been trying to say, but no, she wouldn't bring it up in the car. Not yet. She was exhausted, and ooof, needed a shower. She eyed herself in the rearview mirror. Soon her hair would get greasy. She had no other clothes.

Her mind drifted to her three pieces from the fashion show.

What would the school do with them? What would they think happened to her? Poof, Maya Silva vanished. The school. Mama's job. What did the bride think of her altered wedding dress? And Lisbeth! Their house . . . Luna. Her throat ached with forcing down emotion. *Don't think about it, don't, don't,* she willed herself. Instead she stole looks at Sebastian. Studied his profile. What he'd told her about the cops . . . What *else* did he know? Why had he waited so long to tell her any of it? And what were he and Oscar even doing in Puerto Barrios, anyway? And why, on the *exact night* of the fashion show, did they—oh. Of course that was *why.* Maya had been so distracted, her mother too. Their guard was down. They hadn't seen it coming, none of it. Goose bumps suddenly covered her arms. She hated herself for being so naive. When was she going to get that the world was not a piece of fabric she could manipulate to her liking?

That evening they stopped at a restaurant. Fernando treated them all to a meal of tacos, rice, beans, and even ice cream. He insisted that Mama have a margarita, though he refused one himself. She drank it in three gulps, it seemed. But instead of helping her relax, it made her more paranoid. She side-eyed every person who entered the restaurant—she'd make a horrible detective. Maya remembered their meal in San Marcos—was that really only two weeks ago? What she would give now to return to that table instead of this one. Sebastian accordion-folded a straw wrapper, unfolded it, accordioned it again.

Fernando, perhaps trying to make Mama chill, said, "Guess

what tune this is." He drummed his fingers on the table.

"Let me guess. 'Despacito'?" Sebastian offered. And Maya genuinely laughed, almost spitting out her horchata. Mama pressed her lips together, shaking her head at Maya. But her eyes were smiling.

Fernando put his palms up. "Guilty, chicos. Bueno—how about one more?" Maya looked at Sebastian, then looked away. It was so weird to be in this alternate universe now, where she hated every last bit of his being, but also . . .

This time Fernando drummed a different tune—one that clearly her mother knew, because she pushed her fork around the rice on her plate and blushed for the second time that day. Then they were all taking turns "playing" songs with their fingertips.

Once they'd finished the ice cream, her mother told her she needed to speak to Fernando in private.

"Okaaaay." Maya inched out of the booth. Sebastian followed.

Outside, on the way back to the car, he pulled her aside, spoke on fast-forward. "Maya, we really need to talk. I'm really, really sorry. But I need you to *hear* me. I should've told you. I had no idea that they were planning to go so far . . . I truly did not. So, that cop, he called Oscar and told him that you seemed okay, but your mom seemed skittish. He wasn't convinced she wouldn't make trouble. Oscar was telling *me* this in Puerto Barrios, and Martín overheard. We didn't know he was listening. But he was. And Martín—Martín is . . . ruthless. And then, like I said, your mother went to the police asking all sorts of questions, and that was it—Martín said you and your mother had to . . . that they had to . . . that . . ."

"¡Chicos! ¡Vámonos!" Don Fernando called.

Maya glared at Sebastian. "Pft! So why didn't you warn us?"

"I *told* you," he said, not flinching. "He would've seen the text on my phone. Martín trusts *no one*. Most suspicious dude I've ever met. We had a job to do out by Puerto Barrios. That's all I can say. But I really planned on being there for the show! Until Martín overheard . . . I'm going in circles. Look—you won!"

"I did win," Maya snapped, and spinning away, she rushed toward the running car.

They rolled down the windows, the starry night all around them. But Maya couldn't sleep. Neither could her mother. "Why don't you let me drive, Fernando?" Mama said. "You're going to nod off. You've been driving forever. You need a break."

Fernando hesitated, but then pulled over and let her take the wheel.

So it was Maya's mother driving, and Maya sitting up front. Sebastian and Don Fernando slept like babies in the back seat. To any outsider, the four of them looked like a nice family on an overnight road trip.

Maya embraced the quiet around them—Fernando's gentle snoring joining the hum of crickets outside—to ask some of the many questions that were electrifying her brain.

"Mama, when we cross . . . after we cross . . . Well, what happens next? I mean, remember what señora Pérez said? About people not being able to get asylum?"

Her mother was silent. A bug splattered against the

windshield and Maya squirmed. The coincidence was chilling. "Bueno," her mother said at last, reaching for Maya's hand. "Whatever happens, we'll be together. And we'll pray to God for guidance."

"So that's our plan B? That's not a plan!" Maya glanced toward the back seat. "Sorry, sorry, I'll keep my voice down," as she dropped to a whisper. "But seriously, Mama—once we cross, where are we going to go? Where are we going to live? Am I going to go to school? What about money?" And there were about fifty other things on top of that!

Her mother gripped the wheel. "Maya . . . ," she sighed. "I have much to tell you. And you need to listen. And you need to remember that there has been no time to . . . plan *anything*! Do you understand?"

"Sí, Mama."

"Remember Fernando has a sister, Isabel, the one you remind him of? Isabel Sánchez. She was actually born in the States. Fernando's mother gave birth in Texas but moved back to Guatemala with the baby. It's a long story. Anyway, she will be our sponsor. Fernando already spoke to her. He called her immediately, when we were still at his house. Anyway, when we get to the United States, we're going to seek asylum, like I told you. Are you with me so far?"

With her? Was she kidding? "No."

Mama laughed. Maybe for the first time in days.

"Mama, now I have even more questions."

"Okay. Let's take it one step at a time. When Fernando and I were—when he was—"

"When you two were dating?"

"Sí. Eso. Well, his sister would come to Guatemala to visit once, twice a year. You probably don't remember her. We'd go to Antigua for the day, or to the zoo."

"Oh yeah . . . I do remember! She has a mole on her forehead, right?"

"Sí, sí. Like I said, she was born in the US, she's a citizen—she's going to be our sponsor. Remember her name. Isabel Sánchez. It's very important. Without a sponsor, they'll send us right back."

Maya looked out the window. Unlike the city, they'd passed very few lit houses, lit anything. They could have been driving to the ends of the earth.

"Maya, are you listening?"

"I know, Mama."

"So, Isabel lives in New York."

"And that's where we're going to go?"

"God willing. We'll probably take a bus there. It's a long way from the border, and we'll be safe." Maya watched how the headlights illuminated the path right in front of them, the only light around. She tried to imagine herself in the United States, in New York. What she pictured: enormous buildings, people who looked like models, English everywhere, from the billboards to the magazine covers to the radio. Her English sucked. Why hadn't she paid more attention in English class?

"Then what?"

Her mother adjusted her seat belt. "Then we begin again."

Maya huffed. "That's so . . . specific."

"Ay, mija. What do you want me to say? I don't have an exact plan. Hopefully you can attend a school, learn English. I can work." The car veered to the left, but Mama straightened the wheel just in time to not hit a passing van.

"Mama!"

Fernando stirred. "¿Qué pasó?"

"Nada. It's fine. Go back to sleep." Mama gripped the wheel tighter. She glanced at Maya. "Enough. You should sleep while you can too."

The moon spilled light over them, and in her mind, Maya could picture the car inching its way up a map, in the only direction that mattered now. Going north.

28

They drove and drove. Mama and Fernando continued to take turns at the wheel, Sebastian and Maya sleeping in shifts too. Maya tried to time it so she'd always sit up front with Mama driving, but now, it was just her and Fernando facing the wide-open road. It was almost five in the morning, according to the clock on the dashboard. He fiddled with the radio station. Settled on reggaetón, probably for Maya's sake. She liked that he was so often thinking about others' needs, like when he tried to calm Mama down at the restaurant by drumming tunes on the table. She remembered how, whenever the three of them were together in the capital, he always walked on the part of the sidewalk closest to the cars. How he stepped into a room first—a party, a comedor, a store—surveying it, before taking Mama's hand and guiding her inside, Maya holding on to Mama's other hand. Maya wondered what it would've been like if he and Mama had stayed together. What would Fernando be like as a stepfather? Lisbeth hated her stepmother. Lisbeth . . .

Maya suddenly sat up straight, turned down the radio with just a couple of taps of the button, and turned toward Fernando. "Can I talk to you about something?"

He glanced over at her, the tiniest flash of panic across his face. How could a grown man—one with a *beard*—be nervous around a sixteen-year-old?

"Claro," he said, sitting up straighter.

As the sun began to rise and Mama and Sebastian both slept open-mouthed in the back seat, Maya said, "I have a friend. Her name is Lisbeth. It would be amazing if— I am worried that— I was wondering—"

"You want me to check on her?"

"Sí, por favor." Maya ached for Lisbeth, who suddenly felt impossibly far away. Would she ever see her again? Would she ever share a cinnamon roll with her again? Of course she would! Right? Maybe not in San Martín, but somewhere . . . else? The last time they'd gone to the café, Lisbeth listened as Maya shared her dream of studying at a fashion school in the United States someday. Lisbeth had barely touched her egg and avocado croissant sandwich, she was so zeroed in on Maya. Now she wished she could stitch that moment into her life right now, have her friend with her this very moment.

"Maya," Fernando said, his voice a mixture of sorrow and concern. "I will do what I can, mija." That word. *Mija*. Maya clung to it. She wrote down Lisbeth's email address and phone number on the back of an envelope she found in the glove compartment.

"Gracias, Don Fernando," Maya said as she put the envelope back. He nodded. Then she turned the music back up.

The drive seemed endless. When they eventually stopped at a gas station, Sebastian went inside to use the bathroom while Fernando pumped gas. Mama slept.

Back in the car, Sebastian let out a long yawn, stretched his arms, and brought a hand to Maya's shoulder. She couldn't stop herself from flinching. He leaned back, squinted hard as she turned around; he was staring out the window, out at nothing. She just couldn't forgive him.

So she was shocked when he asked, "Maya, can I ask you a huge favor?"

Maya couldn't even formulate a response. Fernando focused on the road.

"My jeans . . . ," Sebastian went on, his voice husky. "They're the only pair I have, obviously."

Her neck twitched, but she wouldn't turn around.

He leaned forward again, so close to her ear. "Would you— would you mind sewing them for me?"

Wow. Even if she had a needle and thread, which she *didn't*, she wasn't about to fix his damn pants.

"Here," he said, handing her a mini sewing kit he'd apparently pulled out of nowhere. "I just bought it at the gas station. It even came with this little . . ." He paused, looked right at her, and said, "Carrete de hilo."

Her throat caught. Damn him.

"¿Porfa?" he practically begged. "Unless, I mean . . . do you really want the hole to get even bigger?"

Fernando cracked up, like a lot. *Ugh.* "Fine," Maya muttered. "Give them to me." Sebastian shimmied off his jeans and handed them to her. As she sewed, practically stabbing the fabric at first, her hand kept slipping. Then she remembered the last time she'd touched those jeans so . . . intimately. How could this be the same pair?

As she deftly closed the hole, he leaned forward again, this time positioning his head between Fernando and Maya.

"You know, I've actually crossed before," he said to Fernando, who drummed on the steering wheel. "It's true. I was a baby."

Fernando smirked. "Entonces, you have experience, sí?"

"I guess." Sebastian tilted his head. Maya wondered if he was thinking about his mother. She felt a pang in her chest. Sebastian cracked his knuckles. "You have any advice for me this time? For all of us?"

"Por supuesto," Fernando said. He brought a hand to the back of his neck, steering with the other. "Pero, muchachos . . . it's not funny. It's very dangerous. Border Patrol . . . many of them are real jodidos. They find the gallons of water and cans of tuna that gente leave out for the migrants, and they pour the water out, stab the cans so the food will spoil."

Maya brought her knees to her chest.

"But that's nothing. For women, especially, it's . . ." He sighed. "Just keep your eyes open, especially in the dark."

Maya watched emerald green whiz past, littered with garbage and white crosses and the occasional wooden stand selling avocados and mangoes in dirty plastic buckets.

"But . . . maybe worst of all is getting caught *and* deported," Fernando added. He glanced in the rearview mirror. Mama was still asleep. "You get sent back to Guate and you're—" He made a gun with his hand and pretended to shoot himself. "Those mareros find you, and buena suerte."

Agh! Maya pricked her finger. She sucked it for a few seconds, then kept on sewing, glad she had just made a jean dress, was used to heavy fabric. When she was done, she held on to them a little longer.

Late that afternoon when they arrived at Reynosa, just a few kilometers south of the US border, Don Fernando explained that he would hand them off to a coyote who, along with other coyotes, had groups crossing that night. They were standing outside a McDonald's on a busy street. Cars honking. Traffic. People on the sidewalks selling clothes and food and toys. The sun was beating down, as if charging them like batteries for the final leg of the journey. "You must one hundred percent stay with your coyote," Fernando was telling them with a father's concern.

"Wait . . ." Maya looked from her mother to Fernando. "You're not . . . you're not coming with us? But I thought—"

He rubbed his beard. "No puedo. But listen, you'll be in good hands. I know this guy. And I know how to find him in case—" His throat caught; he didn't finish his sentence.

Maya looked frantically from Fernando to her mother. "Mama? Why can't he come with us? Is it safe? What about—"

"Mija," she said, her voice emphatic. "It's the way it is. He got us all the way here. There's no way we could've— Just, please. Don't be difficult."

"Maya," Don Fernando said, drawing her attention. "You must promise me you'll stay close to your mother and listen to the coyote at all times. ¿Entiendes?"

Yes, she understood. She would stick close to Mama. Everything else would be fine, so long as she had Mama. As for Sebastian, well . . . She wondered what he'd do after he crossed into the US. Could he go *back home*, to his California home? What would he tell his family? They were related to Oscar. It would all get back to him, and his brother. Or . . . maybe he'd try and make it on his own. Change his name? Something?

Don Fernando and Sebastian left to buy food at McDonald's and were back ten minutes later with bags of Big Macs, fries, and water bottles. Maya took fries from Sebastian but avoided making eye contact. Even still, she could tell what he was probably feeling—regret, worry, relief, hope. Just like she was. They ate in silence, not so much enjoying the food as seeing it as fuel for the trek ahead. Maybe she should save half her burger for later, just in case . . . but Maya ate it anyway.

For the next few hours, they waited for it to be time to cross, each filling the time in their own way. Don Fernando smoked cigarettes and talked to Maya's mother while playing old corridos on his phone, and when Mama said she was taking a walk, he watched sports videos. Sebastian tried to nap underneath a tree. Maya collected chip wrappers that were skirting across the parking lot. Using her nails and a sharp stone, she cut them into thin strips, which she then stitched together to make a little purse. It occupied her as much as it pained her—a reminder of her happy place, of the fashion show, and all she was leaving behind. What would Ana say if she could see Maya now?

Then, just after dark, Don Fernando, grimly quiet, drove

them to a motel on a street with motels as far as Maya could see into the night. He wasn't the only coyote. They weren't the only ones about to cross. That was obvious enough. She pressed close to Mama. People *didn't* make it. Fernando's brother . . . What would make the difference between *them* making it across and not?

"¡Oye, cabrón!" a man in an Adidas windbreaker, jeans, and Adidas sneakers called out to Don Fernando. He was shorter than Maya, and his teeth were white as Chiclets. He shook hands with Don Fernando; then they hugged, pounding each other on the back.

"Ernesto!" Don Fernando smiled hard as they pulled apart. He introduced them.

Maya's vision blurred. Was she already dehydrated? She'd heard stories about people dying in the desert, how their bodies turned on themselves, drying and shriveling like a flower petal browning in the intense heat. But, no. She'd just drunk a whole bottle of water, and Don Fernando had bought them a dozen more to pack in their bags. This crossing was getting real. Until now, they were *going* to cross. But now . . . now . . . it was about to happen.

"Don't worry, mija," her mother said, reading her mind. "Come, let's go inside."

As Ernesto walked them across the parking lot—where there seemed to be *way* more people than cars—Maya clutched her mother's arm. The sight of the dingy motel, families with terrified looks, children crying, toddlers clutching their unwashed bottles, their diapers dragging down to their knees, it all made Maya feel claustrophobic. A little girl with a messy ponytail thrust out her palm and asked Maya for candy. Maya shook her head. Where was the girl's mother? Maya scanned the pairs and trios of people leaning against the side of the motel. One man had his head in his hands. She couldn't tell if he was asleep or praying or both. Another woman, pregnant, paced the concrete path as the motel lights shined on her enormous belly. There was a hum in the air, but nothing like when Maya and her classmates would get totally focused on their designs in the studio. Instead the hum here was one of nervous chatter and anticipation. She could tell that for many—like the boys who looked no older than eleven or twelve, in mud-splattered jeans and hoodies, hair slick with grease, faces holding grief—the journey had been less comfortable than a straight shot to the Mexican border. And *here* was a motel in Reynosa, the last stop before the real journey. The crossing.

Inside their motel it wasn't much better. At least forty people occupied the one room that the coyotes had rented, taking up every inch of space on the two beds, rug, and bathroom area. Maya and her mother found a spot and squatted down. Sebastian stood with other young guys who were watching TV, guys with rings of dirt around their necks, grime underneath their fingernails. They were fixated on the fútbol game. Maya didn't have the energy to see what teams were playing. Maya thought of Sebastian's poster, the pang came back. She had her mother. Sebastian had no one. Her body felt heavy. Like she was sinking into the rug beneath her.

"Mama?"

"¿Sí, mija?"

"Where's Don Fernando?"

"He left, mijita."

"Without saying goodbye?" Maya let her head—it seemed to weigh a thousand pounds—rest on her mother's shoulder.

"Shh, mija. He did . . . he tried . . . It's hard for him, you have to understand. Just rest, rest."

"You really expect me to fall asleep, Mama?" They were crammed so close to everyone else, and everyone else's smells and sounds, that even with the television and AC on, Maya felt like everyone could smell *her* breath, hear *her* hushed conversation.

"Vaya, pues." Her mother scooched up against the wall. "Let's play a game."

"A game?" Maya's brain felt clogged. She couldn't stop repeating everything her mother said.

"Sí. Let's take turns saying things we love. I'll go first. I love coffee."

"Wow. You love coffee more than me?"

"No, mija. Not in order of how much you love them. Just . . . things you love. Anda. Your turn."

"I love . . . Lisbeth."

Her mother inhaled deeply, exhaled, then wiped her nose with the back of her hand. "Okay," she said in a wobbly voice. "My turn again. I love . . . zapotes. The ripe ones. When the inside is orange and red like a sunset. Sí. Zapotes."

"Going to the movies," Maya said next.

Her mother added, "The beach." Ah, that was a good one.

"Lipstick," Maya said.

"Special soap! Like with the little chunks of dried fruit."

"Pizza."

"San Marcos," her mother said in a whisper.

"Sewing."

"Sewing."

"Little Luna . . . ," Maya said, the room's edges suddenly going soft as she drifted into sleep.

29

Far too soon, but not soon enough, they at last were instructed to gather their things (all Maya had was a bag and her "new" chip-wrapper purse) and use the bathroom. They would be leaving—walking—for the border in a few minutes. No way Maya was going to use the toilet in the room. It smelled like it'd been clogged for a week! She covered her nose and stood up. Her mother did the same. "Let's use a tree out back. Vámonos," Mama said.

Maya couldn't help it—before leaving the motel room, she scanned the crowd for Sebastian. He was doing the same, for their eyes locked. Could he tell she was scared? Of course. He nudged a couple of people out of the way to get to her, and when he did, a man shoved him hard. Sebastian fell back, but another man caught him. Startled, Sebastian called out, "Maya! Wait." But her mother was moving ahead toward the door. Maya couldn't lose her, not for a second.

After Maya and her mother peed out back, they quickly

gathered around Ernesto, who was instructing people in his group, ones who had paid to be there, to line up, as the path through the woods was a narrow one. Surprisingly relieved, Maya spied Sebastian, front and center. He saw Maya and her mother, and slid back next to them.

"Hey," he said, his voice low. "Can we talk? You know, before . . . I mean, things might get intense, and I just want you to know—"

"Muchachos, now is not the time," her mother scolded.

Sebastian nodded, dipped his head, then, to Maya's shock, took her hand. A bold move, considering her mother was right there. A bold move given how angry Maya still was. And yet, she let him. In fact, she held it right back.

Ernesto explained that the path would be long, that under absolutely *no* circumstances could anyone use their phones. The smallest light would signal to Border Patrol that there was movement, people, and they'd be fucked. Maya could only wish they had phones. He also told them that if they veered off the path, or stopped to rest or use the bathroom or whatever, he would not be responsible for them. Maya held Sebastian's hand tighter. She wished they'd had more time. Why hadn't they talked it out before? He'd tried . . . and she hadn't let him.

And now there was no more time. Ernesto zipped up his Adidas jacket, and just like that, they began to walk. Maya had counted thirty-eight people in total, teens and adults and the one pregnant lady. Ernesto led the way, single file, along a path. The only light was from the moon. Maya wondered what would have happened if there'd been no moon. Then she willed herself to *focus*. One foot in front of the other, stay right behind Mama, don't stop.

They walked and walked. Kilometer after kilometer. Just when she didn't think she could walk any farther, Ernesto urged them to keep walking, don't stop.

So they did; they walked more and more. A branch cracked in the distance. Maya's feet were swollen and aching inside her sneakers. The backpack heavy with water bottles on her shoulders. The smell of dirt and sweat and wood-fire swirled around her. Someone in line called out, "¡No puedo!" and someone else called back, "You have to keep going!" A call-and-response that echoed in Maya's mind for seconds, minutes, maybe longer.

Ernesto hissed, "Silencio!"

Once, Sebastian leaned in and asked, "Are you okay?"

She couldn't stop herself from thinking that he was interested in how she *was*—and he looked so handsome underneath the moonlight, the trees hovering over them both. "Yeah? No," she whispered. He nodded, stayed close behind her. A bat whizzed by and Maya ducked, almost causing her to trip. Mama turned and caught her, squeezed her hand, and kept walking.

It began to feel less like walking and more like floating, trancelike. She'd drunk three bottles of water and still she didn't have to pee. Had it been an hour? Two? Three? Sebastian came up close to her once more and murmured, "Please. Just listen, okay?"

For once, she did not protest. What could she say? This was it. They were here. They were on the edge of a cliff that was her life, before . . . Where had it all started, really? With Lisbeth meeting Oscar? With Oscar introducing Sebastian? With that afternoon on Maya's roof? If she had tailor's chalk, where would she begin tracing this border within the entire fabric of her life?

"I'm really sorry, Maya. For everything. If I had known what my cousins were capable of, if I'd known that you'd be in this situation, I would *never* have brought you into it all. I'd never have tried to meet you. You have to believe me."

She walked, and walked.

"I couldn't sleep that night, the night before ... well, anyway, thinking about Martín and what he planned to do. He almost didn't let me come back from Puerto Barrios. But I did. I was racking my brain for a way—"

She reached behind for his hand. "I believe you."

"You do?" Relief and breath and . . . in the distance, the gurgling of water . . . a river? Was that the Rio Grande?

"I do," Maya said. "And"—she couldn't believe she was bringing this up now, but what if they didn't have much more time? "I wanted to tell you, thanks. For the idea with the balloons. It worked. It really worked."

"Maya . . . ," Sebastian said, his voice heavy, so, so heavy.

But Ernesto's abrupt stop cut him off. The water, Maya realized, was so loud. They were so close! Ernesto gathered them round. "Rest up for half an hour. Then we cross." And he disappeared into the dark.

Maya sank onto the ground. "Shh," her mother warned, even though Maya hadn't said a word. Sebastian squatted down by Maya's other side.

He whispered, "Maya. You have no idea—I'm just so happy

you believe me. I never meant to hurt you. I would never—
and hey, you're welcome. For the balloons."

"¡Patojos!" her mother warned. "We didn't come this far to
have you both . . ." Mama was so tired, she leaned back against
a tree trunk, not finishing her sentence.

Maya looked at Sebastian, and their hands met so fiercely
that it startled her. What would happen now?

What felt like a second later, Ernesto was back. He passed
out plastic bags, like from the supermarket. "Quiet. Undress.
Swim," he instructed them. He was not a man of many words!

Her mother immediately took off her dress. Maya hesitated.
Was Sebastian watching? She couldn't bear to look up. Or take
off her clothes. Nope. Not happening. She compromised by
taking off her sneakers.

A man asked, "That's it?"

"What?" Ernesto whisper-barked. "Did you expect a cruise
ship?" A few people laughed softly. One made a cross on her
chest. "Bueno," Ernesto added. "The water is cold, and deep,
and if you can't swim, then hold on to someone who can.

"Oh—and this is important. The last time we crossed, they
said to watch out for a drop to the right. It gets deep real quick.
So listen up—stay left. And buena suerte."

Stay left. Stay left. Got it.

The water—the Rio Grande!—was colder than Maya had
anticipated. Her teeth were instantly chattering. Stay left, stay
left. In the darkness, everything felt amplified, scarier. The
swoosh of the water. The sounds of people moving through
it. Because her sneakers didn't fit in her backpack, she held
them, tied together, above her head, but it was hard to balance

them. It was all making her move slowly. Age didn't matter in the water.

Her mother, just ahead, turned and whispered, "Stay *right* behind me. And remember—"

"Stay left! Okay, Mama!" Maya whisper-yelled. Sebastian was just ahead of Mama. Together, they were a little train.

Maya willed her mother and Sebastian to not go so quickly, but at the same time, she didn't want to stay in the water a moment longer than necessary. The rocks at the bottom hurt her bare feet, and she kept slipping. A woman moved up beside Maya, a look on her face like she was walking into her death. She was weeping silently. Maya felt spooked; she tried to distance herself from the woman, keep up with her mother. But the woman was like a leech. She wouldn't leave Maya's side.

The river waves grew bigger, louder. Many of the others were already far up ahead. How wide was this damn river, anyway? Maya kept tabs on her mother. As long as she could see her mother's back, she was okay. And as long as Mama could see Sebastian's back, Mama was okay. Just focus. The water grew deeper, up to Maya's waist now. The woman beside her was growing hysterical, waving her arms in the air.

"Wait for me, señorita, por favor," she called to Maya.

Maya kept moving. It was getting harder and harder to balance the backpack and shoes above her head. They were so heavy. Her arms felt like Jell-O.

"Please," the woman begged. "You're going too fast."

Maya turned to her. Damn. She was the last one in the group. Up ahead Maya could see Sebastian, already on shore, reaching his arm out to help others.

"Just keep moving," Maya encouraged her.

"I can't swim," she announced through tears.

"Neither can I," Maya said. "The water won't get any deeper than this, so long as we stay left. Ernesto said the Rio Grande was a shallow river." Had he actually said that? Was Maya making that up? Her head and body and soul—it was all too much to carry. But she had to keep going.

And then she truly couldn't compute what she was seeing. Mama. Up ahead. Dropping into the water.

"Mama!" Maya rushed, but it was like trying to wade through cement. And the rocks were like sharp daggers on her soles. "Help her! Sebastian!" She didn't care that she was supposed to be quiet.

Sebastian looked up and instantly dove into the water, swimming toward Mama. And a thought flashed through Maya's head—it was impossible for him to have saved his own mother, but now he was helping hers.

"Mama!" Maya yearned to cry out. But she knew she couldn't. She'd put them all at risk.

Then, coughing. Lots of coughing. Mama gasping for air, Sebastian trying to pull her onto shore, Mama looking out of her mind with panic.

To make things worse, the woman who had been beside Maya now waved frantically, the river threatening to pull her under. "¡Ayúdame!" Her voice sounded garbled. "¡Ayúdame!"

And that's when the riverbed underneath Maya fell away completely.

As she went under, Maya grasped her backpack, tried to use it as a float. It didn't work. The water whooshed it away instantly.

She opened her mouth to call for help, swallowing water.

Somehow, Maya found purchase again. She coughed and spat, then gasped and gasped. Her shoes were long gone, floating on to another life. The river was anything but shallow! It was high and swirling. She spied the woman who'd been calling for help a few meters away, her head bobbing, her hands clawing at the line between water and sky, between life and death. Maya reached out for her. But as she did, she slipped right back under. The swirl of water filled her ears.

Maya kicked and kicked. She could barely keep herself above water, never mind help carry this poor woman, who somehow caught hold of Maya's arm and clutched it. Still, she kicked and kicked toward shore. *God, please. Please!*

They were almost there. They were almost there.

She'd choked down so much water. But she kept moving.

"Go! Yes! Go!" people called from just a short distance away, ignoring the coyote's rule to be quiet. "Maya!" her mother cried. Sebastian—he had finally managed to pull her mother safely up onto the shoreline. Thank God! Oh, thank God.

"We're almost there," Maya assured the woman. The water, miraculously, became calmer and shallower.

The people on the shore waved them forward. Maya could see her mother's lips moving, almost frantically, like she was warning Maya of something.

"Just a little more," Maya, now standing again, told the woman encouragingly. She caught her breath. Moved through the muddy water as if tires were tied to her legs.

"To the left!" she heard her mother say, along with Ernesto and Sebastian and a few others. "Left!"

Then, mud.

It pulled at her. Like quicksand. She whipped around to warn the woman but couldn't see her. Maya started to sink.

Her feet were not hers anymore.

"Here!" someone from the shore called. "Grab this!" A vine.

But the vine hit Maya in the face, and when she opened her eyes, it was gone. Her ankles were now deep in the mud. The sand yanked at her calves, sucking them farther down with each movement.

"¡Señora!" Maya called out to the woman.

"Another vine! It's coming! Grab it!" a man yelled.

This time Maya caught it. She gripped it so hard it almost fell apart. She let the others guide her carefully, slowly, to the edge of the river. It felt like years until she touched the shore. There, Maya fell to her knees as her mother's hands reached for her.

When she'd caught her breath and had coughed out a mouthful of water, Maya sat up. "The woman," she sputtered. "We need to help that woman."

"Mija . . . ," her mother said in a way Maya had never once heard her say it.

"The woman!" Maya gagged on the river left in her throat.

"Madre de Dios . . . ," her mother said.

Then, a guttural sound from someone else in the crowd.

Maya reluctantly looked to the river. There she was, the woman. Her body bobbed like a cork, facedown.

Maya's mother led her to a patch of grass, rocked her back and forth. "It's not your fault," she repeated. "It's not your fault.

You tried your hardest." And as her mother wiped Maya's tears, she realized—they were in America. And that poor woman— she'd been alone . . . and now, she was gone.

Then Maya thought about how here she was, in America, with absolutely *nothing*. Not her sneakers or backpack. Only the clothes on her back, the jeans on her legs. She had refused to strip down to her bra and underwear. Maybe she would've moved faster in the water, if she had? It was too late now.

Her mother quickly got dressed, and suddenly groaned, "I'm going to be sick." She rushed behind a tree. Maya could hear her vomiting.

Sebastian squatted. "Maya . . ." Before she could think not to, Maya hugged him.

The rest of the group was crying and breathing hard and praying and putting dry clothes back on, at least those who had managed not to lose their plastic bags while wading between countries. Then Maya spied a flash of light. Oh no, oh no!!!! Her alarm grew when she realized it was a flashlight. The sound of tires against the dirt immediately followed. The crack of branches. A microphone. Someone saying something in English.

Sebastian pulled away from Maya. "Run!"

But her body locked. She looked desperately in the direction of her mother. "I can't leave Mama!"

He grasped her elbow and tried to get her to move.

"No!" She pulled her arm back.

He looked at her, his face anguished. They exchanged a look that had a thousand more looks inside it before he let go and bolted into the darkness of the woods. A thousand heartaches.

That was what it felt like. Goodbye, Sebastian. Goodbye, first kiss. But the thoughts couldn't linger—she had to get her mother. They had to *move*! Like the others, who were now running like ants in the night when someone turned on a light switch. Every which way. A voice yelled into a microphone. Impossibly loud. But Maya couldn't understand what he was saying.

Suddenly two white vans pulled up. The sun was just rising, its caramel-colored light enveloping them all. Maya shivered in her wet clothes. "What are they saying?" she asked a man who hurried past her.

His face looked stricken. "It's Border Patrol."

Maya didn't hesitate. She bolted toward where Mama was, the pebbles and rough dirt piercing the soft, bare bottoms of her feet not slowing her down. Ernesto had agreed to cross them. That was the plan. They'd make their way, fold into the fabric of the United States someway, somehow. But if they were caught—the plan was to seek asylum, yes. But not apart. They would do this *together*.

"Maya!" her mother screamed.

"Mama!" Maya's voice scared even her. "Mama!"

"¡Mija!"

Maya froze. A man had her mother. He was handcuffing her and shoving her into one of those white vans, one with green letters on the side.

Maya sprinted after her, the pain in her feet making her wince. A female Border Patrol officer appeared out of nowhere. She flung out her arm to stop Maya, then pushed her down and pinned her to the ground. "¡No te muevas!" she ordered.

"Get off me!" Maya yelled, managing to turn in her mother's direction. "Mama!"

Her mother was trying to wriggle away from the officer who was pushing her into the van, but he was literally twice her size. And *he* wasn't handcuffed. Faster than Maya could believe, he had the van door shut and had jumped into the passenger seat.

"Take me with you! Take me! Please. That's my mom!" Maya shrieked, trying to wrestle free.

She could just make out her mother's face in the window, as her mother screamed and writhed and mouthed, "Maya! Maya!"

Another officer dressed in green hauled Maya up by one arm—and a searing pain jolted through her shoulder. She felt ice-cold handcuffs snapping around her wrists, and just as she was thinking her world was cracking open and she'd surely fall into the deep, dark space within, the officer opened the white van door and shoved Maya inside too. Her shoulder burned. She felt convinced it was broken. But then, "Maya! Gracias a Dios! Maya!" and her mother's voice eclipsed the physical pain. Her mother, maneuvering her way over to Maya inside the strange, dark van, which, upon closer look, resembled a dogcatcher vehicle. Her mother's head beside Maya's head. Kissing Maya and praying, *Thank God. Thank God.*

30

An hour later—Maya's jeans and shirt still damp, her feet throbbing and caked with mud—they were inside the very place Maya had seen horror stories about on the nightly news: an American detention center. The walls were white and tan, and the floors, gray. Maya winced as she followed a guard who led everyone from the van down one hall and then another. The smell sterile, not unlike a hospital. So many guards, all with guns. She was so disoriented she could hardly take it all in. The guard instructed them to wait inside a ceiling-high metal cage with dozens and dozens of other migrants. She kept hearing that word: *migrants*. That was what they were now, one of many . . . *migrants*. She wondered vaguely where Sebastian might be. Lights, the bright kind you see at stadiums, stung Maya's eyes. At least she and Mama were here together. In this strange, cold place that was like a prison. And what was that sound she kept hearing? Like static. Or foil being wrapped and unwrapped.

A few minutes later, another guard arrived. He snapped his fingers, and everyone in the cell lined up. Apparently they were going to be "processed." In a bare room with lone benches bolted to the floor, a woman—an agent—wearing a green uniform and holding a clipboard took notes with little interest. She handed Maya a pair of canvas sneakers—gray, used, no brand name, no laces—and in Spanish demanded that Mama take the laces out of her own sneakers. Whaaat was happening?

"Now!" she barked. A short man with a buzz cut, maybe in his twenties, looked like he was about to say something, but the uniformed woman glared at him, so he stayed quiet.

Her mother did as she was told. Then the agent said to Maya, "Your hair tie too." She motioned, robot-like, for Maya to drop the hair tie into the garbage bin, making it clear there was no way *she* was going to touch it.

"Why do they want my hair tie?" Maya whispered.

"Shh!" The agent pointed at Mama. "Yours, too."

"Just do what she says, Maya." Her mother hesitantly pulled the band out from her hair and tossed it into the trash.

Maya's hair was still wet and tangled, and though she tried to remove it, the tie was stuck.

The guard came over, yelled, "Do you understand Spanish? Or do you speak one of those other languages?"

Maya's chest heaved. What if she had? Clearly, she was *trying* to get the tie out. Couldn't the agent see that?

"¡Vámonos! Hurry up!" she yelled.

Maya tugged harder, but the tie would not come loose. Would the guard cut off her ponytail? She pulled and pulled, ripping her hair, only making it worse. Mama tried to help, but the guard slapped her hand away.

"Wait a sec!" Maya insisted.

"Gentle, mija." How could her mother stay so calm?

Maya massaged the coiled hairs around the tie, managed to loosen it, then pulled it free at last. She felt like she'd just run a race. And lost . . .

Now the agent wanted their names, Mama repeatedly saying, "We are seeking asylum." The woman barely acknowledged them. A buzzer rang and a new batch of people were brought in. Apparently, Maya and her mother had been "processed."

Maya and her mother were led to another cage, a massive one, and told to wait.

"For how long, sir?" Maya's mother asked, but the officer ignored her.

Thin, army-green mats had been strewn across the flooring, which was vinyl laid over concrete; Maya could see the concrete peeking through a curled piece of flooring. Everyone— hundreds of people, from what she could tell, from babies to grandparents—had been given "blankets," aluminum sheets, like giant pieces of tinfoil. That was it! That was the sound she'd heard earlier. Maya and her mother were given one as well. What did that make them? Burritos to be wrapped, and then what? Discarded? Her teeth chattering, she tried to make sense of all that had happened in the past few hours, never mind the past few days. Sebastian. Had he escaped? Had he made it into the woods beyond the Border Patrol's reach? Maya now fully understood his terrible predicament—he could not seek asylum; he'd already been deported once. No question he would be sent back to Guatemala like returned mail, if they caught him. And that could be a death sentence. If he was going to make it in the US, it would have to be on his own, no doubt. She shivered just considering his situation. She genuinely felt sorry for him. Even after everything. She pulled that stupid silver burrito bag around her.

People clustered together in the cramped space—daughters and mothers, sons and fathers, and lone teenagers. One man rubbed his stomach and kicked at the floor over and over, the rubber of his also laceless sneaker making a *squeetch* sound. A girl, maybe nine years old, wept in a corner, clinging to the chain-link, pleading with a guard who lazily paced the area to let her see her mother. The guard didn't even turn her way, stared instead at the television mounted in the corner. An episode of *SpongeBob*. In English, of course. Maya couldn't bear to look at the girl any longer.

No one deserved any of this, she thought as she wrapped the aluminum sheet tighter around her. No wonder this place was called la hielera—a nickname for the detention center, because it was always freezing. "Why is it so cold?" she asked her mother when they'd first walked in, and a woman near them answered, "They think it will keep our diseases from multiplying." Another man had interrupted, "No. It's to punish us." *Punish us? For what?* Maya didn't ask. She only leaned closer to her mother. Her shoulder throbbed. She asked the guard to see a doctor, but he'd only sucked his teeth and given her two ibuprofen with no water. She choked the chalky pills down anyway. They didn't help.

So—the other weird thing was, no one looked anyone else

in the eye. And why would they? Also, where *exactly* was she? In the United States. She knew that much. Names were called over the intercom periodically. It reminded her of school.

Two other guards announced a bathroom break. Maya and her mother clutched hands and joined a line with the other women and children. They followed the guards to a room called LADIES—no mirrors, no paper towels, just sinks and toilets and hand dryers. Back in the hallway, they lined up again as yet another guard distributed ham sandwiches wrapped in clear plastic. A woman next to Maya tore open the plastic and began eating right away. Then she gagged and spit the mush out of her mouth. A long black hair. The woman hesitated, then, removing the hair, continued to eat the sandwich. Maya ate only the bread and tossed the rest in the trash. Later, she learned that if you were in the bathroom when they passed out the food, that was your bad luck. You didn't get a sandwich. So, Maya and her mother began using the bathroom at different times, just to be certain they'd get *something* to eat. And it was . . . something. Something gross and wobbly and nasty. Those dry, cardboard-tasting, practically frozen sandwiches didn't count as food. And they weren't even offered mustard or mayonnaise.

Several hours later—Maya didn't know if it was day or night or what—after she and Mama took turns using each other's laps as pillows, her name was called over an intercom. At first, she didn't register it as her own. A voice repeated, "Maya Silva."

Maya looked to Mama, whose face was puffy with exhaustion. *Isabel Sánchez,* Mama kept repeating. *Remember.* Right. Their sponsor.

"Mama? They're calling my name. Come on."

"Of course, mija."

They both stood. But when her mother tried to follow, the guard stopped her. "No. Only her."

"But . . . I'm her mother!" Mama looked incredulous and, Maya thought, so weak. And instantly hated herself for thinking it. Mama, in her navy-blue sweatshirt. Her dirty jeans. Her sneakers without laces. Her hair tied in a braid behind her neck, with a piece of string from her sweatshirt. Maya had tied it tight for her. She had to do it when a guard wasn't looking, because they'd surely be punished for it. Sent to solitary confinement, a place she had learned was called la loba, the hole. Yet what was so wrong about a girl wanting to braid her own mother's hair?

"Only her," the guard said, his voice expressionless.

"I'm not going, then," Maya said.

"Fine by me," the guard said, and clicked the cage door shut. "No me importa."

No *way* was Maya leaving her mother's side. So, wrapped like silver burritos, they sat, and sat.

Another mother-daughter pair had noticed Maya's hair tie trick and asked her to make them one too. She did. And doing so on the cold floor in this strange place brought the first smile to her face since . . . well, a long time. So she made some more hair ties. Then she fixed a little girl's jacket zipper by using her nails and a tiny safety pin that another woman let her borrow, not keep. She felt glad to be doing something. It took her mind off everything, including her own smell.

While they were making the journey north, she'd worn pads

in her underwear to keep fresh, but at this point, Maya couldn't stand her own stink. What she'd give for a shower. And her hair was even worse. Despite how tightly her mother had braided it to keep it clean, her scalp itched with sweat, stinky and greasy and impossible to ignore. Everything built up—the wax in her ears, the dirt underneath her nails, the itch between her toes. But Border Patrol didn't let migrants shower in the detention center. They probably washed their dogs more often, she thought, anger again surging.

Luna.

No—no—she could *not* go there.

Just then the man who had been clutching his stomach began writhing in pain. "Por favor," he said to the guard. "I need to see a doctor. Something is wrong."

"All we can give you is ibuprofen," the guard said impassively.

The man was near tears. "Por favor," he begged.

Mama prayed under her breath "God help him."

The guard walked away with a shrug, tapping his fingers against his gun holster.

"Mama? That poor man. What can we do for him?" Maya asked.

"Nada, mija. Just pray in your head." She caressed Maya's cheek.

The man curled into a ball and kicked and kicked.

Maya tucked herself into her mother's shoulder, wanting, with every atom of her being, for this all to end.

The next day—or so she assumed, it was impossible to tell—a guard called Maya's name again. And the day after that, too.

Never her mother's. She and Mama became dizzy and mad and feverish and thirsty (she couldn't stand to drink the chemical-tasting "water" at the fountains they were allowed to use every few hours), but being apart was not an option. Still, Maya hated the question that swelled in her mind—what would be the breaking point? What would make it so one of them actually followed the guard out of the cage when one of their names was called? What would bring them over the edge? Maybe these damn always-on lights! The guards left the fluorescent lights on twenty-four hours a day. When Maya had asked a guard about it, she'd glared at Maya. "What? Do you want them to turn off the lights so you can be raped?" Maya had gasped.

For the next two or three or four days—it was all a blur—people shifted in and out. Maya couldn't stop herself from hoping one would be Sebastian. She knew she'd likely never see him again, and she also knew that getting in touch with him on Instagram or whatever would only make her a target for the maras . . . again. Still, she searched every face.

Mama spoke to a few others when she summoned the strength—asking about the asylum process and timing and laws and if they would ever let them shower. But no one seemed to know any more than she did.

Then one day, when the guard called Maya's name, the woman sitting beside them suggested in a low voice, "Go with the guard. Trust me. I mean, you don't have to. You don't even know me. But I think they just want to interview you for asylum. Can't enter the United States without the paperwork. So, if I were you . . ."

No. The woman was just trying to trick them. Don Fernando

hadn't said anything about this part. An interview? Sounded like a trap. Or had he? Mama couldn't remember. Really, Mama didn't look so good. Her skin was pale and her lips were dry.

"Maya Silva," the voice over the intercom repeated.

This time, her mother nodded. Maybe the woman was right? What if this *was* the way out? Mama clearly agreed, because she said in a low voice, "Remember, when they ask, Isabel Sánchez is our sponsor. Your 'aunt.' If we get separated"—here Mama made the sign of the cross—"we'll meet in New York."

"What! Meet in New York? Mama—"

"We talked about this, Maya," her mother said, then broke into a cough. She looked so frail.

"Okay, Mama. Okay. Rest." But first, Maya hugged her so tight, she could feel her heart pounding. *Don't cry. Don't cry.*

"I love you, mija. Everything will be okay."

A guard smacked the chain-link fence. "Hey! No hugging!"

"I love you, too, Mama."

"Remember everything I told you," she said, as Maya let go bit by bit.

Was this really happening? She was so delirious, so desperate. She didn't know what was real anymore. She kept tripping in her canvas shoes, which flapped open without any laces as she followed the guard.

When she stepped into the small office, she never expected that she would be sitting in that chair alone for hours upon hours, no one to tell her they'd be with her in just one moment. Eventually, someone came in and shoved a paper at Maya. Took a pen from behind her ear, clicked it once, and handed it to Maya. Ordered her to sign the paper.

262 · DE LEON

Maya scanned the document. "What is this? What does it say?" she asked.

The guard, a woman in her fifties maybe, her gray roots a stark contrast to her dyed chocolate-colored hair, stared at Maya as if seeing her for what she was: an actual human being. Or so Maya thought, because she abruptly asked, "You can't read?"

Maya's breath caught.

"Says here you're from Guatemala. I know a lot of people there can't read."

Was she testing Maya? Seeing if she'd snap? Throw a chair? Because that was what she wanted to do! Instead Maya channeled her mother's calm and said, "It's in English, señora. I would like to read a copy in Spanish. Por favor." She looked her right in the eye.

"Solo firmalo," the guard said, almost sounding annoyed that Maya wouldn't just sign it. Or bored. Or both.

"But what am I signing?" Maya tried to make meaning from the words. She knew some English, yes, but this was full of legal terms. Plus, her stomach was rumbling.

The guard snatched the pen back, wiping it with a tissue before tucking it behind her ear once more. Left without a word. It was torture, staring at the one poster on the wall. An image of the solar system. It seemed almost deliberately cruel to offer her a picture of a greater universe.

After who knew how long, a new guard came in. Younger. Red lipstick. Hair in a top bun! She shut the door and sat across from Maya and handed her some graham crackers.

"Thank you!" Maya said, immediately opening the package. "Please. Do you have any water?"

"I'll see what I can do," she said. She sent a text on her phone. The sight of the phone made Maya immediately think of Lisbeth. Was she safe? Would Oscar really not hurt Lisbeth? Maya had been praying for her whenever she remembered . . . but somehow seeing that phone felt like science fiction, a portal to another world. How many texts had she and Lisbeth sent back and forth? *Meet you in five. TTYL. K. Oscar has a cousin . . .* Maya's fingers practically ached.

The woman looked up. "I need to ask you some questions about why you're seeking asylum." She opened a notebook, pulled out a long form.

"Okay," Maya said, nodding, hoping to appear helpful.

Someone walked in without knocking and handed Maya a bottle of water. "¡Gracias! ¡Gracias!" she said, before gulping down half the bottle in one huge swig. The person left.

"Well, I hope now you're ready to talk," the guard said. Hold up. Was she a guard? Or a lawyer?

The woman barreled through question after question. *Do you have any family in your home country? Has anyone in your family ever applied for asylum before? Do you fear returning to your home country?*

How was Maya supposed to adequately answer that last one? Yes, she feared returning to Guatemala. Yet she also feared *never* returning to Guatemala. Because, she was now learning, that was what asylum was, among other things. An agreement never to return to your homeland.

"Señorita. I need to record your answers."

"Sorry." Maya shifted in the cold chair. "No, no, and . . . yes."

The lady scribbled on that long form with so many lines and

boxes and small print. It was impossible to determine what she was actually writing.

She went on. "Who harmed you, or put you in fear of harm? Was the government involved? If not, did they do anything to try to stop it?"

Maya used her finger to gather the graham cracker crumbs on the table, assembling them into a little pile. How could she summarize it all, like in a short essay at school? *Two gang members named Oscar and Martín tried to kill my mother and me in our kitchen.* Would that be a good topic sentence?

"¿Señorita?" A mix of sympathy and impatience layered in the officer lady's voice. Maybe she was on Maya's side. Maybe . . .

"Two gang members . . . they tried to murder my mother and me, in our home. Mama . . . my mother . . . she had gone to the police, but . . . no, they didn't help us at all. Actually, they—"

"Bueno." But . . . Maya hadn't finished!

Maya leaned forward. "Did you write that down? Two gang members—"

The lady slid the paper closer to herself and made a little wall with her hand. "Can you live safely somewhere else in your country, even if a move would be inconvenient? You must know that you might not qualify for asylum if you could live safely in another part of your country." She looked up, searching Maya's expression for an honest answer.

San Marcos, San Marcos, San Marcos, flashed in her mind. The lavender sky. The horchata. The mountains. Abuela . . . If only Maya had listened to Mama early on, if only they'd moved there immediately. If only . . .

"I know it's difficult," the lady said, again with that layer of sympathy. "But the more specifics you can give me now, the better your case will be." She smiled. She really smiled. And that was when Maya noticed the red lipstick on her teeth. La directora! The fashion show! Her shoulders sank and sank, along with her heart.

"Do you have anything else you would like to say to me today?"

Maya opened her mouth, but could not utter a syllable.

The woman sighed, crossed her legs. "This is your last chance."

Maya dug for the right words, but they were out of reach. Besides, how could that paper, that *form*, hold all that she had inside her? If she had only told her mother the whole story of what was going on, what she'd seen, then they might not be here right now. If only she'd told her??? She thought of her father, how he would never put voice to his story. But Maya could. She could. . . . So in that freezing room, she cleared her throat and told the officer lady everything—from the local gangs to señora Pérez to the . . . murder Maya had witnessed. She urged the lady to look up news articles and Daniel's obituary on her phone, which the lady promised to do. Maya must have said "Isabel Sánchez" a dozen times, for this name, this woman, was a life raft out of this room, this hell.

Afterward, the officer left and had Maya wait some more. She wondered whether—no, she *prayed* that Mama was in another office just like this one, telling the same details about the gangs and signing the same forms. Maybe they'd be released at the same time and they'd be able to travel to New York together, after all! Maya decided to dare to be hopeful.

The waiting went on forever. Finally someone new showed up, simply to say, "Vamos. You're being released."

Maya looked at her, stunned. "I *am*? But—but—what about my mother? Is she released too? Her name is Carmen—"

The officer had already pivoted, was already walking swiftly down the hall, leaving her question unanswered. Maya had no choice but to scramble after her. The next thing she knew she was being ushered onto a large bus with others who were clutching plastic bags full of their belongings. A guard handed Maya a similar plastic bag. All it held was Maya's paperwork. Not one thing more. She'd lost everything else in the river, even the chip wrapper purse.

"Wait! Is my mother on this bus? I can't go without—" she cried in alarm as the engine of the tall, wide bus revved. No response. Just a no-nonsense nudge forward, up the steps.

A rush of warm wind enveloped her as Maya reluctantly boarded the bus, looking around for Mama. She sank into a seat a few rows from the front—at least the leather was softer than the cage floor—and blinked away hot tears, frantic to see if maybe her mother was walking from that drab concrete block of a building at this very moment. Was her mother still inside?

As she looked through tears out the window, she couldn't resist wondering, *Is this really it? Los Estados Unidos?* The avenues were wider, much wider, than in Guatemala or Mexico. Everything was so . . . flat. And yes, clean, but in a soulless, empty way. Where were the mercados? The women selling papayas and mangoes? The men with the white buckets full of fresh marigolds and roses? Where were the street vendors sizzling carne asada and ladling steaming, sweet atole de elote into Styrofoam cups? Oh, how she ached for a cup of home right now as the bus maneuvered through these foreign streets. Welcome to America.

31

Wind. So simple, invisible, and yet strong enough to break glass. From her seat, Maya could hear it howling. Funny how the wind could travel freely from one country to the next, without so much as a glance from the men with guns at the border. Through the tinted windows, she watched it yanking the leaves on the trees this way and that, this way and that. She was about to undo her itchy braids, pull her hair into a ponytail—was *about* to—when she realized that her hair tie had not been returned.

They'd taken so much.

Mama . . . Please be wherever we're headed. She whispered this little prayer over and over as she scanned row after row of passengers, other migrants like her. Then a bold gust rushed through, almost knocking over a sign that said WELCOME TO McALLEN! like a punch to its back.

Not ten minutes later, the bus hissed to a stop in front of a building. The driver, in the same hideous green as those who'd ordered her around in the detention center, picked his teeth, jerking the toothpick in and out, not even glancing at the passengers. At the *migrants*.

Maya pressed the back of the seat in front of her. Come on, come on. How long did it take people to get off a bus? She sent *Hurry up, hurry up* thoughts at everyone in front of her. Gaaah! Mama might be in that building! What was this place, anyway? The building—one level, painted white with two large purple columns, wide front doors, bushes lining the paved walkway— was it another kind of detention center? It didn't look like anyone's home. Maya pounded on the seat.

The woman right behind her, who appeared much too old to have made this trip alone, pushed her gray hair behind her ears before placing a wrinkled hand on Maya's shoulder. "Breathe, mija. Let go, and let God." She made a half-hearted sign of the cross, not even touching her forehead.

Breathe? Maya's lungs were threatening to choke her until finally, slowly, the people started to move. She clutched her plastic bag.

"Welcome to the Humanitarian Respite Center," an older man in a navy-blue baseball cap with a red *B* on the front, smiling wide, greeted them once they were off the bus and lined up on the sidewalk. "Come inside. God is with you. Welcome."

His Spanish was perfect, no accent like the guards inside the hielera had. But he also looked estadounidense, like an American in the United States, with his blue jeans and Nike sneakers and button-down shirt. A sweatshirt, too. He looked like a fit grandfather, yet moved like a teenager. "This way," he beckoned. "Inside, we have a hot shower, hot food, and a change of clothes." He waved them along. "This way. God bless you."

Maya looked uneasily, hopefully, at the others taking hesitant steps along the paved walkway, entering the building like ghosts. She'd felt like she was floating into another world. And so this simple "welcome" went a long way. As did the words *shower* and *hot food*. Maya's mouth watered, imagining a piping-hot bowl of arroz con pollo. Guilt immediately washed it away. What if Mama wasn't here?

Maya turned to the man. "Excuse me, sir?" She smiled her best smile.

The man looked at Maya. Really looked at her. Maybe the first person to do so in days.

"Señor, I'm looking for my mother. Her name is Carmen Silva. She has long black hair, but she usually wears it in a braid tied in a bun behind her neck. She's a few centimeters taller than me, but we have the same dark skin and eyes and our shoulders measure the exact same when we stand back to back when I am wearing tacones and—"

"Mija," he said kindly, earnestly. "We will find her. Do not lose faith. First, come inside."

Maya managed to nod. "Gracias."

She wondered why he kept mentioning God. This place didn't really give off religious vibes. Plus, it looked more like a community center or a bank than a church.

A lady with super-stylish short dark hair stepped out of the building and joined him. "Carlos, they need you inside." Her eyes were heavy with blue eye shadow and a bucket of mascara, and she tapped her nails against the laptop she was holding. "I'll welcome everyone."

"Ahora voy." The man, Carlos, nodded toward Maya and the others, and just as she thought he was going to leave her there, he pivoted and said, "Come with me, señorita."

32

The lobby, with its low ceilings, was a quiet chaos. Maybe it was the volunteers in teal aprons milling around holding clipboards, or the man calling names into a microphone, or the sheer number of migrants here, hundreds of them, seated on the floor or standing in lines to use the phones or the bathroom. Some waited their turn to talk to a lady in a magenta T-shirt and faded jeans who sat at a table with a laptop. Was she a volunteer too? Where was her apron? In a soft voice, she instructed everyone to wait calmly. "You'll *all* get your turn. We'll work with each of you individually. We'll help you contact your sponsor and we'll get you transportation—a bus ticket, a plane ticket. Whatever you need. We'll get you to your sponsor—don't worry."

But worry was all Maya had. She scanned every small crowd, every face, looking for the braided bun—even a loose one—at the back of her mother's neck. She walked down one tight hallway—America was made of hallways, it seemed to her—then another, peeking inside rooms without doors. Blue mats were scattered on the floors. One woman breast-fed her baby. Another bit her nails. A family of four huddled together, a toddler asleep across both his parents' laps. Maya kept moving. Another hallway. More rooms. A maze, in and out, and she quickly lost track. She passed a kitchen where two men wearing hairnets stirred something in a huge silver pot. The smell—was it spaghetti and meatballs?—made her stomach clench. She could hardly remember when her last *real* meal had been. She lingered for a moment, enraptured by the smell, then forced herself onward. There, in another hallway, a man was pounding—but gently, as if he couldn't make up his mind between anger and patience—on a mostly empty vending machine. The only items left were Diet Coke. Ew.

No music, no games, no television of any sort. She peeked into another room. A mother was helping her young son with the Velcro on his sneakers. A toddler played with his father, trying to zip his papa's jacket all the way to the neck, both of them laughing. But no Mama. Then, back at the entrance—somehow she'd made a full circle—she noticed a shopping cart full of red flannel blankets like the ones Maya had seen people use on airplanes in the movies, and a bunch of string backpacks, like the kind they gave out when you bought a Tigo cell phone.

A hand tapped her arm, ever so lightly. Maya swung around, hoping against hope. But it wasn't her mother, it was a baby, held by *her* mother, a baby who now grinned at Maya, having gotten her attention. In the woman's free hand was a tan envelope with a white sheet of paper stapled to the front:

PLEASE HELP ME. I DO NOT SPEAK ENGLISH. WHAT BUS DO I NEED TO TAKE? THANK YOU FOR YOUR HELP. ☺

Maya figured this paper was her way of asking for help from strangers in case she got lost along her journey, after the volunteers helped her board the right bus. Words in English. Would Maya get a similar envelope? Would the words be enough? *Focus, Maya. Find Mama.* She smiled at the baby, told the mother how cute it was, and resumed her search.

On the other side of a pair of blue doors, she heard the sounds of children laughing. Maya pushed through the set of doors into a courtyard. Outside, two toddlers played a game in the dirt, something with pebbles and an orange-and-yellow plastic car, while a woman in a teal apron spoke to another woman with silver hair.

Maya's head began to feel impossibly heavy. She felt empty, spooned out, drained. Sit—she needed to sit down, just for a moment. . . . Was she fainting?

"Mama . . . ," she murmured. "This is when you say, 'I'm right here, Maya Luz. I'm right here.'" She sat on the concrete, curled herself into a ball.

The tall lady hurried over, looking alarmed. She gently touched Maya's leg. "Miss? Are you okay?" she asked in Spanish. "We need to get you processed. Then you can take a warm shower and change your clothes and we'll get you some hot food. How does that sound?

"Miss?" the lady repeated when Maya didn't respond.

Maya sat up, centimeter by centimeter. Her body felt like packed dirt. "I'm . . . I'm looking for a woman named Carmen Silva. Have you seen her?"

The lady squatted, took Maya delicately by the elbow. "Are you traveling alone? Is your mother with you? No—I'm sorry. I didn't mean to upset you. We'll find her. What's your name, honey?"

"Maya Silva."

"I'm Ingrid. I'm a volunteer here. Been here about a month. Probably stay another. I'm retired. My kids are all grown up. Lived in Oregon all my life. Figured I'd come and help out where the help is needed. Where are you from, Maya?"

Maya blinked—the woman's Spanish was great. It made Maya feel like she could answer her truthfully, and so she did. "Guatemala."

"Ah, Guatemala. What a beautiful country, just beautiful," the lady, Ingrid, said, pushing up her glasses. "Now, let's get you checked in, yes?"

Maya nodded, and got up shakily to follow her back to the lobby. There, Miss Ingrid pulled out a little spiral notebook and flipped to a blank page. She pulled out a pen, wrote something. "Maya *Silva?*" Maya nodded. "Sounds like someone famous." She winked. "You an artist?"

Maya frowned. She didn't know how to answer that, not anymore. "Sort of."

"Sort of? Well, I'm sort of an artist too. I like to paint birds. My walls are covered in paintings and postcards and calendars—all birds."

"Oh." Maya wanted to tell her about the national bird of Guatemala, the quetzal, but she just didn't have the energy.

Miss Ingrid explained that this was where migrants met one-on-one with volunteers, who, with cell phones and laptops, helped connect them with their family members or sponsors in other parts of the US. The sponsor would pay for the bus or plane ticket to bring the person to them; the volunteers helped make the purchases.

Well, at least this system made sense, Maya thought.

Ingrid was looking her up and down. "Normally we ask that you contact your sponsor first, but you know what—let's change it up. Come with me, honey."

As they walked, Miss Ingrid hummed a tune, helping Maya feel brave enough to ask, "Miss Ingrid, can you explain . . . what comes next?" Maya was half-scared to hear the answer, but she was tired of not knowing what came beyond what the car headlights showed.

"Of course. It's so much to take in! So, just like you and your mom, many people cross, get detained, seek asylum. But it's far from over—the process, I mean. You can live with your sponsor, but you still have to appear in court periodically. Oh my, look at me. Chatty Kathy."

Maya didn't catch that last part about someone named Kathy, but it didn't matter. She had a far bigger question. "But what if a person's not granted asylum?"

Ingrid's eyes filled with sympathy. "Well . . . then they're deported back to their home country . . ."

Maya rubbed her temples with her palms.

"We'll talk more," Miss Ingrid hurriedly assured her, "but first, how about we get you a bottle of water, and then some new clothes."

"Clothes?!"

They paused at the kitchen, where Ingrid found Maya a cold

bottle of water, then continued to a large room where two folding tables were nearly buckling from the weight of enormous stacks of clothes organized by pants, tops, coats, and undergarments. Maya's heart lifted at the sight. So much fabric! Her brain churned; she couldn't stop it. She could cut parts of shirts and pants and sew them together in a crisscross pattern, make a dress from shades of blue, or a long jacket. Yes! Maya pulled forth several items, her old self magically eclipsing her current situation.

"Take one from each pile," Ingrid instructed, her voice sounding like a big bite had been taken from its otherwise kindly tone. Just like that, Maya's old self retreated as well.

"Oh . . . sorry."

Maya kept looking, just in case there was something better than what she'd already pulled out. She dug through the mound of tops—turtlenecks, V-necks, tank tops, faded T-shirts. What would she need? Was New York hotter or colder than here? She had no idea. Most of the tops looked too big, but she settled on a lavender sweater. Better to be too hot than too cold, her mother always said. At the next table she picked out a pair of jeans that looked almost new. Where had they all come from? They were in a lot better shape than the clothes at the pacas in the markets at home. Maya lifted up a sweatshirt. This one read SMITH COLLEGE. Where was that? And another: INDIANA UNIVERSITY. And another: GAP. She imagined one with the words SALOMÉ FASHION INSTITUTE. In the end, she decided to keep the lavender sweater.

"All righty," Ingrid said, now handing Maya a fresh packet of underwear. Three to the package—one blue, one yellow, one pink.

"Thank you," Maya said, avoiding the woman's eye. She figured what would probably come next.

"And here you go." Yup. Maya was right. Ingrid passed her a loose bra. Not in a package. "It's all we've got in your size, honey. You're a tiny thing."

Maya accepted the bra, curled it into a ball, and hid it inside the sweater, embarrassed by this exchange of intimate clothing with a stranger. She'd only ever passed a bra back and forth with her mother at the Laundromat on Sundays. A tsunami of grief washed over her. Her mother wasn't here, that was clear. Mama should be here with her, not some random lady from—where was she from again?

But it wasn't Miss Ingrid's fault that her mother wasn't here. "Thank you," Maya said, trying not to sound ungrateful.

"Oh, let's not forget about shoes." Miss Ingrid pointed to the huge pile in the corner while she opened a package of fresh socks. Maya dug around for sneakers. Anything would be better than the canvas ones she was wearing! There was one glittery purple pair, but she decided on a more practical pair of black Converse. Gently used, which was fine—at least these had shoelaces. Most of the other shoes looked beat up, or were winter boots, or for men. The sight of some Vans made Maya think of Sebastian. For the twentieth time, she wondered where he was. If he was okay. Or was he still running somewhere in the desert, living off sugar cane and prayers? Tears pricked her eyes. She really, really hoped he was okay.

"Here you go!" Miss Ingrid held up a pair of fresh socks. "Come on. You'll feel better after a hot shower."

Hot. Shower. Maya had yearned for these words, together.

33

Ingrid led Maya to . . . the backyard? These words didn't fit together; they were like two mismatched fabrics—shower, backyard. Was she missing something? Maya looked around and didn't see any other buildings. Okay . . . so, was she supposed to wash outside like a dog?

Ingrid pointed to a row of six aluminum closets, each one like a porta-potty. "Voilà! The showers. Inside, you'll find soap and a pile of clean towels." A piece of paper with the word *mujeres* was written in black magic marker and taped to the front of each door beside a red cross and letters in black: AMERICAN RED CROSS.

"When you're done," Ingrid continued, "you can put on your new clothes, and just toss your towel into the bin that says 'Dirty Towels,' and your old clothes into the bin that says 'Trash.' I'll meet you back in the courtyard in ten minutes. Okay?"

Maya nodded. But . . . her mind raced. The clothes she was

wearing were the only things she had left of home! Throw them away? No. No. She couldn't do it. She wouldn't do it.

Still, the lure of a hot shower—what had it been, almost a week?—beckoned. She couldn't begin to imagine how badly she must smell, must look, but she realized Miss Ingrid hadn't so much as flinched. Who *were* these people? Carefully, she opened the door to the second silver "shower." Inside was indeed a showerhead and a knob with a red and a blue dot on either side of it. A container labeled BODY WASH sat in the corner. Maya undressed, turned the knob to the red dot.

As the hot water cascaded down onto her head, neck, shoulders, she wanted to cry, it felt so good. She gave in, fully and wholly, to its power. Lifted her arms. Opened her mouth. Turned her head this way and that. Then she pumped the body wash container three times onto her palm and massaged the silky soap into her hair. She could spend hours in here, making and washing away designs with the soap on her arms, legs, and stomach. She spiked her hair as high as it could go before it collapsed to one side. Then she let the hot water run on her sore shoulder for a long, long time. As she did, she shut her eyes and made a prayer. Please God. *Please bring my mother back to me.*

Miss Ingrid knocked on the door. "Don't take too long in there—you'll turn into a prune."

"¡Un momento, por favor!" Maya rinsed her hair. Lathered her body once more. Let the water fall all over. She watched as the drain sucked down the soapy brown water, every last drop of her treacherous trip. Somewhere in that mucky water was the sweat she shared with her mother. Down went the water that held their fears, dreams, and everything in between. It didn't matter to the guards or the government or whoever was running things on this side of the border; they didn't seem to care one iota if two people belonged together or not, she thought angrily. Mother, daughter. Father, son. Wife, husband. Sister, brother. It was like—it was like they weren't actual people to the guards. They were animals. But even animals could find their way back to one another. Wasn't it true, what her science teacher had said once? That a mama bat could locate its baby in the darkest, most crowded cave. How? By its smell. And Maya's smell had just spiraled down the drain.

Reluctantly, she shut the water off, reached for a clean towel from the stack. She wished she had a brush. Instead she combed her fingers through her hair as best she could. Then she dried off and dressed in her "new" clothes and shoes. The jeans pretty much fit, just a little loose around the waist. And it was bliss to wear new socks and sneakers with actual laces again, even though they were too big. Next, she took up her pile of dirty clothes. But as she held it above the bin labeled TRASH, she hesitated. Images from the fashion show flooded over her. It was too much. Her heart literally hurt. Then, she gave a fierce nod, y con todas sus fuerzas, she started dropping article after article in, until all she held were the black jeans with pink bleach blotches. Choking back a sob, she let them go too, listening as they made a quiet thud when they hit the bottom. How would her mother find her now?

"Miss Ingrid—can you . . . can you see if my mother is still in the detention center? Or maybe they transferred her to another place like this? Maybe you can call?" Maya suggested as she left the silver box, trying not to sound overly desperate.

"Sure thing. We can call first thing in the morning. But let's see, it's almost five o'clock. We need to process you and get ahold of your sponsor, but"—she paused, that sympathy back in her eyes—"let me first show you where to eat and then where you'll be sleeping tonight."

"Just tonight? You mean until my mother comes, right?"

Ingrid did that same little lip twist thing that Lisbeth did, and Maya instantly braced herself. "Well . . . no . . . Migrants are allowed to stay here for one night, and then we help you get on the right bus or airplane to meet your sponsor. . . ."

Hold up. Had she heard Miss Ingrid right? She reached for Miss Ingrid's arm. "You mean . . . I have to leave? *Tomorrow?*"

"Well, you don't want to stay here forever. What kind of life would *that* be? This is just a place to get yourself back on your feet. Eat a warm meal, take a hot shower, put on some fresh clothes. It's why it's called a respite center. We give you respite along your journey." She gave Maya's hand a quick pat. "And then, yes, you'll be on your way. Maya, remember. You're one of the lucky ones; you're seeking asylum. Your case has been registered at least. Otherwise, you would've been sent back to Guatemala already. Your sponsor is your lifeline. Now, who is sponsoring you?"

Asylum, detention, sponsor, court dates—the words tornadoed in her mind. So different from *slip stitch, Velcro, embroidered.* Thing was, these new words had been hypothetical, sort of. When she and her mother said them in the trunk of Don Fernando's car, when her mother gripped the steering wheel and drove into the darkness, yes—they were possibilities, but more like doors they'd never have to open. And here she was, suddenly standing inside all the rooms at once. Alone. She swallowed. "My aunt." Exactly as her mother had instructed Maya to say.

"That's good! Where does she live?"

"Nueva York."

"Okay then. Maya goes to Nueva York. It'll be a great next chapter. You'll see. I told you your name sounded like a star!"

"But—what about my mother?"

Ingrid's brow furrowed. "Like I said, we'll call in the morning. Right now, though, let's call your aunt. Come on, now. Don't make a face."

At that moment, Maya's stomach gave a long, low grown. She gripped it, embarrassed. "Do you think, Miss Ingrid, that we could possibly get something to eat first?"

"Oh, of course—I'm trying to do everything at once," she said with a laugh.

They came to a kind of cafeteria, where folding tables (they sure loved their folding tables in this place) had been lined up in a rectangular shape, and other people were already sitting, eating quietly.

"Have a seat right here. I'll get you something," Miss Ingrid told her.

As Maya waited, she stared at a calendar hung from a gold tack. The picture on it was of pine trees covered with snow, something Maya had never seen in real life, only movies. Everything felt like a movie right now; how could this possibly be her real life? As she sat there and stared, she realized she needed to stay at the respite center for as long as it took for her mother to arrive. She couldn't possibly leave for Nueva York without her. Go all that way? Start a new life with an "aunt" who wasn't even her aunt? Nope. She had to stall.

34

But first, beef chili. It was, no joke, the best thing Maya had ever tasted. Well, in the past week. Steam spiraled from the top of her plastic spoon as she savored each and every bite. Only thing better would be if they had tortillas, but she couldn't complain. There were rolls. Maya took two—Miss Ingrid told her to eat as much as she liked. She looked around to the others at the table, but it seemed like everyone kept to themselves.

After a third roll, Miss Ingrid led Maya back to the front lobby, over to the tall countertop. "What's your aunt's name, honey? We'll give her a ring."

"Shouldn't we wait in line?" Maya gestured to the crowd seated in plastic chairs.

Miss Ingrid winked. "You're with me. It's fine."

Maya reached for a Post-it on the countertop, wrote down the name and phone number she'd memorized, and handed it over. As Miss Ingrid dialed, Maya looked around the lobby. Well, this place might be a respite center, but it didn't look like anyone got much rest—nearly everyone looked as though they hadn't slept in days. Even the toddlers looked wiped, most not even playing, as if it wasn't worth the energy. Maya waved at a little boy in a yellow-and-blue-striped fleece. Instead of waving back, he ducked his head behind his papa's leg.

"It's ringing," Miss Ingrid said happily.

Maya felt torn. She wanted her "aunt" to pick up, and yet she didn't. What if this Isabel Sánchez person didn't really want Maya to come to New York? Didn't want, out of the blue, to take care of someone she barely knew? What if she wasn't willing to be her sponsor anymore?

"Still ringing," Miss Ingrid said, her voice singsong.

Maya leaned against the countertop. What had this building been before it was a respite center? It smelled like a nursing home. It had that look, too—the linoleum floors and the rooms missing doors.

"Maybe she's not home," Maya suggested hopefully, yes, hopefully, more enthusiasm in her voice than she'd intended.

"Perhaps . . ." Miss Ingrid wiped her glasses with a little cloth. "Let me try again. Sometimes people don't recognize the number and so they don't pick up the first time."

Maya gave a half-hearted nod. Miss Ingrid was just trying to help—she knew that—but, well . . . *could* Maya really see herself in New York? With Mama, absolutely. They'd work as seamstresses, take on odd jobs, whatever. Eventually, Maya would finish high school. They'd both learn English *for real*, for real, and maybe . . . maybe they would still start a fashion line, open a store.

Dreaming usually made her feel lighter, happier, but instead she let herself slowly slip down the counter's edge until she sat on the floor crossed-legged. That was when she noticed another teenager with the ends of her hair dyed ocean green, their eyes meeting. Something passed between them. Like, if they were anywhere else, they might be friends. But here, there wasn't any more to give, nothing left to stretch, even for friendship. The girl turned away and wandered out of the lobby. As she did, Maya noticed she had a monitor strapped to her ankle. Whoa. Why? That seemed so . . . so . . . degrading! Like crossing the border wasn't traumatic enough? Maya wondered if they'd run out of monitors at the detention center, because she hadn't seen anyone else wearing one. Were they battery-operated? How could they tell if you sawed it off? And what if—

"Maya! Someone's picking up!" Miss Ingrid whispered excitedly. Maya rose to her feet as Miss Ingrid started talking into the phone.

"Yes, hello. My name is Ingrid and I am calling from a humanitarian respite center in McAllen, Texas. I am here with your niece, Maya Silva. Is this—oh, good!" Miss Ingrid covered the phone with her palm, mouthed, "It's her," and put her on speakerphone.

It's *her*. Maya was supposed to pretend to know this . . . *her*. She leaned toward the phone. "Hello?" She tried to sound excited, or at least like she'd actually spoken to this person in the last decade.

"Maya . . . oh, Maya . . . thank *God* you're okay. I mean, you are, right?"

How could Maya possibly answer that? No, she wasn't okay.

She wasn't remotely okay. She had no idea where her mother was, and she was allowed one single night to stay at this shelter before being booted out. But there was only one acceptable answer. "I'm okay," Maya said softly.

"Please, please know I will do everything I can to help you. My brother . . . Fernando . . . Your mother—" She cleared her throat. Let out a long breath. "Maya. You have to listen super carefully, okay? It's going to take months for me to legally sponsor you, but in the meantime, I pulled some strings. You're being transferred to an Office of Refugee Resettlement near me. But first, you're going to take a bus from McAllen to New York City. It's for tomorrow. It's a three-day ride. Do you understand?"

"But what about my mother? She's . . . they—separated us. I have to wait for her."

"Maya, sweetheart, listen—"

"I can't get on any bus without Mama. I won't. You'll have to drag me." She felt the muscles in her neck tighten.

"Bueno . . ."

"I'm not trying to be rude, really I'm not, but I'm not leaving here without my mother."

"Let me talk to the lady." Her "aunt's" voice suddenly sounded like a teacher's.

Was Maya in . . . trouble? She nodded reluctantly at Miss Ingrid, who took the call off speakerphone. The two of them spoke quickly in English, and Maya tried to make out a few phrases, but she could barely hear this woman, Tía Isabel she would call her, through the phone. Maya *did* hear Miss Ingrid repeat bus information, which she wrote down in her little notebook. They said goodbye and Miss Ingrid hung up.

Maya needed to explain that she couldn't possibly get on a bus to New York tomorrow. No, no, no. "Please . . . I need to stay here longer, miss. My mother, she might be on the next bus. I can't—I won't—"

Before Miss Ingrid could respond, a nun with short gray hair, Latina—what was up with women with short hair in this place?—strode into the lobby. Immediately, migrants who had been sitting against the wall stood up. Those who were seated in chairs stood up. Everyone seemed to be standing up. Who was she? Miss Ingrid wrote something else down in her notebook, then turned as well. Even a baby in her father's arms took her thumb out of her mouth and aimed it at the woman, the nun.

"Don't point," her father whispered.

The baby kept pointing anyway. It made Maya smile. The baby didn't know it was rude to point. In fact, the baby didn't know anything—what a nun was, what a respite center was, what legal or illegal meant. Those were just words.

The nun cleared her throat. "Hello, hello, everyone! I'm Sister Nadia Hernández. I want to welcome you to the respite center. May you remember what it means to be respected, to be treated as a person with dignity. Know that God is always with you, wherever you step." She folded her hands. "Let us pray."

Her habit was navy blue, with a white collared shirt underneath it, sleeves rolled up, and she wore an ornate cross around her neck. As she led the group in a prayer, Maya couldn't help it—she stared at Sister Nadia. Her side part. Her kind face.

Her round pinkish cheeks. Soft-looking skin. Her dress was actually more stylish than what the nuns in Guatemala wore. And why was Maya thinking about this right now?

Sister Nadia continued, "Let us pray, too, for those who are not here, for those who have lost their lives along this treacherous journey."

Maya's mind trailed to the image of the woman gasping for her life in the river. What about *her* family? What happened to all the wishes that woman had made while blowing out birthday candles? Did she have kids? Would they—would they ever know what happened to her?

Then a woman standing near Maya suddenly started crying. Should Maya place her hand on the woman's back? Comfort her? She didn't even know her. Maya placed her hand on the woman's back anyway. The woman only cried harder. Oh great. That hadn't exactly helped.

And yet the nun said, "Yes. That is exactly what we should be doing during this time of strain."

Was she talking about Maya?

"You, young lady," the nun said as if she'd heard her. "I thank you for comforting your neighbor in this dark time. This will give rays of light, little by little. Trust. Have faith in God. We will get through this, and you will have more light than darkness someday. God bless you, young lady."

Maya's face flushed. Everyone was looking at her now, including Miss Ingrid. "Gracias," she managed to reply. Miss Ingrid whispered that she'd be back in a few minutes.

As the crowd dispersed, Sister Nadia scooped the infant who'd been pointing from her exhausted-looking father. She nodded and cooed at the baby. She *truly* cared, Maya could tell. She would talk to Sister Nadia. Convince her to allow her to stay longer than one night. She *had* to. But already a mini line had fanned around the nun, pressing close, yet leaving her space at the same time. Maya eyed them nervously. Were they going to ask her the same thing? Maya rushed to join the line. Then, to her amazement, Sister Nadia called her over.

"Ah, you are the young lady I was just speaking about," she said, her smile wide. "May God bless you, señorita. How can I help you?"

"Thank you. If I may—with all respect, may I ask you—may I stay here longer? A few days? I can clean. Cook. Clean . . . I know it's special consideration, but, well . . . I'm in a unique situation. My mother—she hasn't gotten here yet."

Sister Nadia's whole spirit emanated comfort, sorrow, understanding, and regret. "I'm so very sorry, but that is not possible, señorita."

"But I need to! I have to—" She wanted to scream. Why was all this happening? She just wanted her mother. "Please—"

Sister Nadia took Maya's hand in hers. "What is your name, my girl?"

"Maya. Maya Silva. I'm waiting for my mother. Carmen Silva."

Someone else interrupted. "And I am waiting for my husband, Ricardo Fuentes."

"And I am waiting for my daughter, Olga Santos."

"And I am waiting for my sister, Eloise Pérez."

"And I am waiting for my son, Edwin Espinoza."

"And I am waiting . . ."

"And I am waiting . . ."

"And I am waiting . . ."

"And I am waiting . . ."

"No!" Maya covered her ears from the heartbreaking chorus and sank into a crouch.

Sister Nadia handed the baby back to its father, then gently lifted Maya's chin. "Come, child." She led her to a cozy room by the lobby. "Sit, please." Maya did. Sister Nadia tracked down a nearby volunteer and asked her to please get them some water.

"Thank you, Sister, but I don't need more water. Or food. I just need to wait here until my mother arrives. Please. Please! I beg you. I will pray every hour on the hour. I will sort clothes, make sandwiches, give bottles to the babies, anything you need. I *beg* you." This time Maya reached for Sister Nadia's arm and clutched it. Her shoulder throbbed in protest, but she held on.

The sister sighed. Leaned back in a chair that looked like it belonged at a barbecue, not inside a small room in an old building—the chair looked much too festive, with its pink-and-green-striped design. Maya sat in a similar one, only the colors were gray and blue.

"Señorita Maya," she said. Her voice was like honey. "Let us pray."

And they did. Maya prayed like she'd never prayed before.

35

When the volunteer reappeared with a small paper cup of water, despite her earlier protest, Maya gulped it down. She set the cup on the floor, and Sister Nadia took Maya's hands into her own. "You are a strong young woman. You will be more than fine. This I can tell. You need to keep faith."

"Thank you, Sister. But please—" She raised her hand as if in class.

"My dear, there are rules we must follow. Yes?"

"Yes, *normally*." Maya kept her hand in the air.

Sister Nadia laughed. She gently lowered Maya's hand. "Maya, sí? Do you know you're actually one of the *lucky* ones? You could have been transferred to one of the camps—at the army base. Or at the converted Walmart. Listen, your case has been processed. You have a sponsor waiting for you. Right now! You are one of the lucky ones, indeed." Why did that last part sound like she was announcing that Maya had won a brand-new car?

Just then the woman with the heavy blue eye makeup approached. "Pardon me, Sister. But there is an issue with the food donation. The pizzas arrived, but there aren't nearly enough. And the chili . . . it's all gone. People were even hungrier than we anticipated. What should we do?"

Sister Nadia looked heavenward, as if asking God himself what should be done. "Let me think. Is there any money left in the petty cash fund?"

The eye makeup lady shook her head. "We used the rest of it for baby formula yesterday."

"Multiplying loaves and fishes would almost be an easier task," the nun murmured.

As they talked, Maya's eye wandered to a woman slumped against the wall across from the doorway. She clutched a wrinkled piece of paper so hard her knuckles were white, and was rocking back and forth ever so slightly. She gazed at the scrap as if fixating on a memory, like it was a screen only she could see, a hint of a smile yet eyes full of tears. On the paper were two tiny pink handprints. Oh . . .

Maya approached her. She wasn't sure whether the woman was married, so she didn't know whether to use *señorita* or *señora*. She didn't want to assume either way. Age was deceptive on this journey, she was realizing. Some looked older, some much younger. Lack of sleep, ill-fitting clothes, worry, regret, fear, and intense hope—all of it could shave off or add a few years here and there. So she said, "¿Seño?"

The woman continued to rock. Maya squatted down next to her. "My name is Maya." The woman looked over, startled.

"What do you have there?" Maya asked gently.

"My daughter," the woman answered. "Sus manos."

Maya gasped. Her daughter's hands?

"Her name was Rosalie."

"Oh . . ."

Whenever Maya and her mother were at the sewing store, just past the train station, they'd see dozens of mothers carrying laminated pictures of their missing children, stapling flyers on bulletin boards. Women chanting, "¡Dónde está!" Mothers haunted the station, looking haunted themselves, desperate to make their children's faces known, in case someone recognized them.

Maya felt a pit in her stomach. "Rosalie is a pretty name," she blurted out, trying to get a grip. She didn't want to upset the woman any more than she already was. No. She would do what Sister Nadia did. Listen. Listen to her story.

"What happened?" Maya asked, in her most polite voice ever.

A thousand emotions crossed the woman's face. Then she began. "Fuimos a la policía." She swallowed hard. "Like that would do anything. But still, we filed a report. The pandilla . . . the gangs . . . they wanted my husband to join them. They threatened him. Me. Us. Ha! Going to the police—just saying that now . . . seems so naive."

"No, no," Maya protested. "You did what you thought you needed to do. You know, to protect your family." She pictured the officers in her living room. It had all been a setup. Oscar had paid them. She, too, had been just as naive.

The woman finally turned her gaze directly to Maya. "They killed him. My husband."

Now Maya's stomach dropped. Oh, this was a bad idea. She wasn't Sister Nadia. She didn't have the same healing and peaceful effect. This was . . . not good.

"So we left. I took Rosalie and we rode La Bestia through Mexico. Me and a two-year-old. Can you imagine?"

Maya bit at her bottom lip. "But you're here now. Right? You made it."

"I made it. *I* did."

"Oh Lord. Oh crap." Maya slapped her hand over her mouth. "Forgive me, Father, for saying Lord like that—and crap like that—oh shit."

The woman actually smiled.

"I'm sorry," Maya blurted. "I just . . ." She laid her hand gently on the woman's arm.

"My baby was congested, had a really bad cough, too. Then a rash. She stopped eating. And you know what the guards gave her? Vicks. Vicks VapoRub."

Maya again covered her mouth.

"Later, the doctors said, no, no. She had a viral respiratory infection. So they put her on a ventilator."

"Ay . . ." Maya didn't know what else to say.

"But in the end, all the hard work of these doctors came too late." The woman looked down at the paper in her hands. In a shaky voice, she said, "Rosalie died on my birthday. When I walked out of the hospital that day, all I had with me was this piece of paper with Rosalie's handprints." She lifted the paper for Maya to see. Sure enough, two small pink-paint handprints seemed to reach out to her.

"It's all I have left of her. . . . And soon this will probably be gone too, because I can't stop holding it. But I can't help it. I just can't help it." She slowly tipped her head back against the wall, closed her eyes.

Dazed with grief for this woman, her baby Rosalie, Maya simply sat beside her until Sister Nadia's voice talking about vendors and restaurants who might provide dinner pulled Maya's attention back to the small room.

"Well, then, that is what we'll have to do for now," the sister was saying, finality in her voice. "Cut the pieces in half, give them to the women and children first, and in the meantime, hopefully, the tamale delivery will be here."

"Thank God she's letting us give her an IOU. A small act of kindness can move mountains."

"Yes, thank God."

Maya turned back to the woman, Rosalie's mother. Wait— that was it. An act of kindness. This poor lady needed *something* to hold on to . . . and Maya had an idea. What if—

"I'll be right back," she told the woman, scrambling up.

All she needed was some string, a needle, and . . . a pencil. Even yarn would do. There must be a sewing kit in some closet somewhere. Maybe Miss Ingrid had one. Maya rushed to find her.

Sure enough, Miss Ingrid was sorting through piles of boxed clothes in one of the rooms off the main hallway. She held up a purple T-shirt.

"Well, hello, Miss Maya," she said brightly. How did that woman stay so cheery, cheery? Maya wondered.

"Miss Ingrid, do you happen to have a sewing kit? Or even a needle and thread? And a pencil?"

She blinked behind her glasses. "There *may* be a sewing kit in the supply closet right at the entrance. You'll find pencils there too. Let me check."

"I can check! No problem!" Maya bolted away, then pivoted. Grabbed a scarf. "I need this, too! Thanks!"

And boom. There it was, behind some laundry detergent—a sewing kit. Maya ran back to the woman holding her little daughter's handprints—she'd never gotten her name. "¡Señora!"

The woman looked up, her eyes questioning. Carefully Maya said, "May I see your paper?"

The woman's questioning eyes went frantic.

"Please—I won't damage it. I promise."

Hesitantly, the woman passed the paper to Maya, hands trembling.

"Look," Maya said. "I'm a clothing designer." She pointed to the scarf she'd just grabbed. "I can embroider the handprints here, using the paper as a template. That way you can carry your daughter with you wherever you go."

The woman gaped at her in disbelief. Maya nodded. "It's true, I can do this."

Instantly, her eyes grew wet, and she at last nodded too.

"Please, señora, don't cry. Here, I'll sit beside you. You can watch!"

And she did. First, Maya lightly penciled the handprints, using the paper as her guide, onto the silky fabric. Then, as she wove the needle up and down, this way and that, she felt her own hot tears collecting. Her fingers moved—no, they danced—across the fabric. They were so happy to be holding a needle. But of course, she couldn't not think of Mama. Was someone, right now, helping *her*? She prayed, so hard, she prayed, yes. Please yes. Maya kept sewing. With each stitch she reached for Mama, her abuela, their country. Her home. Whatever came next, Guatemala would remain her home. The silky fabric felt familiar in a way she realized nothing else had—nothing—since they'd left their house. Maybe . . . maybe, she could stitch her way through this nightmare, find light somewhere on the other side. Maybe.

Not fifteen minutes later, the woman was wrapping the scarf around her neck, her daughter's tiny handprints close to her chest, the worn paper back in her pocket. "Gracias," she said to Maya, clutching her hands. "May God bless you. Truly, we must go on and live. Even when . . . the unthinkable happens, we must try. Maya, sí?"

Maya nodded. "And may God bless you . . . I'm sorry I never asked before . . . What is your name?"

"Yazmin," the woman said, stroking the scarf softly. "Yazmin Rosalie Rodriguez."

"A beautiful name," Maya said. "No wonder you used it for your daughter."

36

Maya needed to walk around, clear her head after that. Her brain was buzzing in every direction as she roamed the hallways. Eventually, she sat outside in the courtyard. A woman in a hairnet and a teal apron handed her half a warm tamale on a paper plate.

"Thank you," Maya said, her mind flashing to the woman who'd sold her all those chuchitos for the corset dress. Would she ever make something like that again? What would she find in New York?

"Dios te guarde, and remember, miracles can happen, mija," the woman said before returning to the kitchen.

That one word, *mija*, was too much to hold.

Maya ate her tamale carefully, savoring each bite, surprised that she could possibly still be hungry, wishing both for the time to pass and for it to slow down.

When it got dark, she went to one of the sleeping rooms and dragged a blue mat toward the wall. She reached for a blanket from the stack against the window. No human burritos here! The blankets were individually wrapped in clear plastic. Other people, especially those with young children, had already gotten both. They all exchanged nods and silent smiles to express what they could not, or would not, say: good night. Maya closed her eyes. Someone turned off the light. There were no doors to the rooms, so a soft light glowed through from the hallway, but it was far better than the stadium lights in the detention center. Maya exhaled. She heard a toddler do the same across the room. Then another. A yawn here. A yawn there. Maya reveled in having an actual blanket for the first time in days. She pulled it up to her chin, and in her head said, *Good night, Mama*.

But sleep didn't come. Maya tossed and turned. She stared at the white wall, the paint chipping here and there, making a design of its own. *Everything has potential*, she thought. Anything can become art if you look at it long enough. So she closed her eyes once more and willed herself to think about designs.

It didn't work. Water. She needed water.

In the hallway, an orange-and-white water cooler with the words HOME DEPOT sat on a folding table. Maya filled a paper cup from the stacks beside it, brought it to her mouth. She drank four cups in a row.

What she really wished for: Big Cola. Which made her think of Lisbeth. When she saw her again, this bizarre time when she stood in a random hallway and filled cup after cup of water, how it was nothing like the soda they shared at the tienda after school, where Lisbeth could laugh so hard that bubbles would come out of her nose. Maya felt a surge of love for her friend.

Her best friend. She prayed, fiercely, that Lisbeth was okay. Oh! Maybe her rich tía in Mexico would let her come live with her. Oscar wouldn't find her there! That she'd graduate and run a company someday. That Oscar would leave her be.

Like the tamale lady had said, miracles could happen.

In the morning, hunger was her alarm clock. As was the crick in her neck from yet another night with no pillow. She followed the smell of hot coffee and warm syrup to the cafeteria, where she joined a few other early birds at the folding tables. Pancakes and egg sandwiches made pyramids on plastic platters. An old señor with super-white hair was laughing uproariously, pointing at the egg sandwich on his plate. What the heck was so funny? "Oh, man." He slapped at the table, he was laughing so hard.

"What is it?" Maya asked him as she reached for a couple of pancakes. Normally she wouldn't talk to strangers, especially a grown man. But so many rules had gone out the window.

"Nothing." But a moment later, he started laughing again.

Maya did too. His laugh was contagious. Loud and stretchy, like taffy. "No, really. What?" She sat down across from him.

The man caught his breath. "It's just that I was remembering the last time I had an egg sandwich. You know, in the hielera. I guess it was . . . just yesterday, technically."

"That's what's so funny?"

He sighed. "No . . . it's just that, the last time . . . the egg sandwich. I had been looking forward to it, you know? I don't think I'd eaten anything in twenty-four hours. They'd called me in for questioning, and of course, they don't give you snacks."

Maya nodded, poured syrup on her pancakes. A little bit of heaven.

He went on. "So at mealtime, I reached for an egg sandwich, you know, in line, with the tray. I sat down, and even though I would've given anything for hot sauce, I said to myself, well, you know, at least I'm getting some eggs. Protein. No cheese, but así es."

At this point others at the table were listening. One woman, nursing a baby who couldn't have been more than three months old, scooched forward in her chair.

"So I sit down. I take the egg sandwich in my hands and I bring it to my mouth. I bite into it." He paused. But he wasn't laughing anymore. In fact, he looked suddenly solemn.

"Then what?" asked the nursing mother.

"Then I hear a crunch," the man said.

Maya raised an eyebrow.

"It was a cockroach," he said. "A damn cockroach."

Maya couldn't stop herself—she gagged.

"So I spit it out. Actually, now that I think about it, it probably had more protein than those fake eggs they use from the carton. ¡Diablo!" He started laughing again. But now the laugh sounded haunted, delirious.

A couple of people laughed in solidarity; others shifted in their seats. Maya picked at her pancakes with the plastic fork. They weren't amazing, but the old señor was right: anything was better than the food in the hielera. Especially cockroach sandwiches. So she ate the pancakes.

"But you know, that wasn't even the worst part," the man started up again.

"It wasn't?" Maya asked.

"N'ombre. The worst was that those bastard guards—they started singing, 'La Cucaracha'!"

"Estupidos," another man, wearing the same red GAP sweatshirt Maya had seen yesterday, said.

The old señor raised his eyebrows, bit into his egg sandwich like nothing had ever happened. Maya gulped down another gag.

GAP sweatshirt man shook his head. "Over there, you're treated like dogs, not humans."

The nursing woman corrected him, "No. Dogs are treated better than humans, vos."

The old señor added, "You complain about an illness and they do nothing."

"Or they send you to the loba, you know, the hole."

"Ay, no." The woman took her baby off her breast and began to burp her. "Once, I complained that they didn't have fresh water for us to drink. And I'm nursing. I need to drink a lot of water. So one of the guards said, 'Why don't you write to the president?'"

"Terrible," GAP sweatshirt man said.

Maya agreed. Then she felt a tap on her shoulder.

"Miss Maya?"

Maya looked up.

"Oh, good morning, Miss Ingrid," she said solemnly, the vibe at the table still lingering.

"Maya, if you've finished eating, Sister Nadia said you are to help out in the kids' room while we wait for your aunt to make the bus arrangements. As soon as we get word, I'm afraid you'll have to be on your way."

Maya bit at her lips to keep from protesting, gave a nod. There wasn't anything Miss Ingrid could do, she realized that now.

"Here, I'll show you the way to the day care."

"Buen provecho," Maya said to the others at the table, wishing them a good rest of their meal.

"Gracias, joven," the woman with the baby said. "May God bless you today and always." As she made a cross, her baby tried to grab her finger. But missed.

37

The kids' room was in the back, across the courtyard. Maya welcomed the morning air—far less windy today—as she hustled to keep up with Miss Ingrid. Did all Americans walk so fast? They seemed to! When they reached a door marked LA CLINICA on a piece of yellow notebook paper, Miss Ingrid pulled out her keys.

"I thought I was going to help out in the day care?"

"You are. This is one of the only rooms with a sink, though. So, kiddos have to share." She was humming a tune that sounded like a bird. She must really love them.

"With *sick* people?"

Miss Ingrid unlocked the door. "Better than putting the babies in the kitchen, don't you think? We do this to give parents a break, to let them organize their plans, and sometimes, to sleep."

Maya was about to respond, but Miss Ingrid continued, "And there usually aren't truly sick patients in there, mostly just people needing aspirin for headaches or Gatorade for electrolytes."

"Oh." Wow, Miss Ingrid sure had an answer for everything.

In the distance, cars honked and lawn mowers roared. The sun was actually out this morning, unlike yesterday, when the day seemed to be stuck inside a cloud. So this was Texas. So this was the United States. What would New York be like? She'd seen the tall buildings and busy city streets on Instagram and in movies, but actual *life* life? She couldn't picture it. Not yet.

Inside, the faint sound of music came from a radio in the corner. Was that . . . Luis Fonsi? Sure was . . . "Despacito"? *"Quiero respirar tu cuello despacito / Deja que te diga cosas al oído / Para que te acuerdes si no estás conmigo . . ."* Don Fernando's favorite song! Maya would give anything to be listening to it again, with him and Mama and Sebastian in the car.

"We have lots of kids coming in today. The early bus apparently had a dozen toddlers. Their parents just finished washing and feeding them, but now they will need to get in touch with their sponsors. And it's much easier to do so without kiddos on their laps."

"Makes sense," Maya said, looking around at the office desk and chair, two bookcases, countertop and sink, and faded orange rug.

Miss Ingrid turned down the radio, then handed Maya a container of Clorox wipes. "We clean the toys before each new group of children arrives."

"So—this is the makeshift day care?" Maya didn't mean to sound rude; it was just that . . . well, it was so sad. Everything about it. From the drawings on the wall made with faded markers, to the puzzles that looked to be peeling apart and probably missing lots of pieces.

"It's something," Miss Ingrid said, as if reading her mind. She rubbed at a silver-chained necklace that dangled just below her collarbone. "And something is better than nothing." True, Maya thought. Miss Ingrid let go of the necklace as she reached for a wipe. And Maya did a double take. It was—was it—no—yes, a bird that looked like a quetzal dangled from the silver chain.

"Miss Ingrid?" she had to ask. "Is that . . . is that a quetzal? On your necklace?"

"It is!" She beamed, giving the necklace another rub. "One of the most beautiful birds in the world, in my opinion." And in Maya's.

"It is . . . beautiful!" Maya said. *And lucky*, she thought. A good sign—Mama would say a great one.

Now Miss Ingrid took a cardboard box labeled TOYS and tossed the contents on the rug that didn't cover even half the floor, puzzles in tattered boxes, half-filled coloring books, a deflated ball, plastic blocks, and a bunch of Barbies with really messed-up hair.

As Maya cleaned each one, she thought of birds at home, the parrots and owls, the ones in San Marcos, the ones in the capital. As she assembled the dolls into a neat pile, an idea came to her. "Is there any chalk in here?" she called over to where Miss Ingrid was counting bottles of aspirin and jotted down numbers in her notebook.

"Chalk? Hmm . . . I believe so. Why?"

"I was thinking—we can have the kids color on the pavement in the courtyard. Get them some fresh air at the same time?"

"Great idea; I like the way you think. Chalk is in the bottom drawer there. I'll go get the kids. Be right back."

Maya lingered on the words, *I like the way you think*. But Miss Ingrid would never have said it if she knew the reason she was *here*. All the reasons. All the reasons, which if Maya was being truly honest, were ultimately all her fault. There was no sugarcoating it, Maya knew. It was her *lack* of thinking that had gotten her here. Her mother? Sebastian? Lisbeth? Who knew where *they* were. Would she *ever* know? And so the compliment, intended to make Maya feel good, did the opposite.

She would never forgive herself. Never.

38

Fifteen minutes later, Miss Ingrid returned with six toddlers, though they sounded like a dozen! There were crying ones, laughing ones, skeptical ones, and straight-out rebellious ones who started running in the opposite direction down the hall.

"Oh, boy!" Maya exclaimed, breaking into a trot after two squealing escapees.

"Don't worry," Miss Ingrid said with a laugh. "Once they're inside, they can't go anywhere. *Luckily!*"

Yeah. *Luckily.* Not quite! Maya instantly pictured the metal cages in the detention center. But *no.* This was different. So very different. Besides, there was no time to think. Only act. Maya tucked an escape artist under each arm, set them in front of the blocks in the room, then scooped up a little, little boy, the one wailing the loudest. Uh . . . so much for being *easy.* He wore the smallest pair of baby jeans she'd ever seen.

"Hey, come here, niño," she said. "It's okay. It's okay." She walked back and forth with huge, exaggerated bounces until the toddler began to laugh.

"You're a natural!" Miss Ingrid remarked, her face alight.

Some kids pulled at Maya's sweater. Others ran toward the toys. One little girl had already fallen asleep on the rug.

Then an older man, maybe in his sixties, carrying a yellow plastic bag with the letters H-E-B on it, poked his head into the clinic-slash-day-care doorway. "I need more Band-Aids. Please."

"No, Hector," Miss Ingrid said patiently. "You don't need any more."

Maya cocked her head. What if the man *did* need more Band-Aids?

"Maya, honey. There's apple juice in the fridge. Pour cups for the kiddos, okay? Only halfway—they tend to spill whatever you give them."

Maya nodded.

"Please, señora," the man pleaded.

"Now, Hector, we went over this," Ingrid said. "You have a first aid kit. I trust that's all you'll need for your ride to Oklahoma City. You're not even going as far as others. Barely seven hours away. Listen to me, Hector. Hector, please."

The man clearly did *not* want to listen. He entered the room anyway and started reaching for items on the counter—Q-tips, a container of Vaseline, cotton balls.

"Hector!" Miss Ingrid took him gently by the shoulders. "I know you've been through so much, you have, you truly have. But you can't take all the supplies. Other people will need them. Let's go."

Maya ached for him. It was how she'd felt when she'd first arrived and saw those piles of clothes on the tables. She'd wanted them all. She could never get enough.

It was only after Miss Ingrid left with Hector that Maya realized she hadn't mentioned the bus ticket. Damn. Could she at least ask her aunt Isabel to make it for tomorrow? Would she really have to go *today*? What if her mother was on the very next bus? She might be, right?

At Maya's feet, a little girl in mismatched sneakers was struggling to put a dress on a naked Barbie—a naked Barbie who was missing an arm.

"Here," Maya said, taking the doll. "I can help."

As she shimmied a sparkly lavender dress over the doll, a sorrow as sharp as a knife sliced her in half. The fashion show. Fashion. Clothes. Sewing. Lisbeth. Sebastian. Even Ana Mendez. What would happen to the prize money and the reward of having her clothes sold in La Fábrica? It would probably go to the second-place winner . . . Ana Mendez. Maya could feel the knife's edge.

The little girl looked at her quizzically. "Are you my new teacher?"

"Me? Oh . . . no." Maya forced her hands to cooperate. "There." She handed the Barbie back with a smile. "All better!" The girl smiled in turn and skipped away, clutching the doll close.

Oddly, most of the children huddled together in a group, almost as if they didn't know how to take up space anymore. So, actually, not so odd, now that she thought about it.

The apple juice! Maya had almost forgotten. "Who wants

juice?" she asked. Instant swarm. Guess they did. "Uh . . . okay, give me a sec. One at a time."

As she filled tiny—*tiny!*—paper cups with apple juice from a huge carton (harder to do than it looked), Maya wondered how it was possible to feel so many things at once. She knew the respite center was a place run by volunteers who were trying to help people, migrants—people like her. But why are they trying to get us on a bus so quickly? Like, one minute they're welcoming us, but then they're kicking us out within twenty-four hours. Why *couldn't* she just wait a few more days, just in case? She could work in the day care. They clearly needed her. Yes! She would ask Miss Ingrid. But first, chalk for the niños.

When Miss Ingrid returned, she was with another volunteer—another older American woman who said she'd take over watching the kids. Maya didn't bother asking why; she practically pounced on Miss Ingrid. "I was thinking, you need help here. I'm a natural, you said." Here Maya smiled her most dazzling smile. "So I could help out here. Stay longer."

Miss Ingrid's blue eyes went soft. "You *are* persistent, I'll give you that. And I admire that. But no, missy. You know the rules. Besides, I have some news—"

But Maya wasn't going to give up. "Like, I could even change diapers!" she blurted out. What had she just offered?!

"Listen to me, Maya."

Maya barreled on. "That way, I can wait for my mom and then we can ride to New York together. What's a few more days, really?"

"Maya." Now Miss Ingrid was gripping Maya's shoulders,

but nothing like she just had with Hector. Her eyes were filled with sadness. "I'm so, *so* sorry to tell you this, but I just found out—your mother has been deported. She's on her way back to Guatemala. *She was not granted asylum.*" She seemed on the verge of tears herself when she added, "Oh, Maya, I can't tell you how sorry I am."

And just like that, the room blurred. Maya took a step backward, then another, away from Miss Ingrid. Away from the news. *Away.* She backed all the way into a wall, and only then realized the children were all staring at her.

"But—but—why? How? She's—she's in as much danger as I am! The maras . . . they'll find out about her being back in the country. . . ." Maya twisted away angrily as Miss Ingrid reached out to console her. "So . . . then, what does this mean now? Am I— Is she—?"

"I realize this is a lot to take in. Again, I'm so sorry. As you can see, you staying, waiting for her, is not an option. Having a place to go to next, where you are with family and safe, is the only option now."

Maya glared at her. "You really expect me to leave? To . . ."

"To the bus station and then, well, yes, to New York, to your sponsor. In fact, Carlos has just arrived with the shuttle van to take you and several of the others you came with to the bus station."

Maya had to get some air or she would surely faint. She stalked into the courtyard. A few kids were playing with the yellow and white chalk, drawing circles and triangles.

Miss Ingrid spoke cautiously, like someone talking to an angry tiger. "Miss Maya, let's not make a scene and scare the children. Your aunt is waiting for you in New York. At least you have someone."

But that someone was a stranger. In a place Maya had never been to, like a thousand miles *farther* away from her mother. There was no question, suddenly, as to what Maya needed to do.

Return to Guatemala.

She cleared her throat, collected herself, calmed her voice. "Miss Ingrid, I'd like to turn myself in . . . to ICE . . . to whoever I need to. I'd like to be deported, please. Where do I go to do that?" She wanted Miss Ingrid to take out her little notebook and write this down. Why wasn't she?

Miss Ingrid pulled at her necklace. Pulled at the quetzal. "Maya . . . I think you'd better . . . sit down. You're not thinking clearly. Hold on. Let me get Sister Nadia."

Maya shook her head, hard. "Please, don't bother her—she's busy enough. There's nothing you or she can say that would change my mind. I belong with my mother. We'll . . . we'll . . . figure it out. Move to San Marcos. Move to Mexico. Try for asylum again. But we'll do it *together*. I don't want to be in this country, or anywhere, without her. Please turn me in, or whatever. The United States is not the only place to live, is it?"

Miss Ingrid opened her mouth, then promptly shut it again. For once, she didn't have an answer.

Yes, it was crazy. To some. But not to Maya. She'd put her mother through all this, and *she* was the one deported? *Mama* would have to return to Guatemala, *alone*? Maya, her brain clicking into high gear, knew her mother would find a way— change her name, settle somewhere in the mountains, maybe. Finding a job would be a challenge. Still, everywhere needed someone who could sew. Anyway, all these things were details. They didn't change the fact that the one thing she couldn't ever imagine was actually happening. Right now. Separation. In all the scenarios, even death, they'd been together. If Oscar was going to shoot and kill her mother when she sat tied to the chair in their kitchen, Maya was going to stand in front of her. They'd die together. But this—*this?* It was impossible.

Maya walked stonily to the main lobby, where señor Carlos was speedily passing out food—sandwiches, it looked like— and water bottles to twenty or so nervous-looking people, each holding folders and heading toward a white van, a shuttle with the words HUMANITARIAN RESPITE CENTER in purple letters on the side. After handing a sandwich to a man in an orange windbreaker, señor Carlos headed to the van himself, whistling. He waved at Maya, pointed to a stack of wrapped sandwiches on a table at the entrance.

Maya inched outside and watched the people board the van. They wore mismatched and ill-fitting clothes, but they were clean. Many had scarves wrapped around their necks. All had these blue nylon backpacks that said BANK OF AMERICA on them. One father held a toddler in his arms and another little boy stood by his side. Where was their mother? Just then a woman ran up to them and leaned into the man before bending down and kissing the older boy on his head, then the toddler in the man's arms. Together they boarded the shuttle. The woman held a manila folder, like everyone else, and she clutched it as she settled into her seat. That folder held their paperwork, and that paperwork held their future, Maya now knew. Maya watched them as if watching a movie as she stood at the front entrance of the respite center. She watched and watched until señor Carlos climbed into the driver's seat, honked the horn, and looked at Maya, a question on his face: *Are you coming?* She shook her head no and watched him drive away. Reluctantly, she took a sandwich—for later.

39

Maya knocked on Sister Nadia's office door. No answer. She pressed her ear against the wood and could hear the nun talking to someone in English. Maya would wait. She'd waited this long. . . . Still, it was probably rude to like, wait right by her door. So she sat in one of the blue chairs in the lobby.

A few minutes later, it was Miss Ingrid who spotted Maya and practically yelled, "Maya! What are you still doing here? Your bus leaves in less than an hour. Where's Carlos?"

Maya stood up. "He left. Thank you for your help and everything. I mean it. But I just couldn't . . . I . . ."

Miss Ingrid placed her palm on her own heart. "Honey, when Carlos returns with the van, you must go with him. You're going to land on your feet. I promise you. You'll see."

Maya looked down, clenched her toes. How could Miss Ingrid possibly understand? Then, as she looked up, she saw her pull at her necklace. That woman loved her birds, Maya thought bleakly. "Miss Ingrid?"

"Miss Maya?"

"In Guatemala we call the quetzal, the national bird, the god of the air. The legend is that it cannot be held for any long time in captivity. When it is caught, it chooses to kill itself rather than be caged."

Miss Ingrid lifted the necklace, the bird, to eye level.

Maya continued. "My abuela in San Marcos used to tell me the story of the quetzal. This guy, a prince named Tecún, fought bravely for his people, the K'iche' Maya. Anyway, one day he lost to a Spanish conquistador named Alvarado, and apparently there was a quetzal flying overhead. When Alvarado totally gutted Tecún—he ran a spear through him!—the quetzal was said to have flown down and landed on Tecún's chest and dipped its own chest in his blood. That's why the quetzal's chest is red. I thought you would want to know . . . because you like birds and everything."

"I didn't know that," Miss Ingrid said softly. "I'm very glad I do now." Then, to Maya's utter shock, Miss Ingrid unclasped her necklace and pressed it into Maya's palm. "For you," she said.

"For—me? Really?"

Miss Ingrid nodded. "For you." Maya opened her palm, took in the flash of green that was the quetzal.

"Thank you—thank you so much. I'll take the best care of it!" Maya said at last.

"I know you will." And Miss Ingrid pivoted, disappearing toward the sound of the toddlers.

Maybe ten minutes later, Sister Nadia suddenly appeared. "Hello, Maya," she said, oozing calm.

"Muy buenas tardes, hermana," Maya said, rubbing her new quetzal necklace.

"Miss Ingrid caught me up on your situation." Maya's first thought was, *Man, news travels fast here!* Her second was, *Situation*—spiraling her back to Mama, to all the times she'd used that word to describe their life in Guatemala. The situation, the situation, the situation.

Maya launched right in. "You're not going to change my mind, Sister. They deported my mother. So they can deport me. I'm not staying in America without my mother. I'm hoping that, well—can the van bring me back to . . . that place? Where I was first?" It was too horrible to name, that place, never mind something to say aloud, but it was what she wanted. It was.

Sister Nadia was nodding, nodding. "Fine, then. If it's truly what you want."

Maya wasn't sure she'd heard the nun correctly. She said *Fine?*

"But first I need to drive the next shuttle to the bus station. I can drop you at the detention center on my way back. It's only a twenty-minute detour."

If this was the only way to get back there . . . she'd agree. Plus, she didn't have any idea where it even was. So Maya agreed.

They waited in silence by those purple pillars, Maya with her own folder now in her hands, for señor Carlos to return. She tried to ignore the pull in her stomach as Sister Nadia texted nonstop on her phone. Then señor Carlos drove up with the now empty van. Without a word he handed the nun the keys, and she beckoned to Maya to sit up front beside her. More people came aboard, including the woman she'd sewn the scarf for yesterday, Yazmin. She waved at Maya with the end of the scarf. Maya returned the wave. And then they were off. She braced herself, never looked back.

The bus ride was not long at all, and unlike what she'd seen on the ride from the detention center, this part of McAllen had stores, sidewalks, people—just like Guatemala. It didn't look *that* different. Same with the bus station. Inside, though, could not be *more* different! The high ceilings and slick maroon benches made the place look clean, orderly. No one was selling tamales or mango slices or toys for the kids. From what Maya could tell, there was only one sandwich shop, called Subway, in the corner. When she stepped closer, the place glowed neon and it smelled like detergent, not food. Maya didn't have an appetite anyway. But yes, the bus station seemed so . . . *empty*. That was the word that floated to her as she shadowed Sister Nadia.

The sister was giving blessings to the people holding folders waiting on the benches, and praying with them, holding their children, offering them cough drops and Chapstick to take with them on their journeys, reiterating the destinations that were on their folders: Atlanta, New Jersey, Kansas City. Some places Maya had heard of, others she hadn't. But when Sister Nadia announced San Jose, Maya felt an instantaneous raw thudding ache. Sebastian. He had no home in Guatemala. And no home in San Jose, either. Yet he was smart and kind and talented. Surely others would recognize that. Maybe he *had* made it past Border Patrol. If he was able to blend in with other *Americans* in McAllen, lie about his name, he could find his way to California;

he could be okay. She was in this nightmare in part because of him—but he was also in it because of *her*. But she couldn't deny the difference. She was here because of her bad choices. He was here because . . . he had chosen her. Except—it was getting confusing—she had chosen him, that's what *led* to everything, so they'd chosen each other for better, for worse. She said a quick prayer that for Sebastian, it wouldn't be for worse.

When she opened her eyes, Sister Nadia was handing a granola bar to a woman seated on one of the maroon benches. Yazmin! Yazmin noticed her as well and flapped the scarf at her again, the little embroidered hands almost seeming to wave. Sister Nadia called Maya over.

"*Surely* you two remember one another," Sister Nadia said. Was it just yesterday that Maya had sewn that scarf?

"Claro," Yazmin said, a shy smile on her face. All around them people waited to board big, purring buses headed toward places they'd never been. The faster the people boarded the buses, the faster Maya and Sister Nadia could go back to the hielera, and then she'd get on an airplane and land back in Guatemala City and find her mother.

"Señorita? Did you hear me?" Yazmin was asking Maya. "My bus broke down. So I'm waiting to board the next one. Will you sit with me?"

"Oh, sorry . . ." Maya felt so rude for spacing. . . .

"Yes, sit with her; I'll be through in a few minutes," Sister Nadia said.

Yazmin moved her bag from the seat beside her as Sister Nadia moved on to a young father and toddler. She reached into her purse and pulled out two more granola bars.

Maya sat. The sooner this was over, the sooner she could leave. So she'd be polite and talk to Yazmin, like Sister Nadia wanted, even though that pulling feeling filled her stomach again. Across the bus station a woman fiddled with an ankle monitor.

Yazmin rubbed at her knuckles—it was then that Maya noticed how thin her hands were . . . how thin she was. As Yazmin delicately ran her fingers along the scarf's fringes, Maya thought of Mama. She wished she would've given her something, her sweatshirt, *anything*—before . . .

"Voy para Chicago," Yazmin said. "They say it's really cold over there."

Maya nodded. She didn't know where Chicago was in the United States. She wondered, though, if her fashion career would ever take her there, or Los Angeles, or New York, or even Europe. First, she supposed she'd need to finish high school. But one thing at a time.

"Where are *you* headed?" Yazmin asked, now patting the scarf.

Maya looked up. The ceilings were so high a pigeon was perched on one of the beams. "Me? Oh . . . I'm . . . I'm supposed to go to New York, but I'm actually returning to la hielera."

Yazmin's eyes went wide. "¿Cómo?"

"Sí . . ." Maya wiggled her toes inside her two-sizes-too-big sneakers. "I'm going back . . . to Guatemala, to be with my mother. We crossed together, but they caught us, then separated us. They deported her. She's already there." Just saying these words aloud made it feel so cruel, so real.

Yazmin stared at Maya with laser-like intensity. Even when

Maya turned away, she could still feel her looking. It wasn't so much shock or judgment, as awe. Maybe. Maya didn't mean to bring up her mother, especially when . . .

After an awkward silence, Maya said, "Excuse me. I need the ladies' room."

Yazmin dipped her chin. But then she blurted out, "And you've made up your mind?"

Oh God. This was the part where Yazmin tried to convince her to go to New York, wasn't it?

"Yes," Maya said, shoulders already tensing.

"Vaya, vaya . . . You are strong, I can see that."

Around them, families sat together, sometimes one adult and one child, reading over paperwork, looking into some far-off distance, sharing food. People were so quiet. So very tired. All Maya could hear was the occasional announcement made over the loudspeakers.

"But . . . ," Yazmin said. "If you get on the bus, then you could find a future that may be different. Not necessarily better. *Maybe* better. But for certain, different. More opportunities in the United States, that's for sure. And you left in the first place to leave things *behind*. If you go *back*, mija, you're not going forward."

"But my mother—"

"Sí, sí, sí." Her eyes instantly watered. "But if my daughter had an opportunity like this . . ." She swallowed. "I would want her to take it. I would want to know she was safe, first and foremost. Even if . . ."

Maya raised her eyebrows. A part of her appreciated Yazmin's honesty, but she also didn't know what Maya had been through.

They called the next bus. Her head throbbed. "Well, it was nice talking to you. Good luck, I mean, with everything."

Yazmin pulled at her scarf. "Good luck to you, too. Adiós, Maya."

"Adiós, Yazmin."

In the bathroom she stared long and hard into the mirror. *I look like hell.* Her cheeks looked sunken and her hair flat and brittle. But it was still her. Still her dark eyes, her puffy—Lisbeth said she was so lucky—lips. In her face there were parts of her mother, her father. Yazmin called her strong. But her mother—what kind of monumental courage her mother must have had to leave behind her own mother in San Marcos, to search for something more. And her father? To stand up to a man with a gun because of his ideals? His values? Maya didn't have a fraction of their strength. She hadn't been strong enough to listen to her mother. She hadn't been strong enough to give up Sebastian. Or the fashion show! But—at the same time, she had come in first place in the fashion show. And she had made it across the river. She had survived things. She was surviving them right now.

It was unreal how just a few weeks ago she'd been hanging out with Sebastian and Lisbeth and Oscar on her roof, looking out at her sweet and complicated city. She pictured Sebastian plugging her cell number into his phone. And what was he doing right at this moment? He had sacrificed so much for Maya and her mother. Would she ever see him again? Probably not. She knew that, too. But she also believed he would see her, her designs. She imagined him scrolling through the designers at Parsons and finding her name. Maybe. And Lisbeth . . . her

best, best friend. Maya would pray for her, and for their friendship. Figure out a secret address, or an app where they could
chat under fake names, something, anything.

It was all too much; she felt dizzy with it all. She bent over
the sink to splash water on her face, saw her warped reflection
again, this time in the curve of the metal faucet, a version of
herself she didn't recognize, but was still her nonetheless.

She thought about Yazmin. What about her? She was literally
moving on, despite the worst of the worst having happened.
Would Maya do the same with her last yard of fabric? Do something useful with it? She would like to think so, yes.

With her strength on its last ember, she willed herself back
into the waiting area and searched for Sister Nadia. There she
was, consoling a young couple. The woman wore her hair in
a braid, curled into a bun at the back of her neck . . . just like
Mama. They didn't look much older than Maya. Or . . . Mama
at Maya's age. It could've been her, standing beside Maya's
father. How could Mama have left San Marcos? Left her
mother? For the unknown, no less! Yes, she had Maya's father.
But . . . after he . . . Maya's mother could've gone back to San
Marcos.

But she didn't.

She made a way for herself.

A new home.

She strived for more, not just for herself, but for Maya. She'd
sacrificed so much for her.

So maybe Maya could . . . too?

Sister Nadia approached Maya. "I can see you are contem-
plating, mija."

"I was so sure . . . but now . . . I don't know." Maya's voice had become a silvery whisper. Her chest felt fluttery, like a bird was trapped inside. "I don't know if I can go on without my mother."

"Mija," she said, placing a gentle hand on Maya's shoulder. "Don't you know? You are your mother's daughter. You are always with her and she is always with you. You have faced so much heartache. But trust that God will help you move through this next chapter." And the nun wrapped Maya in her arms. Maya hugged her back.

And in that moment of calm, of safety, something huge occurred to her! If her mother was sent back to Guatemala City, she would immediately find her way back to Don Fernando. And without a doubt, he would help again. Maybe . . . maybe he would even come with her. And! How had she not thought of this?! At the very least, Isabel, Maya's "aunt," could get in touch with Don Fernando—and Mama would know Maya was safe! Maya knew Mama would do whatever she could, however long it took, to get back to her. Yes. Yes! And then, like a thunderbolt, something else struck her. What Sister Nadia had just said: *You are always with her and she is always with you.* The words pulled Maya back to the table at the outdoor restaurant in San Marcos—was it *really* only a few weeks ago?—where Mama ordered a beer and Maya, a horchata. Where the sky had swathed them in purple as they talked about moving there permanently. Maya had to laugh, how at the time, *that* had seemed something beyond her imagination's reach, and now . . . well . . . now was now. Different. So, so different. At the restaurant—among the spicy smell of marigolds blooming around them, mixing with the vanilla and cilantro and savory tomato from their meals, all of it wrapped around them. And in that conversation, at some point, her mother had said those exact words. Hadn't she? *I'm always with you, mija. And you are always with me.*

So, maybe it *was* true. Maybe this was when Mama would say, *Anda, mija. Get on that bus. Or else . . .*

And so, and so, with a deep breath, Maya walked toward the purring buses, then toward the one that said NEW YORK in orange letters across the rectangular strip at the top of the bus. DEPARTS IN 5 MINUTES. A few steps and she was on it, this vehicle that would take her to a new place, a life that she would stitch from her previous one. And from where she stood, with the vibration of the engine beneath her feet, she could tell she would make something of it, like with all the scraps from fabric otherwise unwanted, make something unexpected, but true.

Something she couldn't wait to show her mother.

Acknowledgments

In the summer of 2018, when I was pregnant with my second son, I could not keep my eyes off screens that showed children being torn away from their parents, especially mothers, at the US-Mexico border. It pained me not to join others at rallies to protest the "zero tolerance" immigration enforcement policy, which affected many Central American people. My people. For me, the news was personal. Both my parents are from Guatemala. And while they moved to the US in the 1970s, Guatemalan culture was always in our home—from the tortillas con queso we ate to the Spanish we spoke. And of course, in our stories. I grew up visiting Guatemala often, making memories of my own. Although I could not march in the streets in 2018, I decided to begin writing this novel. It was my own way of marching.

I researched and wrote and revised this book with the help of so many people. To Faye Bender—the most amazing literary agent in the world—thank you for all that you do to allow me to do what I love to do! To my brilliant editor, Caitlyn Dlouhy—you inspire me to work hard, and I'm thrilled to to learn from you. To Clare McGlade, I always feel my book is in the safest of hands with your keen eye.

Mil gracias to Krystal Quiles for the stunning cover art (I have never seen a quetzal on the cover of a book; thank you), Michael McCartney for the exquisite design he created with that cover art, Justin Chanda, Anne Zafian, Erin Toller, Emily Ritter, Emily Varga, and the entire team at Simon & Schuster/Atheneum.

Huge thanks to my incredible publicists—Morgan Maple and Beth

Parker—for helping to get this book into the hands of readers. You juggle so much, and I am grateful for you both.

For their stellar feedback—Jenna Blum, Christopher Castellani, Mark Cecil, Chip Cheek, Lori Goldstein, Desmond Hall, Calvin Hennick, Sonya Larson, Kimberly Hensle Lowrance, Celeste Ng, Alex Marzano-Lesnevich, Whitney Scharer, Adam Stumacher, Grace Talusan, Becky Tuch, and to all those in Jenna's Novel Workshop over the years.

For their encouragement and enthusiasm—Angie Cruz, Ru Freeman, Hanna Katz, Esta Montano, Mia Narciso, Askold Melnyczuk, Cathie Mercier, Charles Rice-González, and Patricia Sánchez-Connally.

To all my SBORO friends and chosen family—I'm home!

And to my wonderful colleagues at Framingham State University, including Lisa Eck, Desmond McCarthy, and the entire English department. I am also grateful for the CELTSS grants that helped support my research for this book.

To my Queridx Zoom crew—our pandemic Zoom meetings gave me life.

Thank you, Angelica Maria Garcia at South Texas College. When my youngest son was five months old, I traveled to the US-Mexico border and interviewed migrants at a humanitarian respite center in McAllen, Texas. Thank you, Angelica, for believing in this project and for generously accompanying me during my research trips.

For answering my (endless) immigration questions—Heather Yountz, you are a lifesaver. And Camilo Pérez-Bustillo and the essential research and policy work published by the Hope Border Institute (HOPE). Also, for helping to provide context, the following books: *A History of Violence: Living and Dying in Central America* by Óscar Martínez and *A Year Inside MS-13* by Juan José Martínez D'Aubuisson.

I would also like to thank the institutions and professors and mentors and editors who have supported my work over the years, in particular the Associates of the Boston Public Library's Writer-in-Residence program, a life-changing fellowship.

To Francisco Stork and Randy Ribay—thank you for your generous words of support.

For teachers and librarians and booksellers, I thank you!

For all the young people reading this—we need you more than ever before to look beyond the single story of immigration, to believe in a world where it is not a crime to seek a better future. And to all the people making the journey from one country to another, risking so much for the possibility of surviving and thriving—I see you.

Again, to my grande familia all over the country and in Guatemala! If there were too many to name before, there are even more names now. Thank you for your fierce love.

To my sisters, Karen and Caroline—love you! And thank you for putting up with a creative writer in the family, and to my sister-in-law, Guadalupe, thank you for answering all my texts!

For my parents, Luis and Dora De Leon, thank you for showing me what it is to work hard, to believe in the possibility of more, and for teaching me that to live a blessed life is to help others in need. You raised us in so much love, and now you are doing the same with your grandkids.

I remain grateful to God every single day, that I get to do what I love, that I get to show my young sons that it *is* possible. Mateo and Rubén—my love for you can fill a thousand hearts. And finally, to Adam, my best friend, partner, fellow family-calendar-filler-outer, I love you and I thank you, and I can't imagine this journey with anyone else.